Deadish

Alex Lancer

www.alexlancerauthor.com

Cover design by: Bailey McGinn

Library of Congress Control Number: 2018675309

Printed in the United States of America

CONTENTS

Chapter 1. The End.

'Deadish' was the word that emerged in the confusion.

It had all been going so well up until that point.

The patient's daughter pursed her lips and reflexively nodded in agreement. As she tried to grasp what was going on, her pursed lips gave way to a silent *'what?'*, and the nodding slowed to a fixed stare. The two sons were less understanding.

The larger of the two was standing with his back to the room containing his mother who was apparently in an uncertain status, somewhere between life and death. He looked left and right at his brother and sister: their furrowed brows and open mouths told him that he hadn't heard wrong. 'Sorry, just... I'm not sure, you started by saying you had some bad news, but then you said 'deadish?'

'She's dead, isn't she? Please just tell me straight,' said the daughter from behind the shivering white hands that were covering the lower half of her face.

'It's a little difficult, it's not quite clear at the moment,' said Dr Ashley Brown.

Ashley had just been at the point of delivering the look over the glasses, which was due to be synchronised with the end of the sentence '*I'm sorry to say your mother has passed away*,' when she had been distracted.

The interference in her verbal PowerPoint presentation had been provided by Dr Chris Newman from the doorway of the hospital room. He had abruptly appeared, making a repeated gesture waving his hand horizontally at throat level as he shook his head from side to side. She had immediately realised something was seriously wrong. What had been perplexing her was how things could be worse, given that the woman was already dead.

Chris was behind the family and invisible to them. As they focused upon Ashley she bobbed from one foot to another. Her eyes flitted from the family to Chris and back again. Using sign language, he was failing to convey to Ashley the message that elderly dead woman, who had refused to co-operate with their textbook cardio-pulmonary resuscitation, had now, rather inconveniently, started to breathe again.

The harsh corridor light seemed to be rebounding off the sterile white walls and focusing just on her. It had rapidly changed from being a spotlight on a stage to something more like one in an interrogation room, Ashley's slim runner's figure made her look taller than her five foot six. Her shoulder length blonde hair normally rested on the collar of her white coat, but now wisps were overflowing forwards contrasting against her black Versace. She dressed in a way as much as a statement of professionalism as of fashion. Unfortunately, now that the going had got difficult, the Versace wasn't covering the rising sense of chaos.

Pushing back her hair she fixed her glasses and wiped her brow, where she could feel beads of sweat forming. The small scar at the edge of her right eyebrow was normally invisible, but as she blushed its white raised ridge stood out. As she sharply inhaled the familiar disinfectant hospital smell, it reminded her of her starring role in this real-life drama. She wrapped her sharp crisp white coat to hide the Versace as she felt she didn't deserve its suggestion of professionalism anymore. She sought reassurance in fiddling with her ID badge and wrapping her stethoscope around her fingers.

Medical school role play had certified Dr Ashley Brown as being competent to deliver the 'death of a loved one' dialogue. She had even acted it out alone in her mirror to perfect the performance. She had executed all the steps in turn, the head tilt, and the wise and gentle compassionate look over her glasses. She omitted the option of the human touch on the hand or the arm from her script. Not because she wasn't empathetic or that she was autistic. It was more because she had sufficient doubts to not exclude herself entirely from either of those categories.

Dr Chris Newman had none of those doubts. His short, black, gelled, hair was normally as fixed as his stare and as unruffled as his composure. His brown eyes, tanned complexion and calmness contrasted with Ashley's ashen face and anxious shivering. With the three possibly soon-to-be grieving relatives oblivious to him, he began making very clear gestures towards Ashley. Chris was usually unflappable in a crisis, but the intensity of his gestures were now definitely elevated into the red zone. He was normally easy-going and always on the point of smiling or making a joke, so when he put on his serious head and bobbed up and down behind the relatives, Ashley was unnerved.

Her speech really was more of a script, rather than an outpouring of raw human emotion. At the moment of interruption her internal hardware had substituted *passed away* with the harsh word she had been avoiding, *'dead'*.

Her brain software attempted to revise this, but it wasn't configured to instantly recall the '*dead*' word into her psyche and instead had simply modified it to *'deadish'*. As this spellcheck error was transmitted to her mouth on autopilot, it had only compounded the issue. It wasn't a word she had ever used, or indeed heard before. However, as her confidence and professional façade began to crumble, the new word evoked sufficient confusion and distraction among the relatives to give her a few seconds to try and regain control of the situation.

Ashley abruptly suspended the conversation with a rushed 'Yes, I'll update you on the specifics shortly.' The bewildered family, who had previously believed that death was a binary yes or no condition, were unable to express any emotion beyond vacant incomprehension.

Chris and the nurse moved to the right side of the patient's bed to make room for Ashley. Littering the bed and floor were IV tubing, defibrillator pads, empty medicine boxes, tape, plastic wrapping, and syringes: the usual aftermath of a medical cyclone.

The patient's white hair was creeping erratically across the pillow, framing an equally white face. Her tongue was protruding from the side of her open mouth, forming a Q shape. Her thin arms were notable for the many irregular purple patches. She looked all of her 95 years.

Trying to regain her composure, she hissed at Chris.

'What? You, what?'

The turmoil in her brain was rattling down her spine and she began to shake. She stamped a foot to release the static in her limbs and focused on Chris again.

'What could possibly…? What do you want? For the love of God, I'm trying to tell them their mother is dead,'

He raised his hands in self-defence and without saying anything pointed at the heart monitor screen with its regular spikes and waves to indicate the beating heart of Mary Kennedy. The noise of the regular bleeps prodded Ashley's ears across the room.

'What, how? You mean she's alive? But she was dead, pulseless, I was breaking the news to them.' She levelled an accusing finger with a Ferrari red fingernail pointing at Chris. Did you just bring her back to life while I'm trying to grieve with the family?'

Chris, who tended to be more sanguine about life and death shrugged and hooked his thumbs inside the draw cord of his green scrubs.

The bleeping of the monitor seemed to be taunting her, with its repetitive sound rattling her brain. 'Can someone turn down the noise of that bloody monitor?'

The nurse pulled a face as if to say, is that really the most important thing right now, as she turned to the machine and lowered the sound.

'Relax, it's okay, nobody's died,' Chris said, accompanying the deeply inappropriate cliché with a reassuring smile.

Ashley was familiar with his use of humour as a defence mechanism, but this pun was too much. Her narrowing lips and widening eyes prompted Chris to try again.

'Right, I didn't do anything… after the electric shocks and all that jumping up and down on her chest, she didn't have a pulse. But then she started to breathe, like that a big sigh just there, now a small breath, now a pause and wait for it …..another big one, there now. It's like the evening of Christmas day when the batteries in the toys are running down and they gradually stop working as the charge goes down,' he said.

'You total moron,' she said. 'Have you never heard of Cheyne-Stokes breathing?' What you're describing and looking at is exactly that… its what people do as they're dying,'

'Oh, okay. I mustn't have been in the day they did that in medical school.' This was Chris's stock answer for numerous situations he encountered in his daily work. Regrettably, although it was delivered as humour, there was a strong element of truth to the statement. 'But that's good news, because if it's what people do as they're dying, then let's just give it a few minutes.'

Ashley couldn't argue with the ghoulish logic and didn't have a 'Plan B' for this unintended situation, so she just hissed; 'Fine.'

Chris knew that this 'fine' meant anything but 'fine'. The pneumatic delivery of the word resembled an engine releasing steam to avert an explosion.

Silence descended in the room. Outside the curtains there was a distant hum of conversation among the relatives. Even without being able to hear the words Ashley knew it wasn't normal background conversation, as the voices were oscillating from hushed to shrill. Each second was agony: the longer this went on the harder it was going to be to contain the drama outside the cubicle.

Chris turned to face her and, once she met his look, said; 'So, "deadish", I don't think I was in the day they covered that either, tell me a bit about it.'

At work, Ashley always tried to be professional and to maintain a neutral facial expression. However, her forehead, eyes and mouth all grimaced independently. Before she got a chance to go any further the monitor's intermittent bleep changed to a constant flat tone.

'Look, she's stopped breathing. Let me just check her heart.' Chris placed the stethoscope over her heart as Ashley looked on impatiently.

'Nothing, she's definitely gone,' he eventually answered. He made an attempt at performing the sign of the cross. As a flimsy, lapsed Catholic, his execution of the ritual was rusty. He touched his forehead with his right hand, but then touched the shoulders in the wrong order. Ashley had her head inclined and was looking at Chris over her glasses with a deeply furrowed brow. He abandoned the gesture and elaborately ran his fingers through his hair as a diversion.

'Thank God she's dead, I'll go and tell the relatives,' Ashley said as she reached forwards to fix the deceased woman's hair neatly around her head. Once satisfied with her work, she turned around, only to face the son who had slipped inside the room when they had been listening for heart sounds. He had clearly heard everything.

He spoke slowly, but even his forced monotone quivered with emotion. 'Can you all please leave? We specifically asked for our mother not to be put through all of this.'

As Ashley passed him by she paused, offered out her hand and said, 'I'm very sorry for your loss.'

He kept his hands firmly by his sides and ignored her.

She withdrew her hand and edged past him with eyes starting to fill with tears. Chris didn't offer his hand, which was just as well, as he had been massaging sticky hair gel between his thumb and fingers.

As they walked side by side down the corridor Chris took the crumpled list of patients from his back pocket. Drawing a line through Mary Kennedy's name without looking up he said 'Well, one down, we still have twenty more to see on this morning's round, room for improvement perhaps.'

The silence from Ashley was uncharacteristic and he turned to look at her face. One of the things he liked about her was her perpetual smile and good humour. Now the smile was replaced with a quivering lip and her head was tilted towards the floor as she attempted to hide behind her hair.

'Ashley it's okay, there was a bit of a misunderstanding there, but don't worry I'm sure it will all be fine. Is everything alright?'

'Yeah'

As they passed the nurses' station Dr Jeffrey Cavendish III was sitting behind the desk. Along with Ashley and Chris he was the third registrar in the surgical department.

Jeffrey's wavy blond hair and ironed scrubs were wrapped in a gleaming white coat which was only matched by the beam off his enormous grinning white teeth. The omnipresent grin of the third incarnation of the Dr

Cavendish line, was a testament to the finest work that expensive orthodontic surgeons and pushy parents could achieve.

'Way to go guys, Professor Stone was just here and got to see all of that going on as well. Ashley have you considered changing from surgery to palliative care? You seem much better at finishing them off,' he said.

'Is that her chart?' Chris said.

'Yeah, I was just checking, Professor Stone was her Consultant. He never actually got around to seeing her, but I told him about her,' Jeffrey said.

'Was she supposed to be for resuscitation, at her age?' Chris said.

'Well, no, the family didn't want it, I guess the Prof didn't get around to signing the DNR order for her chart, so it's not documented. Hey, why are you looking at me like that, it wasn't my job! You should have checked!'

'I thought it was the right thing to do, just to help. Isn't that what anyone would do?' she said. Her shoulders slumped forward and she leaned against the desk. Her stethoscope and lanyard were no longer carrying her like sails but weighing her down like anchors.

'No way, I wouldn't have got dragged into that. Why would anyone go around the place doing things like that?' Jeffrey said.

Chris knew Jeffrey was utterly lacking in empathy, but this was a step to far. Talking to this clown was pointless, he would deal with him later. He steered Ashley away from the nurses' station and into the treatment room.

'Don't worry about him Ashley, we didn't do anything wrong, this will all blow over in a few days.'

'He said Professor Stone saw what happened, he won't like that. I can't believe I messed it up so badly.'

'Listen that could have happened to anyone. On the TV programmes I watch people are always coming back from the dead, or from alien abductions or something. How were we to know she was going to come back to life? So, its fine, the next time we go for a drink, we will be laughing at that. You get a coffee, I'll write up the chart and I'll see you at that hospital induction meeting at eleven.'

'Okay, you're right… I just hope they don't complain. I'll see you then.'

Chapter 2: Conflict

An hour later Ashley had adjusted her make-up and excised any physical traces of the morning's drama. She liked to think she came across as calm and professional, but internally when things started to go wrong she panicked easily and could be flustered for the rest of the day or more.

Outside the lecture theatre, she touched her forehead as she fixed her glasses, then she moved her hand down to check her name badge dangling on its lanyard over her heart. The hand then moved to fix her stethoscope on her left shoulder and finally to the right shoulder. Once her protective ritual was completed, she pushed open the heavy door and stood on the top step looking down over the crowded room. The sloped theatre had semi-circular rows of fixed seating with matching parallel long narrow grey countertop. Chris was in his usual position in the back row and had kept her a seat which she slipped into.

'Who's looking after all the sick people?' asked Chris as he surveyed what looked like the entire staff of a hospital shift. From the back row they could see patches of light blue scrubs marking flocks of nurses. The grey suits, topped with bald heads, nodding deeply at each other, were serious physicians in serious conversations. Pink and navy blue scrubs, casual shirts, excitability and twittering indicated the staff nurses and junior doctors. Managers clutched important pieces of paper under their arms, in lieu of friends. They were scattered individually around the room, industrially studying their phones with the zeal of teenagers, but rather than surfing the zeitgeist, they were probably scouring Facebook for likes.

Jeffrey walked down the steps with the swagger of an athlete, whose excessive protein intake had congealed the part of the brain that does humility. He flashed his trademark white grin at the better-looking nurses. He got two types of responses, some flashed a reflection in white, the ones who knew him better, or too well, kept their dental enamel encased behind telling grimaces. He pointed his finger at a few friends before taking a seat backslapping along a rowdy row of junior doctors: they all had scrub sleeves uniformly rolled back to display their biceps.

Ashley and Chris had known each other through medical school and had hung around with the more introverted half of the class. It was in the years of surgical residency training that the shared experience of years of anxiety, long hours and hard work made them friends. Now in the final year of the registrar surgical training programme, they were reasonably experienced, certainly toughened up and would become fully qualified to be Consultant surgeons in six months if all went well. A Consultant post was the Holy Grail for the registrars, a culmination of years of work and the sacrifice of what might have been in the decade between their twentieth and thirtieth birthdays.

Chris had the confidence and ease of someone who could read situations and people well enough to keep out of trouble. He didn't come from a medical family and was deliberately dismissive of the rules, restrictions and social covenants of the entitled type of doctor. His lack of baggage gave him a clear conscience, a reasonable moral compass and he enjoyed helping people. Unlike Ashley, he had had a city upbringing and had supported himself by working in supermarkets, in a restaurant and finally as a barman, both before and during medical school. Working with all kinds of people had made him street-smart. He had learned to distinguish the tricky individuals, the bully or the thug dressed up as a boss or a customer. Medicine for him was an idealistic choice in life, but as the years went by, he'd also come to understand that in hospitals, amongst patients, medical staff and managers the lunatics were present just as much, if not more, than in the real world.

In contrast Ashley was unfailingly open, pleasant and professional, but utterly incapable of seeing anything bad in anyone. Chris almost felt the need at times to shelter her from the turbulence and storms that could blow through the hospital. He looked over and saw she was drawing a grid on a sheet of paper. Chris switched from people-watching to focus on the drawing. She drew two columns down and three rows across. Column one was headed Ashley, column two Chris. In the first column's second row she wrote *going forward*, then for the third row she *wrote blue skies/green fields*. She passed the grid to Chris.

'I don't get it, what does this mean?' Chris said.

'This is good, it's called bullshit bingo. We get to pick two clichés or phrases each and each time one of them is used, you get a point. The winner is the person who gets the most points at the end. So, if the people at the lectern use *going forward* or *blue skies/green fields* more than the two phrases you pick, I win,' Ashley said.

'Hang on *blue skies/green fields* is two phrases you cheat,' Chris said.

'Stop making excuses, loser, and pick your two,'

Chris intently studied the sheet. He was competitive, maybe too much so. It had helped getting into medical school, but he also always had to beat traffic lights and never, ever, stepped on cracks in the pavement. He also was relieved that Ashley was back to normal and her odd reaction to the earlier death was over.

He contorted his facial features in parallel with the rummaging in his brain, selected his options and wrote *with your support* and *touch base offline*.

'Not bad, now to make it interesting 20 bucks each, winner takes all,' Ashley said laying down and smoothing out a note on the desk.

Chris slapped his note down with the kind of smack that would be designed to intimidate a cage-fighting opponent. Ashley gave him the look any four-year-old in a sweet shop would immediately recognise as a cease-and-desist order.

Serenity Hospital's chief executive and ex-nurse, Mary Gallen entered from the side door and took her place at the lectern. The noise volume in the room dropped from chattering to mumbling. As soon as her underlings took their places she addressed the crowd.

'Can everyone hear me alright?' Mary's peroxide blonde hair was tied back so tightly that it gave her face a feline expression, not unlike a facelift gone wrong. Her grey jacket had clean sharp lines that suggested an inflated price tag. The bulges that the fabric was attempting to conceal however, gave the overall appearances of a life jacket two sizes too small. Chris guessed she was in her fifties.

She looked around the room and began 'I would like to welcome you all here, as you know every six months, we have this induction meeting to welcome all new staff and to remind everyone of the key hospital policies. In addition, I'm delighted, as manager of this Serenity Hospital, to announce we have signed off on a corporate strategy going forward for our healthcare group.'

Ashley, high up in the back row made a subdued punch into the air and put a tick alongside *going forward* on the scorecard.

'We are amalgamating all services under a single governance structure to enhance the patient journey and to improve patient flow pathways. This new model will enhance entry point access and broaden care conduits.'

Mary looked up from her cue card and was rewarded with serious nodding agreement from her supporters. She moved onto the next card oblivious to the blank responses of the cynical senior doctors and the fidgety insolence of the eye rollers at the back of the room. She had relentlessly climbed the corporate ladder from nurse, to supervisor, to hospital manager. In an organisation without strong morals, promotion was easier for everyone rather than confrontation. As she had departed from each level in the workplace, her co-workers had heaved a sigh of relief. She had pursued each step and promotion as persistently and enthusiastically as a dog fetching a ball. In the corporate world of hospital management, persistence and eagerness were often confused with ability. She now found herself in a powerful position without any guiding principles or ideas beyond chasing the tail of power.

'This new structure will allow us as corporate management to interact with clinical services holding them to reaching a high standard. With your support we will have a world class healthcare facility. '

Chris reached across to register his score next to *with your support.* Ashley growled at him and he quickly withdrew his hand after ticking his square.

'Most importantly today I wish to draw your attention to our hospital policies and procedures. On every computer in the hospital, you will find the mandatory policies folder. These policies define how the hospital is to be protected in all situations. The new 'Policy on Policies' sets out how all the 2,500 policies should be implemented. As staff you need to know all of these policies to avoid any difficulties for the hospital. Any deviation from these policies will be a serious disciplinary issue.'

She paused for dramatic effect and without moving her head darted her eyes right and left to let everyone know she meant it.

'Obviously our people are our key resource and in order to ensure that we meet maximum efficiency we need leaders who will deliver on our key performance indicators. With this in mind we have decided to appoint a chief of hospital clinical governance who will oversee all aspects of medical services for the hospital. There really was only one candidate for the post: Professor Stone. You will all know him as a fine surgeon, researcher and influencer at the hospital and university. He is a member of many boards and charities and his reputation precedes him. I believe that with Professor Stone as our chief the future is bright and he will bring blue sky thinking to our development. If I can ask him up to speak…'

'Blue skies, two nil, I win,' Ashley said sliding the money into her pocket.

'Hold on, double or nothing on Professor Stone, same clichés?' Chris said.

'No way, I won,' Ashley said sitting back savouring her small victory both against Chris and Mary's clichés.

Two rows in front, sitting together, two of the Consultant surgeons, Dr Claudia Rossi and Dr William Attwood shared a look, not of victory, but of horror at the unveiling of the new chief of clinical governance.

Dr Rossi leaned over, her facial muscles taut and she whispered to Attwood, 'This is going to be trouble. He'll have her eating out of his hand in a week. He has too much ego and too many agendas for him to be quiet in that job. Image the ability he will have to interfere and create mayhem in a post like that where you get to look over everyone's shoulder.'

'I know, but it's a done deal,' Attwood replied.

On the stage, a beaming Professor Stone walked to the lectern closing the buttons on the front of his suit to hide his paunch. He strode with purpose and jumped his six-foot frame over a step to emphasise that, even though he was in his sixties, he still considered himself a player. Although the jump was strong evidence that he retained the physical ability to walk, the unintended consequence was that it disturbed his comb over and left a large tuft of dyed brown hair askew. It was sticking up at 45 degrees, somewhat like a neglected Mohican. The bushy brown moustache hadn't been dyed at the same time as his hair and its much darker colour stood out as he stroked and preened it before he spoke.

Against the background of junior doctors and younger nurses there was no denying that he was of a different generation. His pinstripe suit and bow tie were the uniform he had inherited from the great surgeons he had trained under. Now, nobody but he, even remembered their names. He desperately wanted his name and legacy to be remembered. He inhaled the air and the atmosphere, as he puffed out his chest and leaned over the microphone.

'It's a great pleasure to be here, I'd like to acknowledge the great work of Mary Gallen and everyone in the executive for putting this together. They're all doing a great job on the sixth floor. I believe that we can now show everyone what success looks like, in our new hospital structures.'

Dr Attwood noted Mary Gallen beaming at the compliment from the Professor. She had the smile of an Oscar winner, which Attwood thought was ironic, as it was Stone's praise for her which was the award-winning performance.

'We are committed to developing a caring institution where the patient is the centre of everything we do. This new model of care will have a motto: *Our Patients' Treatment Is Central in Serenity*. We will brand this as the OPTIC programme of care. As a driving force of all strategy, care delivery and guiding moral ethos this will be our reference point back to what's best for the patient and only the patient. As part of this, I fundamentally believe in the apprenticeship model of training and healthcare delivery. That relationship between a mentor, who is a totally unselfish guardian and teacher for their trainees, is our key resource. We have a great bunch of guys and girls working here that can deliver a world class service.'

Dr Rossi clenched her fists on the desk in front of her. Her knuckles took on the appearance of distant snow-covered mountain peaks. She had had a career's worth of being talked down to as a *girl.* Even when she had qualified, wearing a stethoscope and a doctor's ID badge hadn't protected her from being called 'nurse' for years. She seethed when patients, especially women, looked over her shoulder for the boss, who was always expected to be a man. As a Consultant she was acutely sensitive to her clinical opinion being ignored because of her gender. It was probably just as well she didn't own a gun.

'As chief of clinical governance I intend to get under the hood of all aspects of the hospital and deliver something spectacular for our organisation. I have a vision for our organisation that is centred on a Serenity Hospital brand, of rapid access, quick, efficient healthcare. Thank you all for coming and I look forward to touching base with you offline over the coming weeks.' Stone said.

'Oh, and one last thing, as I will have more of an administrative role there will be a vacancy for a new Consultant surgeon on staff and I know we have a number of excellent candidates ready to step up for this promotion.' He scanned the rows and on reaching Jeffrey their eyes met in a silent, secret accord.

The rest of the room was oblivious and even indifferent. To Professor Stone, the title and the position were everything. He had become heir to his current position from the previous Professor and assumed that he had also inherited the respect and loyalty the old man had enjoyed. As the years had gone on, he had forgotten that the old Professor had earned respect by selfless, skilled hard work, teaching, and attention to detail and empathy for patients, staff and students. Stone had assumed that respect and loyalty were as solid as family ties and genetics. In a previous generation he would have been right. In a generation of internet influencers and trends that changed and sprouted like weeds on an unkempt lawn, he was a relic. In older, slower times Professors had control of careers and promotions, and dictated the narrative in a long game played out at leisure. Deep thought and contemplation had been made redundant in a world where choices and emotions were expressed with a click on an appropriate plant emoji.

'Wow, a permanent Consultant job here. That's incredible, I thought someone would have to die before that happened. I guess it's you, me and Jeffrey that are the possible candidates he's talking about. What do you think?' Ashley said.

Chris wasn't listening as he unfolded the crumpled scorecard and jabbed a finger at his *touch base offline* selection.

'Look he said it, it's a draw. Give me back my 20 bucks.'

Ashley shook her head, stood up and ushered him out into the aisle where they joined the departing crowd.

Rossi and Attwood remained seated, silent and contemplative. When they were able to talk it was in a sombre mood.

'Maybe it won't be too bad,' Attwood said.

'I could just about put up with him when he was tied up with the university and didn't get too involved with us. It always annoyed me when he took credit for everything that everyone else in the hospital did, in teaching, in research, in developing anything,' Rossi said.

'The difficulty is that he's very good at all that. He's a performer, a self-promoter and a very credible one. The hospital management aren't capable of seeing beyond that veneer of charm and bluster. Good luck if they think he's capable of delivering any change.'

'Don't get me wrong, I don't underestimate the guy,' said Rossi. 'He's great company. As a fund raiser and working a crowd he can kiss babies better than anyone. He's useful to the department. He gives great committee and can schmooze funding and jobs as well as the best of them. The difficulty is that at the end of the day he's out to make money and climb the corporate ladder. If he was just teaching it wouldn't matter. If he starts meddling in patient care, letting his self-image outstrip his clinical ability and scoring points by belittling others it's going to get nasty. It might kill careers and maybe a few patients.'

Attwood raised his eyes to the roof and exhaled as he digested the ramifications of the new appointment.

'I know we've talked about this for a long time. Is this the time and the opportunity to finally trip him up using his own web?' he said.

'Absolutely. It's about time, I've wanted to for years. I know it's more personal for you because of what happened when he operated on your wife, but I'm ready,' Rossi replied.

'I've tried not to let that influence my judgement. You do know, if we start this and try to get rid of him, once we start this, there will be no going back, we could lose control.'

'Look, there have been too many incidents, so many problems, and so many questions. We can't stand by anymore.'

'All right, the only thing we haven't factored for is this new Consultant job. I guess there will be external candidates, but we have our own three senior registrars who could apply. Where will they fit into all of this?' Attwood replied.

'I know the third-generation inbred cliché that Stone will want for the job. I don't like Jeffrey, but I could get over that if he was any good. He's the most dangerous kind of surgeon, that type whose confidence grossly exceeds their ability.'

'I know what you mean, well we know how to deal with that, just skew the job description requirements, get the right people on the interview board and create the different background stories that will need to be fed to the relevant people.'

Outside the lecture theatre Ashley and Chris were queueing at the coffee shop, unaware that they even were background stories.

'I like your bullshit bingo. It was the best part of whatever that meeting was about,' Chris said.

'Listen, this just got serious, there's going to be a Consultant job interview coming up. We need to make sure we don't have any more disasters like this morning, or we won't even be shortlisted.'

Chris nodded and his face lengthened as he realised how a Consultant job might change his entire life.

Ashley turned to leave 'I have an emergency case I need to operate on now. That Johnson man who came in last night, he's got an acute abdomen, very tender and sore. The scan shows free air in his abdomen, so he must have a perforation somewhere. I'll have a look inside and see what we can do. It's good just to be able to do some operating.'

Chapter 3. Green.

Everything was ready for Ashley's operative encounter with Mr Johnson. It mattered to both of them, she was struggling to prove she could be a Consultant, he could die if she couldn't. He had signed the form consenting to her taking a knife to open his belly to see if that would help the awful pain he had been in for the last twenty-four hours.

The form was the last piece of the jigsaw of tests and checklists. It normalised and legitimised what, in the street would be considered assault with a deadly weapon, into what might be the subject of heroic TV series set in a hospital.

Ashley wasn't sure which was more bizarre: people willingly allowing someone to use a knife on them, or the fact that there were people like her who relished the prospect of doing it. She had always recognised that medicine wasn't a career for everyone. Choosing to deal with the sickness, injury and people in their most troubling times was somewhat of a vocation, choosing to add on opening people up and it wasn't hard for her to see how some surgeons self-conferred themselves with divine traits.

The long black operating table was the venue for the contest between Ashley and the malevolence that was trying to kill her patient. It was framed on all sides by the shining chrome of the anaesthetic machine, X-ray viewer, the silver trolleys, and control panels. The instantly recognisable smell of actichlor and chemicals was tinged with the undertones of whatever human scent it was masking. The senses were always more intense in the operating theatre. For Ashley this was as invigorating as the smell of a new car. Even after five years, she hadn't lost that tingle of excitement when the trolley banged through the double doors to wheel in the next patient.

'Mr. Johnson, we'll move you over on to the table now and the anaesthetists will have you off to sleep in a jiffy. Don't worry. We'll look after you well and all that pain will be better when you wake up,' she said as she placed a hand on his trembling, cold, tightly intertwined fingers. His eyes had been flitting around the room, taking in the foreign environment. He focused upon Ashley. Her eye contact and touch were a lifeline of human contact that visibly relaxed his anxious expression and distracted him from the gnawing pain in his belly.

'Thanks doctor, just make sure I don't wake up dead,' he said.

'You're funny, really, we're not going there. I'm absolutely certain you'll be absolutely fine,' she said.

She turned away and felt bad for lying. It was only a white lie: she sincerely hoped he wasn't going to die, but nobody could truthfully guarantee that. It was just easier for everyone not to discuss that possibility with him.

He had what surgeons called an acute abdomen. It was a term that covered many possible diagnoses. The unifying thing about all the causes was that the patients were in so much pain that they would consent to anything to get rid of the intense pain.

She left the operating theatre to let the anaesthetists do their thing. As she walked, she visualised the operation. As her clogs clipped down the corridor she went through her checklist. She rehearsed what steps to take: she needed to remember the antibiotics and the anticoagulants, and to check how he was lying on the table, so he didn't get pressure sores or a burn from the equipment. She mentally walked through the key technical parts of the operation. Then she let her mind wander from the things she could control to the things she couldn't. Hopefully, he wasn't going to start to bleed: it would be better if it weren't a hidden perforation of the gut, one that she wouldn't be able to find. He had better not have a heart attack or stroke under the stress of the anaesthesia and surgery. That wouldn't be her fault, but she would feel responsible and it would attract the kind of attention she could do without.

The unknown unknowns were the ones that really worried her. Her patients needn't worry about terrifying outcomes because Ashley had more than covered all the horrible possibilities that could occur. Her paint box of possible scenarios was coloured by the apocryphal tales that doctors share with the glee of children telling ghost stories at Halloween. By the time she reached the window at the end of the corridor she had worked herself into a level of anxiety normally seen in a swimmer confronted with a triangular fin.

She fixed her glasses, tied her facemask in position and then put the visor over her head and fixed it in position. She had kept using the visor beyond when it was mandatory for Covid cases and now adopted it into her routine for every operation. She liked to think it protected her from what people might think or say about her.

She placed both elbows on the windowsill and looked out. The familiar scene calmed her nerves: she'd spent many moments at this window waiting for operations to start. From the fifth floor she could see across the road to the bell tower of the medical school. The road between the university and the hospital was a neon jungle of coffee shops, snack bars and convenience stores, serving the finest combinations of carbohydrates, fat, sugars and preservatives that could be eaten and drunk without needing more than two minutes and a microwave oven.

Scanning the Glasgow skyline, she passed over the grey, red and sandstone buildings. A haze lay over the city blurring the edges and colours into a pastel of calmness over the hubbub of humanity below. People were out and about living their lives carrying on oblivious to Ashley's impending struggle to save one of them.

She looked beyond the concrete towards the distant hills. Her refuge was to remember home. Imagining the countryside of her childhood was her safe space to escape this level of anxiety. She recreated the smell of hay and animals, and the sounds of her playing there with her two sisters.

Once she had restored balance she came back to the here and now. Serenity General Hospital was protected and overseen by a large concrete cross outside a church on one side of the entrance with a simple message urging patients to put their trust in God. This was balanced by an advertising billboard on the other side encouraging the population to trust their healthcare insurance to the private hospital wing of the Serenity Group. Over its six floors with 500 beds, those two images of religious icons and insurance payment income were intertwined and intermingled. Under this umbrella the hospital was a temple run by the merchants with the financial controllers playing the role of moneychangers. Like all hospitals Serenity was composed of different wards, clinics, offices and services. They all had their own little communities with relationships and character. Below the administrative level, the hospital had always been welcoming and friendly towards Ashley and supportive in all its niches.

Ashley's memories of college and her first jobs ran through her stream of consciousness. The friends, the events, the bright days were framed in her mind as a permanent photo album of uninterrupted bliss. She had an ability to filter out and even entirely delete from her memories the unpleasant, the difficult, even all the toil and hard work. In dealing with people, the experiences, memories and recollections that informed her personality and actions were unfailingly open, optimistic, and benevolent. Whether it was a coping mechanism or a life strategy, it was an effective shield against past and future unpleasantness. From the utterly pure to the entirely self-serving ones, her experiences had taught her that people weren't easy.

Shortly afterwards she was gently stroking the scalpel across the bare skin of the patient's abdomen. In the bright theatre lights the cold, sharp steel cut through the skin as easily as paper. The edges fell backwards exposing a layer of glistening yellow fat beneath. She paused, as she habitually did in those milliseconds between creating an incision and the body realising it was injured and began to bleed. In that fraction of time, she marvelled at the change from a blood free wound, to one when the surprised body began to respond, and multiple dots of capillary blood began to appear as its first defence and repair response.

She extended the incision from the bellybutton up as far as the lower end of the breastbone, noting with satisfaction the pinpoints of bright red blood, the clean yellow fat, and the pink skin. The profusion of bright colours, like a flower bed in spring, told her a lot about the health of the patient. Dark, almost blue blood would have told her the patient's oxygen levels and circulation were impaired, mottled purple skin would tell her the blood pressure was falling. A white or grey tinge to the fat would tell her she was too late, that this patient was in irreversible shock and would die irrespective of her best efforts. When asked about her favourite colours she would always choose reds, yellows, and pinks, however she never shared the macabre reasons for these choices. Dark blues, purples and grey or black colours abhorred her: she fervently hoped that if she ever had children, they wouldn't turn out to be Goths.

Now that she had a pleasingly geometrically precise vertical incision, 10cm long, along the abdomen with a sharp 90-degree right angle as it wound around the umbilicus, she was getting into her rhythm.

'Diathermy please,' she asked of the scrub nurse, reaching out with her open left hand and without taking her gaze off the incision. The instrument was slapped into her hand in a firm deliberate manner with the electrical cable carefully draped back along the table with sufficient slack to allow free movement. She could use it to channel an electrical current through the patient's tissues to burn and seal up blood vessels. She closed her fingers around the pencil shaped instrument, noting with satisfaction the fact that she was working with a good scrub nurse who had placed the instrument into her hand exactly the right way up and facing in the correct direction to be immediately used without adjustment.

Ashley relaxed in the knowledge that having a good nurse was critical to the proficiency of the surgery. With an efficient, sweeping, single movement she effortlessly brought the diathermy to the wound and, by touching the pointed metal tip against the exact site where the small blood vessels had been cut, she began to stop the bleeding.

Once the bleeding was under control, she used the electrical diathermy to deepen the incision and cut the layers of the abdominal wall. Using the diathermy to cut tissue used extra current and burned through the tissue like a laser in a James Bond movie. It also produced smoke and a harsh smell of burning flesh. Ashley instinctively looked across the table at the medical student who was there to watch and assist. This was the point in every operation where the visual panorama was flavoured with the scent of burning human. The sights and sounds of surgery being enhanced by the smell of particles, aerosolised as acrid smoke, was a seminal moment in deciding who was fit for a career in surgery. It was also the point in operations where medical students and bystanders most commonly fainted.

This was Ashley's main concern as she looked at the swaying figure across the table. He was a thin pale youth: she could only see his eyes, as he was gowned up for the occasion. She momentarily wondered if he was always pale, but the sheen of cold sweat on his brow as he started to sway told her that he was going to ground. She wasn't as concerned about him fainting, as much as the fact that, if he fell forward, he would contaminate her patient's sterile operative field. She reached across the table with her glove covered extended fingers and with the tip of her middle finger gently touched the middle of his gown covered chest. Much like a tree already cut through by a lumberjack, this final touch was enough to ensure that his direction of fall was backwards, away from the table.

He stumbled backwards, slumped against the wall and slid to the floor. Unfortunately, as he slid down the wall, his back was against the control panel switches and managed to turn off the operating lights. Even unconscious, he was an environmental hazard. As the other medical students removed the casualty from the battlefield, the nurses scrambled to restore light to the darkened room. Meanwhile, by feel alone, Ashley had reached the last layer of the abdominal wall before she entered the cavity itself.

She found this stage almost as exciting as Christmas morning. Once she opened into the abdomen she would find out if her diagnosis was correct, if the scans were right, if it was a cancer, or an infection and ultimately if the patient would live or die. Ashley valued her clinical judgements as much as the items on a letter to Santa Claus, and when she unwrapped an abdomen, she was deeply disappointed if it didn't contain what had been on her list.

She picked up the last layer to be opened, the thin peritoneum which lined the inside of the abdomen. With a scissors she gently cut through the layer of tissue, taking care not to cut through any organ or part of the gut that could be lurking behind it. Once she cut through it there was a hiss and a gush of air. The first sense to be deployed now was smell. She inhaled deeply through her facemask and tested the scent. She sought out the pungent smells of infection, or perforation of the colon; she was satisfied to sense neither. Next, she opened the peritoneum further and looked inside at the fluid. Here again she had a favoured pastel of colours that she preferred to see. A dark maroon colour might indicate a clot in a blood vessel, a light green thick exudate would suggest longstanding infection. But here, to her delight she saw dark green.

'Excellent' she beamed from behind her mask to the students, who were utterly confused and in horror as to how the green fluid sloshing out of the abdominal cavity and pooling on the floor could be described as excellent.

'Can you see the colour of the fluid?' she said pointing at the puddle. 'What does that tell you in terms of the diagnosis?'

Their faces declared that it had told them absolutely nothing. They couldn't have looked any blanker if they had just been asked to explain the Pythagoras theorem. While these millennials were incredibly good on Instagram feeds and social media follower numbers, they weren't great on basic anatomy, physiology or indeed any question requiring an answer beyond an emoji or longer than 140 characters.

Under Professor Stone Serenity Hospital and its medical school had developed an inclusive admissions policy. They were open to anyone who could pay enough, irrespective of ability and especially appreciated students from any country rich enough to pay triple the fees of citizens. One of the consequences of divorcing academic ability from entry requirements was that the offspring of this situation were rich, idle, and possessed of a huge sense of entitlement. As in any financial transaction, over time the balance of control and power shifted from the providers to the purchasers. Ultimately the dumbing down extended to downgraded educational standards with exams that were infinitely easier to pass than a kidney stone.

The process had been so gradual and all-encompassing that the medical graduates' opinions on diseases were little better than an average man in the street. The standard wasn't even that high. It was at the level of the kind of half-wit who appears on CNN, giving a vox pop in the middle of a hurricane, when any sane, rational, person has long since left town. Ashley loved the hospital and the personal and professional relationships and friends she had on every floor, however the medical school decline had changed that dynamic in a way she didn't like. She had become a doctor being taught by doctors who wanted to nurture and develop skill and empathy. Now the medical school was a commercial enterprise devoid of passion and designed to extract maximum revenue from a conveyor belt of students. She missed the human touch of great mentors as part of her growth as a person, now the faceless commercialism of the educators saddened her.

'OK, maybe let's take it down a notch, look at the colour: where in the body will an odourless green fluid come from'?

'Like, maybe it was something, he like, drank, you know?' volunteered one of the more adventurous sheep.

'OK, interesting. But in the normal course of events, can you think of anything that colour that people normally drink?'

'Well, broccoli or a smoothie with…'

'Sorry. Let me just put that a different way. What I'm getting at is that that's not a colour we would normally find appetising on a menu. Could it be something else?' she said.

She was quite disturbed, wondering how he had managed to get through four years of medical school without any knowledge about the colour, location, or nature of bile. However, while this kind of millennial was narcissistic, lazy, entitled, and fragile, they also were aware of the enormous amounts paid to the hospital and university for their education. So, they were pampered and protected by the phalanx of administrators, academics and educationalists who were funded from this trough. This unholy trinity of money-swallowing protectors was viewed by working surgeons, with some factual basis, as largely washed-up or failed doctors who couldn't treat or diagnose patients, or generally cope with working life. So they retreated into cosseted University roles instead of helping patients.

'But it's a good suggestion, thanks for that. Is there anything else it could be?' she asked. She pushed two large hand towel sized absorbent swabs into the abdomen as her mind wandered to broccoli smoothie recipes.

She was wary of upsetting the students, bearing in mind that Professor Stone was particularly protective of them, and the income they delivered.

'Anyone else got any ideas?' she asked with the friendly low tone and low expectations normally expected of a kindergarten teacher.

'Is it like a fungus… or blood poisoning ….or some I don't know….disease,' volunteered another,

'Very good' responded Ashley, 'it's always important to have infection as a possibility in any differential diagnoses. She felt almost dirty for resorting to positive re-enforcement educationalist methods.

She used both hands to sweep the swabs around the inside of the abdomen to mop up the fluid in the abdomen. She mulled how to progress her current teaching interaction with this group of students in which differential diagnoses now ranged from the improbable vegetable smoothie to a, never before described in a human, green infection.

'Could it be bile?' asked the one with fogging glasses balanced on top of his surgical facemask.

'Brilliant' responded Ashley, somewhat in shock that one of them had stumbled on the correct answer. She continued working, throwing the two saturated swabs in the direction of the bins behind her. Then she placed the retractor in the wound: this metal device always reminded her of a car tyre jack as she wound the ratchet and the two metal bars at the ends stretched out the incision until it was diamond shaped and she could see right into the abdomen.

'Now, for a bonus point, how did it get into the abdomen?'

'A perforated duodenal ulcer?' responded Foggy Glasses.

'Correct, that was exactly my pre-op diagnosis, and if you all look in here where I'm pointing, you see that hole just at the lower end of the stomach, at the duodenum: see it bubbling out a little bile? There again, you see it'?

Ashley looked again at Foggy Glasses and mentally filed away his photograph in her brain to ensure she could pick that one sparkly fish out of the shoal when it came to allocating interns after they graduated.

'So, to fix this, it's easy, just take this hanging fat beside the stomach. Like that, and just plug it in the hole like a cork. Now I'll just stitch that in place and this will all heal up in no time. This is what we call a Graham patch.'

'Why is it called that?' said one of the students.

'Well in surgery, often a surgeon who developed, or stole and popularised a technique gave it his own name. We've continued to use their name, sort of as a way of recognising and paying tribute to plagiarising, egotistical, megalomaniacs,' Ashley paused briefly and added 'from the past' just in case they went back to Stone to tell tales about her discussing surgical megalomaniacs.

'One PDS' Ashley said to the scrub nurse and she slapped the suture in its needle holder into her hand. She closed all the layers except the skin with a continuous stitch. Finally, she took the skin stapler and started a row of metal staples to close the skin. This was the reason she loved surgery: she had solved the riddle of why the patient was sick. She had made the diagnosis correctly and executed a perfect operation. She had every reason to think she had cured someone who might have died without her intellectual and technical skills. She took a moment to bask in the sheer pleasure of the process.

It had taken years to get to this level in her training and as many ups and downs as a series of *Friends*. In victorious moments she could forget all the lost nights of sleep, all the financial and emotional cost and the lost social life of a decade which it took to become a surgeon. Now it all seemed worthwhile. However, her daydream was cut short by Chris bursting through the doors of the operating theatre.

'Ash, we're in trouble, Stone's said he wants to set up a meeting with the two of us.'

'What, why?'

'It's the deadish thing, the family complained. He wants to meet us tomorrow morning at eight.'

She put down the stapler: the rush of euphoria after the operation dissipated. A complaint right now wasn't what either of them needed with the job interview approaching.

Chapter 4: Burger

The meeting wasn't as bad as Ashley had expected. Professor Stone met herself and Chris and seemed supportive and dismissive of the complaint. He didn't share the details of the complaint but wrote down their version of events in minute detail. Once they had left, true to his Machiavellian nature, he used the details he had obtained to compose an e-mail to Mary Gallen. In this, he outlined why neither of them were ready to be signed off as being prepared for independent Consultant practice and therefore ineligible to apply for any upcoming jobs.

For Ashley the rest of the morning was hectic, with sick patients, ward work and post-operative rounds. She paused over Mr Johnson, her perforated duodenal ulcer. All the surgeons adopted this sleight of hand, referring not to individual people but to their diseases. Taking the people out of the discussion made things more objective. It also made the process more like a football game where you didn't know the teams and therefore losing wasn't personal.

She was delighted with his day one progress, but made sure chest physiotherapy was ordered for him, to prevent pneumonia. She adjusted his anti-coagulant dose to make sure he didn't get a clot. His blood results were reassuringly normal, but she prescribed intravenous antibiotics to continue for the moment. Early feeding after surgery was her preference and the evidence supported that. But she was worried about the patch she had sutured into his stomach yesterday and decided to hold off on straining, or possibly blowing the repair with food for a day or two. Ashley always felt the first few days after an operation was like playing football in a sparsely laid minefield. Everyone had to play but you never knew when it would all go wrong.

Mr Johnson was tired and grateful, he raised a hand and waved as much as the attached IV line and his energy would allow.

She hadn't left any time to eat and headed straight for the afternoon outpatient clinic juggling in her head all the things that might possibly go wrong with him.

The waiting room was directly across the hall from the nurses' station at the clinic. It was full of silent patients waiting to see Professor Stone. As Ashley arrived he was leaving.

'Ashley, just the person I needed, if you could run the clinic this afternoon that would be great. You're well able to run an outpatient clinic at your stage. I've asked

Chris and Jeffrey to come along and give you a hand. There aren't too many patients due: if there is anything difficult just give me a call' Stone said.

Ashley had nodded and noted that while he had made the offer of being available to take a call, presumably on the golf course, the reality was that it would be about as welcome as a burning sensation when you pee. In an unusual epiphany for Ashley, it dawned on her how offering to take a phone call was a brilliant passive-aggressive tactic. To make the call, would amount to a self-declaration of incompetence or inadequacy, something no surgeon wanting a Consultant job could countenance.

As she machinated over whether this meant that Stone thought she was inadequate, or if it was a test of competence, her high from Mr Johnson's operation evaporated and was replaced by a gnawing unease. Anxiety about her operation resulting in possible post-op complications was exacerbated by a vague unease over the morning meeting with Stone. She lived and breathed her job and found it unfathomable that she might be in a difficult position with the Professor.

The waiting room had grasped that Ashley was currently the only doctor at the clinic and she could sense the disappointment that their afternoon entertainment was with the monkey rather than the organ grinder. Although it was clearly going to be a long afternoon, nobody left. The potential to offload their problems and woes onto someone else was too tempting to forgo. As each patient shuffled across the floor the remainder silently, but intently followed them to monitor their medical conditions, eavesdrop for gossip and assess their prognosis with keen amateur, ghoulish interest. The frequent fliers had a professional interest in making medical judgements on others and taking satisfaction where they felt their own life expectancy was longer than the competition.

Ashley picked up the next chart off the pile in front of Elsebeth, the outpatient clinic nurse, who was gazing into the distance as if she was seated a bar waiting for an offer. Ashley realised she was fixated upon the daytime program on the TV high on the wall.

'Hi Elsebeth, I'll call the next one so,' said Ashley. She responded with all the enthusiasm of a telegraph pole. Ashley wasn't sure about Nurse Elsebeth: she always had a glazed, uninterested, expression and now because of something Chris had said, she suspected that whiff of perfume was actually gin. She walked to the door of the waiting room and called,

'John Collins?'

A patient dutifully stood up and followed Ashley to the consultation room. He was a large man with low hanging, faded, blue jeans on which his white-vested, round belly sat like an enormous egg in a blue eggcup. His open red check shirt and baseball hat were liberally flecked with white paint. With a brief glance, trying to place him in a medical category, she decided he was fifty-five-ish, clearly overweight and a working man. Possibly a painter, definitely more ceilings than Sistine Chapel in that case. When they were both seated Ashley read the letter in the notes, which suggested a possible left inguinal hernia. She nodded with satisfaction: a hernia was more likely in a man occupied with physical labour and in those who were overweight, so fitting nicely with her Sherlock Holmes powers of observation.

She looked up at John: before she could begin to talk to him, she was distracted by the large right hand on the table. He had hands that were deeply brown from the sun, scarred, wrinkled and with fingers that were thick and wooden, like tree branches. But it was the fingernail on the thick thumb that caught her attention. Under the nail was a blue-black swelling. It was bulging and the stain of fresh red blood under the top edge of the frayed nail told her it was a recent injury.

'When did that happen?' she asked.

'Yesterday, dropped a paint can on it. Unbelievably sore, what can you do, just part of the job. I couldn't sleep last night, it was so sore.'

Ashley was delighted that it was a new injury. That meant that the blood under the nail would still be liquid and she could do one of her favourite party tricks.

'I love these, let me fix it for you.'

'Sure.'

Ashley took a paper clip out of the drawer and straightened it out. She wrapped some white tape around one end.

'I'll be back in one minute' she said and went out to the waiting room. She scanned the room, picked out the man she knew would have a cigarette lighter and borrowed it before the patient even thought to ask how she knew he even smoked.

Back in the room, she lit the flame and put the end of the paper clip into it until it glowed bright red. The tape on the end she held, stopped her from feeling the heat.

'Now John just put your thumb flat on the table and I'll just make a small hole and let out the blood'.

John obediently complied and Ashley dropped the lighter and holding the cold end of the paper clip between her thumb and index finger she placed the bright red end on top on the middle of the nail.

A little smoke and a smell of burning filled the space over the thumb. John looked on interestedly, sniffing the burnt-hair smell, but was quite comfortable. It always fascinated Ashley how impressed patients were when treated with a flame, red hot metal and a smell of burning. In medieval times those tools must have been enough to convince patients something magical was going to happen. The modern snake oil equivalents of mentioning a laser or a robot could similarly evoke that degree of excitement in a susceptible audience.

Ashley knew John was in no pain as the surface of the nail had no sensation. In about another second when the paper clip burnt through the nail, she knew to expect a squeal. Experience had also taught her not to stand directly in front at this point and she moved a pace to the side. John squealed, signalling that the pin had reached the right depth, she pulled out the paper clip and a thin jet of pressurised blood shot five feet across the room.

After his yelp John looked down at his nail. The throbbing pain was instantaneously gone and the nail bed colour almost back to normal. The tiny black scorched hole had been a small price to pay. He gave her a broad smile, hugely impressed with what modern medical technology could achieve.

The rest of the consultation was routine. She scheduled him to have his hernia fixed. He left with a cured thumb and utter confidence in Ashley to perform his next operation.

Ashley breezed out to slide the next chart out from under Nurse Elsebeth's elbow. She was starting to lean to the side on the desk but was still watching the TV, but her eyes resembled the last salmon in the fish shop on a Friday evening.

'Dorothy Parks?'

A large woman shuffled forward in her seat. Once she had displaced a sufficient volume and weight of fat over the front half of the chair, her posterior part began to elevate like a seesaw. She rocked back and forward to shift the momentum to the front. She was holding a large bulging, black bag with a multi-coloured scarf emerging from the top. As she swung the bag its added momentum propelled the pendulum arc further. Ashley was mesmerised and had to resist the urge to go over and add her weight to the near side of the seesaw to get things moving. When Newtonian physics released Dorothy, with a gasp from the effort and a sigh, she advanced across the room towards Ashley.

Ashley watched the performance unfold, restraining herself from looking at her watch. She already knew the time, but her subconscious was screaming, *show her you're busy and need to get on with this clinic.*

Once Dorothy was in motion Ashley ushered her towards the corridor and said, 'If you can just walk this way.'

Ashley took off with her brisk, business-like pace with her heels clipping along the corridor. After three paces she suddenly realised the absurdity of expecting Dorothy to walk as that speed. She felt embarrassment flushing across her face. It hadn't been her intention to mock the woman, but now it looked as if she was trying to humiliate her. She instantly slowed her pace, without turning around, to match the velocity she expected of Dorothy. Nurse Elsebeth at the desk furrowed her brow in confusion: watching Ashley's unexpected transition from normal pace to slow motion, she instinctively reached for the TV remote to unpause Ashley.

Ashley painstakingly led the way into the consultation room and walked around behind the desk. She placed the chart in front of her and motioned to the chair. Dorothy placed her black bag on the chair, pulled the chair back and then shuffled around to position herself. Spotting her bag, which was occupying the whole chair, she turned again, lifted the bag and looked for somewhere to put it down.

Out of politeness, Ashley didn't feel it was right to sit down before her patient, so she stood smiling as the seating equivalent of a twelve-point turn took place across the desk.

Eventually the bag went on the desk, the repositioning manoeuvre was repeated and Dorothy parachuted into the chair with a flop. As she landed she spotted the blood splatter across the floor from the previous patient's thumb. Ashley saw it as well and decided to ignore it. 'Well, Dorothy. It's good to see you again'.

'I had expected the wound to be healed by now,' was an indignant Dorothy's opening offer.

Ashley paused to formulate an answer. It just wasn't in her nature to respond to negativity with aggression or defensiveness, so she decided just to pretend she hadn't heard.

'So, tell me, you've been home for two weeks since the operation, how have you been?'

'Terrible, the wound isn't healing. I haven't slept a wink in two weeks. I haven't eaten a thing since I left hospital. My landlord has put up my rent.'

'I'm so sorry, that's terrible,' said Ashley, looking at the recorded observation sheet of the chart which somewhat inexplicably showed that Dorothy, despite claiming an inability to eat, had put on ten pounds in the two weeks since she went home.

Small talk wasn't Ashley's strong point. She sometimes wished she had Chris's gift of the gab and his ruthlessness. She decided to cut short the waffle and move to ground she was more comfortable with,

'How do you mean the wound isn't healed?'

'It's sore, it smells and it's just no good. I'm not happy and my hairdresser says it should be healed by now. She has a sister who knows a woman who had a hernia fixed once and she was perfect after three days.'

'OK, well everyone's different and sometimes it can take a little bit longer.'

Ashley decided not to get into the details with the patient but remembered that the most unpleasant two hours of her year, up until that point, had been this woman's operation.

She had come in as an emergency, with a painful right groin hernia. It needed to be operated on as an emergency. She had gone straight to the operating theatre and the anaesthetist had put her to sleep.

Anaesthetists varied. Much like the proverbial box of chocolates, you might get a soft-centred fudge, or a nut that could trigger a fatal allergic reaction. None of them were ever particularly happy doing emergencies. Urgent cases upset their orderly structure of day-long coffee breaks, reading the paper and gossiping. Gerry was no different. He was tall, loud, bearded and opinionated, but the surgeons all liked him. They could forgive his height, hirsutism and voluminous steam of right-wing diatribe because he was quick. There was no quality prized more by surgeons in an anaesthetist than speed.

Ashley, and even more so Chris, were of the surgical school that felt delays with such minor issues as anaesthetising a patient were complete anathema. Once they decided there was a need for an operation, they required instant gratification, like a dog when food is placed in the bowl. Safety, congeniality, fascism and even bodily hygiene could be forgiven in anaesthetists, so long as they were quick.

Once Dorothy was asleep, Gerry had launched into a politically diatribe, loosely connected to the patient, which Ashley choose not to engage with. She liked to think she was a better person that that, but in reality she feared recorded footage appearing on Twitter, followed rapidly by the loss of her medical licence.

For most of Ashley's hernia patients the problem could be repaired with a finger length sized scar on the belt line. She liked doing the operation as it was quick, technically satisfying and only rarely did anyone die: even if they did, it was probably the anaesthetist's fault.

In Dorothy's case however, to get near the area where the belt line would normally be, Ashley had to wrestle with a belly overlapping like a muffin top just where she wanted to operate. By pushing the belly up with a swab, she had been able to push it temporarily out of the way, almost like lifting up a bean bag to sweep underneath it. This had allowed her to clean and prep the area with her other hand and then apply the green surgical drapes in a square around where she wanted to make the incision. However, once everything had been prepped, the bean bag abdomen had flopped down again over the operative site. Eventually Ashley had managed to stick her left elbow into the belly and, by pushing firmly, keep it displaced enough to see where she needed to operate. The end result had been two hours of continuous elbowing and sweating. It hadn't been helped by the scrub nurse on the far side of the operating table. She had set up with her trolley between her and the table, thus placing a two-foot physical barrier in place, deliberately, so that she couldn't reach the side of the patient being operated upon. Ashley recognised this classic manoeuvre as a statement that the nurse wasn't going to help much with the case. Her impression was confirmed when the nurse called for a stool before the operation even started.

She had had to operate with one free hand and a little help from the hand attached to the elbow embedded in the overflowing abdomen. It couldn't have been more difficult if she had been performing the operation in a jostling nightclub. It was with significant relief that Ashley had applied the adhesive dressing to the wound so she could take her aching arm and elbow out from where it had been propping up the belly. Once she had removed the elbow, the curtain of fat had descended like the curtains at the end of a play and the wound and dressing had disappeared behind the enveloping folds.

'I think you left something inside me, or you gave me an infection'.

'Well, I think that's unlikely, we have procedures, a count of swabs.' However unlikely it was, Ashley felt her heart beating a lot faster and a feeling of unease and anxiety. She tried to remember: *could I have left a swab, oh please God not a scissors or something stupid... what if I left something inside that gets infected and kills her....*

She kept her blank serious doctor face, in spite of her sweaty palms, her shallow breathing and her mental turmoil.

'Why don't we pop over here behind the curtain onto the couch and have a little peek?'

Ashley sat impassively in her chair flicking through the chart. She couldn't focus on the words and used the chart as a prop to distract from her rising panic. She really didn't want to see Dorothy on the front page of the *National Inquirer* holding a two-foot-long piece of silver surgical equipment that had been left inside her in a classic medical blunder.

The meeting over the deadish episode was still hanging over her and she really didn't want another problem. Especially not with a possible job interview coming up. If she had done something or forgotten something and the patient was hurt, she could get sued, or there could be a complaint. She felt a darkness coming over her field of vision and her throat tightening. *You're not having a panic attack, not here, not now.*

She picked up her pen and, holding it like a knife below the desk, she stabbed herself three times on the outside of her right thigh. The sharp pain sent a shockwave through her body and the physical pain won the battle against her mental distress. Once she felt able to focus she stood up and walked across the room and around the curtain to the bedside with a barely discernible limp. She slipped a glove onto her left hand and, with an authoritative snap, settled the right glove in place.

'Let's have a look then…'

The scene of the alleged crime was just as she had left it two weeks ago. The apron of belly fat was covering the belt line so there wasn't any sign of the bandage on the wound. Ashley pushed up the thick apron and, while the smell wasn't great, it wasn't the awful stench of an *E Coli* infection: it was more like a kitchen bin. The lower edge of the white dressing just came into view below the pale pink flesh. She repositioned her hand and pushed to see if she could uncover more. Within the V-shaped valley where the dressing was, she noticed something poking out from the depths on the bandage. It seemed solid and egg-sized with a mixed brown and tan colour. She was perplexed: it wasn't intestine, and it didn't smell bad enough to be gut content or infection leaking from the abdomen. She felt guilty even though she couldn't figure out what she might have done.

'Let me just take this forceps and see what's going on here', she said as she reached with the silvery jaws of the forceps to grab the object.

It was soft, but sufficiently solid to grasp, so she positioned the jaws on either side and started to withdraw it. She still couldn't see what it was but, as it emerged, a piece of paper was revealed with the logo of two golden arches. Ashley was relieved and delighted that the problem wasn't her fault. She lifted it up in the air to show the patient: 'look I think it's a quarter of a quarter pounder.' She was reasonably confident that she hadn't left a half-eaten burger behind when she finished the operation. Otherwise, the operative site was clear and there were no signs of infection or complications.

'Oh, I wonder how that got there, I might have gone through the drive-through on my way home', said Dorothy, eyeing the burger fragment that had been living and fermenting in her folds of fat for two weeks.

Ashley couldn't tell if the look Dorothy gave it was of disgust or hunger, so she quickly dropped it in the bin just in case.

She mulled over assuring her that she hadn't left the burger behind at the time of surgery. She might have a professional responsibility to engage with Dorothy on her eating habits and the effects of obesity on her health. There was also the option of suggesting that she go back to her hairdresser and tell her the truth about the burger.

Hairdressers were like *TripAdvisor* reviews for hospitals and surgeons. It wasn't good for Ashley or Serenity to accumulate negative reviews in their world. She wondered what Chris would do? He definitely wouldn't engage and would probably breeze out of the room at this point. Ashley thought Dr Rossi probably would say something, but she was so polished and perfect she could get away with anything. Dr Attwood would definitely do the professional thing and discuss the obesity problem. Of course, he could combine words and people in a recipe that everyone found appetising.

'Well, I think everything should settle down from here. The operation has been a complete success. I would just like to mention your weight: in the longer term it's a major risk to your health. Perhaps we can help with that. We have a great program at the hospital I can get you into.'

'How dare you, just because I've had such an awful time after my operation, you're blaming me for it? That's outrageous, I'm going to sue,' said Dorothy.

'No, no….. I'm not blaming you, or saying you did anything. I just want to talk about your long-term health. I want to help and see if we can do something for you about your weight.'

'You have no idea…' said Dorothy, beginning to cry.

Ashley didn't have a pre-prepared speech for this occasion. She hadn't expected to be so badly received. She inched forward in her seat wondering if she should go around and hug Dorothy. But it just wasn't her style. It would be as awkward and stumbling as a novice trying to do ice skate.

'I'm sorry Dorothy, it's just maybe it's something we can help with.' Ashley squirmed in her chair and anguished, *why did I start this, I should have left well enough alone*?

'I'm not going to sit here to be insulted.' Dorothy walked out of the room, much quicker than she had entered it, oblivious to Ashley's apologies. As she walked past the nurses' station she was wiping tears with a tissue.

Nurse Elsebeth slid jerkily off her stool, walked around, put an arm around Dorothy's shoulder and guided her to a chair hidden behind the station. In an exchange of sobs and anger for coffee and platitudes, a peace descended. Dorothy drank her coffee and unburdened her woes to Elsebeth, who sipped from her own coffee cup as she listened.

As Ashley walked out to get the next patient, she heard Elsebeth talking,

‘Well, now, let me tell you, if it was me, the best thing to do is to make a formal complaint, let me help you with that, I’ll walk you around to the general manager’s office.’

The waiting room had eagerly absorbed the scraps of the drama between Dorothy and her consoling nurse. They walked down the corridor together towards the administrative offices holding hands. Ashley felt as if the world wasn’t being fair. Either she couldn’t read people and guess their reaction, or her delivery really annoyed people. She wondered if she and the patients would sometimes be better off if she didn’t try so hard to help.

Chris and Jeffrey passed the two women in the corridor. Chris spotted the red-rimmed eyes and looked down at his tray of coffee cups avoiding making eye contact. Jeffrey saw the signs of drama as well and jerked his head around to have another look.

'Did you give the fat woman bad news?' said Jeffrey.

'What? No, I don't, what do you mean?' said Ashley.

Chris shook his head and, after walking around behind the nurses' station, started to place the three coffee cups on the counter.

'You must have done something to her?'

'Why do you talk about patients like that? It's not her fault. She had a hernia for years, she wasn't able to exercise and she put on some weight,' said Ashley.

While Ashley and Jeffrey were engaged talking, Chris glanced up to ensure that nobody could see what he was doing. He took a vial of blue liquid from his white coat pocket: breaking the seal, he emptied it into one of the cups of black coffee before putting the lid back on.

'I guess she's lucky you didn't kill her like that old woman on Monday. But don't give me that '*it's not her fault'* rubbish. People make choices, when I'm a Consultant I'm not going to operate on people unless they are the right weight,' Jeffrey said.

'So, when you get back at your daddy's hospital, you'll only look after perfect people?'

'Guys, let it go,' said Chris as he thrust the doctored cup of coffee into Jeffrey hand. 'You use that room, I'll go over here. Ashley I got you one as well.'

Ashley scowled at Jeffrey, turned around and took a chart from the pile then grabbed a coffee cup from the desk and retreated back to her room. She sat down and opened the chart in front of her. As she read it she picked up the paper coffee cup and, although it felt cold, she decided it was better than nothing and took a sip.

It was cold, bitter and then it began to sting. She leaned to the side and spat the remainder into the bin. She took the lid off the cup and was smelling it when Chris entered the room.

'Are you trying to poison me?' Ashley said.

Chris slapped his forehead with his hand, 'Don't tell me I got the cups mixed up. I put methylene blue in what I thought was Jeffrey cup. You must have picked it up by mistake. Don't worry it's just a joke, it's fairly harmless, but just to warn you, it will turn your pee blue for 24 hours.

I thought it would be funny to have Jeffrey peeing blue and not knowing why.'

Ashley tipped the cup forward for Chris to look into.

'But this isn't blue, this looks like straight vodka.'

'Oh, that's okay then, I must have given Jeffrey the right one.'

'Yeah, but this?'

'There were other coffee cups on the counter, did you take Elsebeth's one?' Chris said.

'Chris, I know I'm a simple country girl, but don't you think all this seems to be getting out of hand?'

'No, don't worry. It's fine, after 24 hours it will be out of his system and he'll be fine. Unless he gets an allergic reaction and he dies or something.'

'Maybe I'm not getting this, but don't you think poisoning your colleague isn't good. And another thing: why is the nurse drinking straight vodka at three in the afternoon? Why do the patients hate me? I did a great operation. I fixed her hernia… I only wanted to get her some help with her weight and she went off the rails.

Maybe being a GP on the islands would be better than surgery for me.'

'Ashley, it's OK, Elsebeth always drinks after lunch.'

'What?'

'No, I'm joking: it's probably her birthday or an anniversary, or the anniversary of her divorce. Either way that's just how it is. But seriously, you're going to be a great surgeon, you know more than the rest of us, you're technically better and a decent person. Jeffrey is an uncaring, inbred mutation who needs a little poisoning now and then. You worry too much about small stuff. Now drink this.' Chris said, pushing the cup of vodka towards Ashley.

Ashley took the cup and poured it into the sink.

'I'm OK for vodka thanks, I've never liked spirits, even at three in the afternoon, but I appreciate the offer. Now, I can't believe I have to say something like this, but can you please go and take the drugged coffee away from your colleague in case it kills him?'

Ashley delivered her instructions with smile, but that façade masked a troubled mind. These difficult patient encounters and complaints could upset all her work in preparing herself for the dream job as a Consultant in Serenity.

Chapter 5: Stone

Ashley rocked back and forth on her white clogs as she stood waiting in the operating room. She was dressed in a green surgical gown, facemask, visor, and blue surgical hat. She held her hands clasped, almost prayer-like, at chest level. With each breath, a thin film of fog condensed on the lower half of her visor, then faded away until the next wave of breath washed over it. Even though the case hadn't yet started, she could feel the sweat gluing the scrubs to her skin. Standing around doing nothing, she felt almost comical, like a clown would feel waiting to come on stage.

Joy Dean was under general anaesthetic and covered in green drapes. Technically speaking, she was a 49-year-old female emergency presenting with bowel obstruction, secondary to possible right colon tumour. Away from the rigid clinical description she was a wife and a mother of three who loved a glass of Sauvignon Blanc in the evenings after the small people had sunk into their beds. The billowing green drapes obscured her entirely, apart from a square opening the size of an A4 sheet of paper which exposed her abdomen. Her belly was coated in a brown antiseptic liquid which bore an uncanny resemblance to fake tan.

Jeffrey was also scrubbed up and was engrossed in conversation with one of the nurses. Absentmindedly staring out the window, she saw Professor Stone getting out of his black Mercedes in the carpark. Like the man, the car was bulky, oversized and expensive to maintain. From the passenger seat descended a woman in a sharp lined dark grey business suit. *Hmm...* thought Ashley.

The anaesthetist had become one with his chair and was settled into his crossword at the head of the operating table. Lisa, the operating department practitioner, or ODP as they were known, brought a stool for Judy, the scrub nurse; when she sat down, they launched into a hushed but animated discussion. The tone of their conversation went up and down: Ashley could tell Judy moaning about surgeons and waiting for them. ODP's tended to be less tetchy than nurses and Lisa just nodded her head and repeatedly mouthed what looked like I *know, I know*.

Stone eventually stuck his head around the theatre door, he hadn't changed but had put a gown over his suit. That immediately told Ashley he wasn't going to do the operation himself, but would delegate it to them to perform.

'OK Jeffrey, sorry I was held up seeing patients at the clinic, but I'm here now, if you just prep and drape for a standard laparotomy.'

Ashley looked at the patient and the scrub nurse standing across the table, who now looked quite perplexed given the patient was already prepped and draped. She wondered if he had been drinking, or just wasn't paying attention.

'OK Prof, no problem, actually I've set up for that approach' Jeffrey said.

'Oh yeah, absolutely good work, that's what I wanted. So why don't you crack on and give me a call if there is a problem,' Stone said.

Stone almost never operated for emergencies like this one for bowel obstruction. The nature of emergency surgery didn't appeal to him. A social calendar of parties, black-tie events and an alcohol intake that could fuel a large SUV, didn't mix with out-of-hours calls to deal with appendicitis, knife wounds, road traffic accidents and the great unwashed public in general. It wasn't only a dislike for the lower orders of society, who had a predilection to stabbings and crashing their cars, it was a simple business decision. If patients weren't insured, then he didn't get paid.

It just wasn't a good use of his time, caring for patients who didn't pay, even if he happened to be sober enough to respond. He had long since avoided this type of activity and, when forced to cover it, he would usually delegate to the junior doctors. Trainee surgeons given an opportunity to experiment with operations have always been as carefree as puppies chasing toilet roll. Giving them access to knives however, does tend to lead to complications and fallout from their well-intentioned but poorly executed efforts. The reality though was that poor people didn't complain or sue as much as the rich. They are too concerned with just getting along and making ends meet to worry about why they ended up where they are in life.

Joy Dean was well-connected, and through social contacts she had asked Stone to see her and operate upon her. Stone had assented, as he always would to requests that played to his self-esteem. Personal requests from appropriate social classes for him to operate on them, as they pandered to his alpha male ego as effectively as their medical insurance plans guaranteed him monetary reward.

However, on this occasion, as organ grinder, he had in Jeffrey an appropriate primate to delegate to.

'OK, let's go' Jeffrey was keen to get stuck in; elbowing Ashley out of the way he reached out his open gloved palm to Judy, 'Give me the knife please.'

He wielded the scalpel like a cavalry sabre and laid open a foot-long gash vertically in the abdominal wall that wouldn't have looked out of place at the battle of Gettysburg. A second slash deepened the trench in the abdominal wall. Ashley kept her hands clasped together for fear of losing some fingers. She remembered a description given to her once, which she hadn't understood at the time, of Stone as being so duplicitous that you should count your fingers after shaking hands with him. But she feared losing real, rather than metaphorical fingers in this knife fight.

A spurter spat some flicks of warm, crimson blood across the green drapes. Behind the blue surgical mask, Ashley could see Jeffrey had his tongue stuck out to the side, almost like a five-year-old doing hard sums.

He now had a rent in the abdominal wall large enough to access the cavity behind. He fumbled to get both his oversized meaty hands and their sausage-like fingers into the abdominal cavity. He briefly wrestled with the intestines and, with a slurping sound flopped the links of bloated pink intestine tinged with blood out of the cavity and onto Joy's abdomen. Behind her facemask Ashley felt as if she was being suffocated. She inhaled deeply but it was as unsatisfying as drinking from an empty glass.

The colon refused to cooperate and remained stuck in the lower right part of the abdomen. In the depths of the abdominal cavity was a section of gut that was bright red and angry looking, with a knobbly, white, obvious abnormality growing out of it. This was the tumour that was blocking the gut and causing her problem.

'Nasty looking cancer, it's a bit stuck down' said Ashley.

Jeffrey nodded and abandoned his two-handed attempt to pull it out. It was stuck down towards the pelvis and draped over the pelvic organs. In front of it was a tight band of fatty tissue with a white line just under its glistening surface.

'What's that?' said Jeffrey indicating the band of tissue.

'Possibly an artery within the fat' said Ashley.

'No, it's nothing, give me a scissors'.

'Jeffrey, you see, I think, is that pulsating?'

'No, it's nothing, it's just in the way I'm going to cut it'.

'Jeffrey, just a question for my own education, could it possibly be the artery to the ovary on that side: would it be worth asking a gynaecologist to have a look?' This was the most tactful way that Ashley could simultaneously express alarm and subservience.

'Nonsense Ashley, if gynaecologists were any good as surgeons, we would let them operate on men,' said Jeffrey, laughing at his own wit. The nurses dutifully laughed along but gave looks that suggested they wouldn't be unhappy if in a tragic accident the knife slipped and amputated enough of Jeffrey for him to require the services of a gynaecologist.

Ashley began to despair: she hadn't operated much with Jeffrey before and she was realising that as a surgeon he was more Budweiser than single malt. In a flash of inspiration, she remembered a Netflix documentary on airline safety. They had a formula, a protocol, a way of ensuring co-pilots spoke up in the cockpit and voiced their concerns. If only she could remember it.

'Jeffrey, I have a fear, no, I mean an opinion, actually, it's a concern. Yes, a concern that if we go ahead and cut that tissue and we're too close to the ground she could crash,' she said.

'You're concerned the operating table is too close to the ground?' said Jeffrey somewhat perplexed as he took a step back and looked under the green drapes to the white tiled floor.

'I think we're OK there Ashley. Judy, can I have a scissors please?'

Ashley decided her role now was as a minor player and she was probably overreacting anyhow. It wasn't as if they were flying a plane anyhow, where hundreds of people could die. She paused to wonder if it would matter to Joy if she died in a plane crash or was killed by a surgeon. Realising she had gone way off reservation, she focused back on the surgery and braced herself for what the junior surgeons called the 'registrar's test'. This was where, if you couldn't identify a structure during surgery, you just cut it anyhow. If it hosed blood like a water main, dripped urine like a leaking tap or oozed bile like a wet sponge then then you had made a serious error. If not, everything was grand.

The meaty hand squeezed the scissors and, at the first attempt, chewed the edge of the band of tissue without making much progress. He grunted and shuffled, repositioning the scissors firmly across the width of the band of tissue. With a satisfied exhalation he closed the blades of the scissors again. Ashley almost thought she could feel the crunch of the scissors splitting the band in two. As she watched the two ends separated and the lower half whipped away like a miniature hose spraying blood. Registrar test result; fail.

'Ashley, there might have been an artery in that band of tissue' said Jeffrey.

Ashley silently nodded in agreement, she couldn't speak, for anything she said would be in the hysterical tones of *'I told you already, pull up, pull up we're going to hit the ground!'*

'OK, so, let's maybe get something, a grasper, a stitch or something'.

'Maybe a clip applier' offered Ashley, barely audible through facemask, gritting her teeth in exasperation tinged with a little satisfaction that she had been right.

'Nurse where's that clip applier?' said Jeffrey.

In the operating theatre it was as if a switch had been flicked and everyone was now on high alert. The heavy bleeding, the alarms bleeping and the loss of Jeffrey's confident bluster all signalled trouble ahead. All conversation had come to a halt. Most disturbing of all, the spray of blood had lashed across the anaesthetist's newspaper and he was now holding it with a disgusted look, shaking off the drops of blood. The pace of the rest of the staff moving around was quicker, deliberate, and focused.

The clip applier appeared and was rapidly conveyed to Jeffrey. It had a straight thin, silver body, two feet long leading to a small pincer-like grip at the top. The pincer tip closed the staples across the blood vessel before being spring loaded with another from the barrel.

Jeffrey pushed the clipper into the abdomen at the third attempt and then looked for the bleeder. The tissues were now covered in blood and congealed maroon clots, obscuring the bleeding artery.

'Should I get the suction and clear away some of the blood, Jeffrey?'

'Let me just get this, I think I can do it by feel,' said Jeffrey as he poked the clot and gut with the tip of the stapler.

Ashley was confused: this made as much sense as assessing the Mona Lisa using your sense of smell.

She reached for the suction. When she had sucked away the blood and clots the artery was still spurting away, but beside it was a large rent in the colon with faeces spilling into the abdomen. Jeffrey's blind application of the clips had missed the artery but managed to tear open the colon.

He grabbed several large white swabs from the nurse's trolley and, flapping them across the table, thrust the entire construction into the abdomen and successfully obscured the mess from the nurses and anaesthetists.

'Okay, I have a trick for this, Professor Stone showed me this one time. If I pinch roughly where the bleeder is with a clamp and twist around and around. That will stop the bleeding and we can just put a stitch under the clamp and then take it off' said Jeffrey.

Ashley looked directly at him, his eyes were narrowed, and his mouth was hidden behind the blue facemask. He sounded confident, but he always did. 'Are you sure? Should we call Professor Stone?'

'No. I've got this, he showed me before once anyhow. He calls it the twist. Artery clamp please?'

The nurse slapped the clamp into his outstretched paw. In the middle of a mess of blood, blobs of fat and intestine there was still a visible geyser. Jeffrey opened the jaws of the instrument and plunged it into the middle of the clutter.

The bump at the lower end of Ashley's facemask showed where it was stopping her jaw from opening any wider. Small animal roadkill was only thing she could recall even remotely resembling this mess.

Jeffrey closed the scissors like clamp shut with a click and began to twist it. Ashley counted out seven twists before the resistance stopped him twisting any more. She used a swab to clean away the blood and clots. The bleeding had stopped. Miraculously he hadn't caught any bowel or other organs with his clamp. The result was a four-inch-long twisted combination of blood vessels, fat and ligaments which resembled a wrung-out corner of a kitchen tea towel.

‘Excellent, stitch please nurse’ said Jeffrey.

With stitch in hand, he tied a knot on the end of his tea towel. The twist now resembles a ponytail with a thin blue string tying it up at the tip. He then began to repair the hole he had accidently made in the colon, while masking his activity with the overlying swabs. Once everything was tied off and the hole in the colon was repaired, he stood up tall again.

He removed the swabs and while Ashley saw the repaired hole in the colon: to everyone else in the room it looked as if this were just a routine if somewhat difficult, operation. He put a hand over the cancer and grasping it like a tennis ball, tried to move it left and right, to little avail. He tried lifting it straight up: only when Joy’s unconscious body lifted slightly off the table did he relent.

‘OK, this isn’t resectable, it’s too far gone and invading into the abdominal wall. Unfortunately, it’s not curable. That’s a pity, I’ll go and talk to Professor Stone. Good work everyone. Well Ashley, maybe you should just tidy there and close up the abdomen. Just keep her on a morphine pump, get palliative care involved and she’ll probably die in the next day or two. Thanks everyone.’

Jeffrey found Professor Stone alone hunched over a computer in the doctors' office.

'Professor, that tumour wasn't resectable. There's just no way I could get it out, I tried everything. There was a bit of bleeding, but I used your twist manoeuvre and sorted it all out. So, I told Ashley to finish and get palliative care involved. There's no need, but do you want to go in and have a look?'

'No, that's fine. If you're happy we can leave it at that. I'll talk to the family in a few minutes. But while you're here and it's quiet I just wanted to talk to you about the new Consultant job. Obviously I will support you, you've worked well in the department for the last few years. I've been impressed with your research output and the papers published with our names on them and all the teaching you've done for the department. I've no doubt you can do the job. Just remember I have your back and I just want to be certain that I can trust on your continued support into the future if I appoint you to the job?'

'Absolutely Prof, you know I'm one hundred percent with you.'

'Good man.'

Jeffrey was standing with his arms behind his back, with the whites of his eyes visible in a complete circle around his pupils, as he focused intently upon the Professor. He solemnly nodded his head deeply towards the floor in agreement.

'I'd want to thank you for your support Prof, it means a lot coming from you and I won't let you down.'

As a third-generation doctor bearing the same name, he understood the importance of loyalty and preserving institutions above all else. He also understood secret initiation ceremonies and was relieved that it wouldn't be an open competition for the job, but a coronation.

'Now keep a low profile between now and the interviews. Just be aware that Ashley and Chris are your competition. I'll deal with them, but be careful about Rossi and Attwood. They're not team players, but don't worry about it, I can manage them, but don't do anything to undermine your case for the job. Alright, we're good?'

'Absolutely,' said Jeffrey as he left and headed for the coffee room.

Stone walked through the changing room on his way to the theatre reception to talk to the patient's family.

He decided to change into scrubs before he met the family to let them know he had just emerged from the coalface. He changed quickly into baggy green scrubs and tied the draw cord tight at the level of his bellybutton. He stopped at a mirror in the bathroom to look at himself and splashed some water on the front of his scrubs creating stains which might suggest sweat, or blood that had been washed way. He put on one of the flimsy blue paper hats and pushed it back to a more world-weary angle then walked out to the waiting area.

'I dearly wish I had different news for you, but the tumour was too large, too advanced and too aggressive to remove. I know it's not her fault, but it's a shame she didn't get to us earlier. I've done hundreds of these operations and I have some of the best results in the country, but this cancer was just too far gone. Don't worry yourselves, there isn't a surgeon or a hospital that could have done any more for her anywhere. If it's of any consolation to you, she won't be in any pain: we will keep her comfortable and let things take their course,' said Stone.

He was sitting in the small waiting room on a row of four cold metal chairs. He had sat immediately beside Joy's husband while her sister was standing across the room. When he finished talking, he placed a hand on the man's shoulder and said, 'I'm so sorry, but life is cruel at times.'

Joy's husband struggled to maintain his composure: his head bobbed around, and he sought out corners in the room to look into, as he gratefully thanked Stone for all his efforts.

*

After Jeffrey had left the operating room Ashley began to tidy up the battlefield. There was still blood oozing from around the tumour where it had been used as a handle to lift her body off the table.

'I don't want her to die from bleeding tonight before her family get to say goodbye, so let's just tidy this up a bit' she said.

The anaesthetist was still aggrieved about the bloodstains on his newspaper: he couldn't concentrate on finishing the crossword, so he flung it in the bin. Once peace had descended on the operating theatre, Ashley gently began to work around the tumour. She trimmed away the bleeding edges where Jeffrey had been tugging and cut and sutured back the surrounding fat and tissue.

His 'twist' had stopped the bleeding, but it looked ugly to Ashley. Reluctantly she had to admit it had helped with the bleeding. She poked a gloved finger at the upturned twisted tissue. It wasn't plaited like a child's ponytail, it was just twisted and matted like a neglected horse's mane. As she nudged it all of a sudden it unwound and the blood began to spurt again. Ashley quickly put a finger directly on the artery and with direct pressure controlled the bleeding.

She lifted her head to look at the nurse. 'Stitch please'

By alternately lifting and compressing with her finger she was able to see the artery and securely stitch it. She was then able to cut out the twisted tissue and tidy everything up. Her pet hate was inelegant surgery. If it didn't look good it probably wasn't any good and that twisting technique appalled her. The fact that it had almost instantly failed, only confirmed her bias.

As the scene became less like a plate of half-eaten medium rare steak, and more like a conventional operation Ashley began to enjoy herself. She flopped the bowel from side to side, divided the attachments and tidied up all the loose ends. After five minutes she suddenly realised that the flopping wasn't just in her mind: the tumour was coming free. She grasped it in both hands and shifted it from side to side: it was definitely freely moving. She lifted it forward with her left hand and, taking a scissors in her right hand probed behind the tumour and was able to divide the last bands holding it in place. It was resectable, it was curable.

'Can you get Professor Stone on the phone for me please?'

Five minutes of fumbling, wrong numbers and different numbers eventually resulted in a message being left.

'Can you try Dr Rossi for me?'

'Dr Rossi here.' she must have been looking at the phone, as it was answered on the first ring. The ODP held the phone to Ashley's ear.

'Dr Rossi, Ashley here, I was just assisting Jeffrey with a Professor Stone patient. We were operating on a 49-year-old female with an obstructing cancer and we thought the tumour in the right colon wasn't resectable. I think he left to talk to the family and I was just finishing up and it turns out I've mobilised it and now it's just there ready to be removed, but I can't get him on the phone.'

'Ok, do you need me to join you?'

'No, it's OK, it's simple from here to do the rest of the operation, I just need a Consultant to tell me if it's ok or not'.

'Ashley, I guess we just need to remember what's important. Do the right thing for the patient, what's the right thing to do?'

'I'll remove it. It's probably curable, if I remove it now. Taking it out is definitely the right thing for the patient.'

'Bingo. Go for it: if there's any problem give me a call. There may be some communication issues to be managed around this, so I'll speak to Professor Stone in the morning,' said Dr Rossi.

Ashley's hands moved economically and smoothly: like a conductor she moved elements forward and back and brought them together. Enjoying the flow and rhythm she soon had the cancer removed and the two ends joined together.

As she patted on the foot-long white bandage at the end of the case she was well satisfied with her work. *What did Dr Rossi mean by 'communication issues?* As she was working through the possible pitfalls, she was interrupted by the circulating nurse.

'Did anyone give her a morphine and not sign for it? There's one missing from the drug trolley.'

Chapter 6: Team Meeting

'So, this morning's meeting. It's like the Colosseum: Nero, also known as Professor Stone and his generals Dr Attwood and Dr Rossi at the top table. They make all the life and death decisions, but the emperor might be assassinated by one of the generals at any time. The doctors, nurses, physiotherapists, occupational therapists, and students in the audience are the public spectators. In the arena are the surgical registrars, who are the gladiators, doing battle with the patients' charts and presenting their cases.'

'Actually, that's not a bad analogy. If anyone asks, you're Spartacus today. I need to keep my head attached,' said Ashley.

'I bet Rossi could take your head off with a little bit of local anaesthetic and some well-chosen words,' he replied, with a disturbed look that suggested he had woken up in terror from that particular nightmare.

'Yeah, and I bet you wouldn't argue with her about it either: she's a bit scary.'

'You think that too? I'm always a bit wary of women over forty: they've seen too much good and bad it makes them full of unpredictable rage. I can't read her at all: some days I think she's a poodle with shiny metal jewellery and then in an instant she changes into a junkyard dog with bits of metal embedded in its neck,' Chris said.

'OK, now you've just gone too far, I'm telling her.'

'What? Was it the junkyard dog thing, or the over forty bit? I can get even more carried away if you want, you know.'

'Yeah, I know.'

They entered the lecture theatre or Colosseum, well before the scheduled noon start. This was the focal point of the week. All patients on the floor were presented by the registrars and discussed. Any errors, identified risks and general gossip might also be aired in an unstructured, wandering mix of teaching, patient management and propaganda.

Chris looked around the old wood-panelled walls and tiered seating and imagined the great whiskered surgeons, teachers and leaders of previous ages holding forth, and expounding their unopposed opinions.

'Did you know that 100 years ago they used to bring the actual patients into these meetings? They used to put them in the middle of the room to be examined, poked, prodded and discussed. They talked in Latin so the patients wouldn't understand,' he said.

'It's no different now: we just use technical terms and acronyms instead' Ashley said.

The others began to arrive and take their places. The laughter and sense of anticipation resembled a crowd attending a play. Professor Stone walked in and took his place in the centre of the front row.

Chris sat at the table beside the lectern noting how well-suited Professor Stone was to the lead role. He could strut and expound on any given topic in any given setting. He never missed an opportunity to give his views or tell an anecdote. All of his opinions were delivered with absolute certainty and conviction.

Dr Claudia Rossi and Dr William Attwood took their places alongside Professor Stone. Dr Rossi eased her tall, slim figure and designer dress into the seat with the precision of a seatbelt clicking home. Dr Attwood, who was in a blue suit and striped tie, slipped into a seat on Stone's other side.

Chris looked at the line-up and thought about the judging panel of *America's Got Talent.* What was it about people's need to sit in judgement? And what did it say about those who were happy to spend their life in a prolonged audition.

It was Ashley's turn to run the meeting: she was standing behind the lectern connecting her laptop. She looked behind her at the screen, then looked down at the computer again and pressed some keys. Chris and Jeffrey were sitting at a small table beside her, with bulging manila folders, ready to record the decisions of the meeting in the patients' files.

Ashley looked behind her at the screen again, she bit her lip and tried pressing two keys together. She shifted from one leg to the other and nervously tapped the lectern with her fingers. She looked pleadingly at the table beside her and Chris got up to help. Jeffrey threw his eyes to heaven as Chris pressed some more buttons.

'For God's sake, just turn it off and on again,' Jeffrey hissed at them.

Inexplicably without them doing anything insightful, the first slide appeared on the screen.

'Good afternoon everyone,' Ashley squeaked at the room. She coughed to clear her throat and to drop her tone to a more sombre note. She used the time while the room was quieting down to compose herself. This presentation mattered to her: how she came across mattered. Technical ability as a surgeon wasn't unhelpful to progression: however, like any talent competition, advancement also required impressing the judges with showbiz skills.

The stakes in this six-year-long beauty contest were high. If the registrar impressed and succeeded, then a lucrative post and a career in a large city hospital could follow. If they failed, then a rural hospital might be their lot in life. Or, if they really annoyed someone in power, perhaps they'd end up in the Outer Hebrides, providing surgical care to humans and sheep alike. The upcoming job interview had made this presentation very relevant and real.

Of the three registrars, Ashley was the most nervous. She cared too much. She cared about the patients. She cared about other people. She cared about doing the right thing. By contrast Jeffrey cared mostly about himself, his pedigree, and his gelled blond hair. His inherited genetic characteristics had already assured him of exclusive golf club membership and a job as a Consultant. He didn't have the pressure of needing to succeed: he was just putting in the time and making the right social contacts. As a human being he was average, but as a schmoozer he had the skills of a salmon finding its way from the ocean back to the stream where it was born.

It wasn't quite clear to anyone exactly what Chris cared about. He was a bit vague about that too.

'OK, everyone: if it's OK, I'll start with the first patient on the list.' She stood with both hands leaning heavily on the table, head down, avoiding any eye contact.

'The first patient is Jack Salmon, 48, he's been an inpatient for three months. You all know his history at this stage, he's a fighter, a great guy. I'm due to present my research paper on his Marfan's syndrome at the conference next week to see if we can get any help with his case. I've prepared some slides to discuss'.

'That's fine Dr Brown, I don't think there's anything to be added here, and clearly if we couldn't help him at Serenity nobody else will have any options either. So just move onto the next one,' said Stone.

Ashley silently clicked through the next four slides. Each click consigned hours of work researching and studying the Jack Salmon case to the recycle bin. So intense was her frustration that a small sigh escaped.

'The next patient is Mr Connors, 57 with a pancreatic tumour and secondary spread to the liver and lungs,'

The standard meeting format was to discuss all the current in-patients and their management. The patient's diagnosis, treatment plan, progress and planned operations were all discussed. Any complications or management problems were highlighted and any learning opportunities from errors were flagged. In reality it was a bear pit in which scapegoats were sacrificed, egos were given an audience and medical politics, rivalries and Machiavellian strategy were played out.

'I have his scan images on the screen here' Ashley said.

Chris sat impassively, feeling sorry for Ashley: he knew that to her this was what it probably felt like to be in the dock at a murder trial. He was laidback and calm in general, but he could appreciate her innate goodness and Catholic upbringing, with its associated guilt whenever anything went wrong.

Chris looked at Professor Stone who, having stretched back in his chair with both arms outstretched on the table in front of him, was in the shape of a pyramid. He never displayed a guilty conscience: he gave the impression of being as pure as the Pope's internet search history. That aura and self-confidence was a big part of the construction of that pyramid of power. He used other tools as well: giving strong opinions on any topic under discussion was a favourite. Any scraps of knowledge he did actually possess he would pepper into teaching vignettes. Magnifying other people's problems was one of his most effective tactics to enhance his persona, by belittling everyone around him.

'So, as you can see, here…' Ashley was about to point out the abnormality on the scan when Professor Stone interrupted.

'OK, hold it there for a minute, from a teaching perspective let's get someone who doesn't know this case to take us through the X-ray. What about one of the students? Yourself?'

The student he had indicated to, turned to the screen and looked deeply into the image.

'Eh, mmm, this is like a CAT scan, yeah.'

'Yes, excellent, well done, that's right, now maybe if we could be a little more specific. Can you see any abnormality that might be a cancer,' asked Stone

The student surveyed the swirling black, white and grey tones on the screen and with all the insight and subtlety of a pig looking into a washing machine, responded, 'Is that supposed to be there?' he said pointing to the patient's heart on the screen.

'Well, yes, good try, if we look down here you see this grey area… just there, that's the tumour in the pancreas, and well done… you can sit down again.'

The student sat back his seat with a smile which suggested he was convinced that his contribution had just saved a life. `

'For the other students, is there a test for pancreatic cancer? Anything to test for? Maybe a blood test… any suggestions?'

He was rewarded with a series of eager faces, but no answers. Chris watched bemused: he knew that this group were about as likely to come up with a clear answer as a Quentin Tarantino movie. They were a pampered product of the system. The traditional model that Chris had endured of rote learning, memorisation, rigid examinations and ritual humiliation no longer existed. Theirs was a world of emotional role play, avoidance of difficult situations and ongoing educationalist assessments of self-absorbed drama that just didn't matter in the real world. *Just don't ask them how they feel about the question, or we'll have two hours of snowflakes' melancholic wallowing in how unfair life is for them.*

Having made the error of looking for facts, rather than feelings, Stone had to fill the silence himself: 'Yes, the Ca19-9 blood test can tell if it's a pancreas cancer'.

Ashley looked around at the silent blank faces and silently hoped that she would die suddenly in old age and not require medical care from any of them. Chris noted how delighted Stone was with himself for having correctly answered two of his own questions. It was astonishing that such a banal attempt at a teaching intervention could fulfil his academic responsibilities and justify his bloated salary.

'So, we'll plan to operate on Monday and remove the tumour,' Stone said.

The sharp crack of splintering wood drew everyone's attention to Dr Rossi's place at the table. Her face was impassive as she brushed the fragments of a fatally injured pencil off her hands and her black skirt. After a long couple of seconds, she spoke. 'Can you just educate me a little here: he already has secondary spread, Ashley you said that at the start. So, if it's spread to the lungs it's incurable, right?'

'Yes, that's correct' said Ashley.

'So, operating will be futile, he certainly won't live a day longer: surgery might kill him immediately, taking away whatever time he might have left. Recovering will be difficult, painful, and will keep him in hospital for a long time. Might he not be better off with a prescription for a fishing rod and a six-pack to enjoy some quality time before he dies?'

In the seconds that followed, any passing observer looking in the window of the room at the silent, unmoving, non-breathing group would think they were looking at a still photograph. Seemingly couched as a simple question, this intervention was anything but. The first shots had just been fired in the battle to take down Stone and get Ashley and Chris appointed. In this forum, with its generations of history, hierarchy, protocol, and pinstripes, this challenge was heretical.

'I find it's the best way to relieve symptoms,' Stone said clearly unprepared for this challenge to the status quo.

'Well, yes, killing him with an operation will certainly make him complain less.'

Stone didn't look at Rossi but scanned the room. He was unused to his infallibility on any given issue being questioned. 'He's very keen on us doing something for him.'

'Absolutely, I get that, it's very important that we don't let patients feel we've given up on them. Maybe doing something like talking to him and being honest about his chances might be an option.'

Attwood slowly straightened up in his seat and looking directly at Ashley he spoke softly but clearly. 'This is a difficult case. I would say that anyone can suggest doing an operation. Good surgeons can do these operations, great surgeons know when not to.'

A medical student with no insight, no people skills and a total absence of appreciation of passive aggressiveness and therefore a fine career prospect for pathology, interrupted the tension. 'What about an Oncology consultation for chemotherapy or radiotherapy?'

Stone turned around in his seat. He clearly welcomed the intervention and pursed his lips in anticipation of delivering a sermon to a more appreciative audience. 'Well, the first thing to realise is that my surgery is the only thing that helps. Oncologists with their chemotherapy, only poison people to a point just short of death and even then, it's never clear what that achieves. As for radiotherapy, invisible rays to cure invisible cells that might not be there at all, that the treatment won't affect anyhow. What's more, is that all their evidence comes from trials that are designed and interpreted by themselves, knowing that a positive result will fund their next Mercedes.'

He paused for a gasp of air now that he had established the supremacy of surgery. Having done everything short of beating his chest to establish his primacy with this display to the students, he turned back to the front of the room and elected not to engage with Dr Rossi's squabbling commentary.

'I'll discuss it with the patient again later. Carry on Dr Brown,' he said with a dismissive gesture.

Ashley carried on.

'The next patient is Louise Stark, 36, Professor you did a laparoscopic appendectomy for her 48 hours ago.'

'Oh yes…she had the worst appendix I've seen in twenty years.'

Chris had been at the operation; he didn't think it had been too bad. He could however decode Stone's speech patterns and this labelling of something as the worst was a repetitive theme. Calling something the worst he'd ever seen, shifted responsibility away from him to the patient, who was clearly responsible for their errant organs, if any problems or complications occurred. Conversely, if everything went well he was solely responsible for saving the day and possibly the patient, despite their awful gizzards.

'Just for the students the big advantage of laparoscopic, or keyhole surgery is that patients recover sooner and get home earlier, so she should get home today' said Stone.

Ashley scanned the room looked for the door, shifted from one leg to the other and then replied.

'Well, yes that was the plan, it's just she's had a lot of pain…'

‘Yes, yes some people just have a low pain threshold, get her up and out today,’ Stone said.

‘Yes, the thing is she had a temperature and her white cell count is raised.’

‘That’s just a post-operative response, which will all settle’.

‘OK, great, it’s just… she also has what looks like gut content leaking from the wound on her abdomen’ Ashley said looking deeply into the computer screen and avoiding eye contact.

A sudden electrical current ran through the room. Everyone was silent, upright, and focused. Even the slowest medical student realised that didn’t sound good. Chris knew just how bad it was: he absorbed the electric energy and felt it concentrating and building in the hairs rising on the back of his neck. After digesting this information for a few seconds Stone lifted his arm off the table and gestured to the registrars sitting in the front row,

‘Chris, did you notice anything when you did the operation,’ Stone said.

Chris felt a cold shiver run up his spine immobilising him rigidly in his seat. He hadn’t done the operation. Stone had. He wanted to object, to jump up and to launch a *you can't handle the truth* speech from the dock, but that wasn't the way things worked in Serenity. While his brain was in overdrive in indignation, all his mouth could do was open and shut like a goldfish and finally eject a less than articulate 'Nope.'

'OK, well I'll see her on the ward round later, who's next,' Stone said.

Ashley clicked onto the next patient.

'Joy Dean is a forty-nine-year-old female emergency presentation with bowel obstruction secondary to possible right colon tumour' Ashley said.

There wasn't any reaction from Stone. Ashley looked to Dr Rossi who was deeply engrossed looking at either the rings or the polished nails of her left hand.

'She had a laparotomy last night.'

'Oh yes, the woman with the unresectable cancer' Stone said.

'Yes, so we…'

'Yes, terribly unfortunate for her, so young and all. Just for the students benefit, sometimes young people present out of the blue, with disease that's just not curable. This woman had an advanced malignancy, one of the worst I've seen. All we can do now is make her comfortable. I've operated on so many of these and saved them, when they came earlier, but the key thing now for her is symptom control, for her last few days. I've already explained everything to the family, and they've accepted the inevitable,' Stone said.

'Professor, I think, perhaps… Did Dr Rossi have a chat with you about this patient?' Ashley said.

Dr Rossi looked up and gave the 'ahhh' sound of someone who just remembered they had forgotten there was something they had to do.

'Yes, yes, that's right, Professor I meant to call you about this case. There were some developments intraoperatively. Dr Brown phoned me last night and, when it became apparent that the tumour could be removed, I told her that was what she should do. As your *OPTICS* program's motto says, our patients' treatment is central in Serenity, so that's what we did. I meant to tell you earlier.'

It didn't require any technology or computerised monitor to see Professor Stone's blood pressure rising. The casual, offhand way that she spoke to him hit hard. A purple haze rose sequentially over each of his three double chins and flushed up through his jowls before enveloping his entire head. From Ashley's elevated perspective she could see the pink bald spot acting like a cork, as it changed colour to match the purple torrent washing beneath and pulsated against the pressure building below.

Stone paused, he sensed that something in the undercurrents at Serenity had changed utterly. He supressed his anger and his immediate desire to attack as the best form of defence. 'Of course, we always do the right thing for the patient. But you know her family will be disappointed; I'd explained she was likely going to die soon. Of course, removing it now just puts her at risk of where the bowel is joined up leaking, or post-operative pneumonia, or sepsis, or a clot. So, she's probably going to have an unpleasant death and her chances are very unlikely to improve.'

'Absolutely, I understand those risks Professor and, just to be clear, I instructed Ashley to do it, so I'm happy to deal with any fallout that there might be. However, Dr Brown has given her a chance of surviving and I think that's fantastic. I'm sure her family will understand.'

The rest of the patients were discussed without any further drama. At the end, Dr Attwood spoke. 'Just before we finish, can I just remind you all about the need for attention to accurate recording of the use of opiates in the patients' drug records. There is some morphine unaccounted for after some cases, from the unsuccessful cardiac arrest on Monday and from the operating theatre stocks. I'm sure it was used appropriately, but whenever drugs are unaccounted for it raises concerns that they could fall into the hands of someone abusing morphine. So just be aware and fill in the records accurately.'

The meeting ended and, as everyone retreated out of the room Chris looked at Ashley grimly gathering up the charts: he went over to help.

Dr Rossi strolled out with Dr Attwood. He lowered his head and turned towards her so that he could see her face and watch her response.

'Did you actually forget to tell Stone about that case?' he asked.

'Where's the fun in warning him in advance?'

'I thought there was something odd about that.'

'Why, did I make it too obvious? I thought I did that really well' she said.

'No, no… you did it really well, it's just that I know you. So, what now?'

'Let me just make my apologies now,' she said: she followed Professor Stone and, once they were outside, manoeuvred him into an alcove under the grey bare concrete stairs.

'I tried to call you about that Dean woman, but I couldn't get you, I knew that you were probably busy, so I didn't pursue it. Sorry about that. But Ashley did ring me, and I told her to go ahead, it was the right thing to do in any case,' she said.

Although the tide of purple that had been covering his jowls had receded, some rogue waves began to flush across his face again.

'I don't accept that. She ignored a direct instruction. She's put me in an exceedingly difficult situation with the family. This is an issue of governance: behaving in a responsible, dependable, safe manner. We simply can't have maverick surgeons flouting the rules, behaving erratically, and undermining senior clinicians.'

'Come on now, you're being unreasonable. She's a fine technical surgeon and she probably saved that woman's life. We can explain to the family that things have changed. Besides, isn't that what it's all about, doing the right thing for the patient?'

'That's not the point, this is the real world, and I decide what's right for my patients. It's not about this patient. Anyone can operate, obeying instructions is the critical skill. Fine, she took out the cancer, but that woman will die of complications or from the cancer coming back so she's only delayed the inevitable.'

'Look, by that reckoning, all operations are futile as we're all going to die of something. She's definitely given her more time and maybe a chance of recovery. But we need to move on from this, can we?'

'Absolutely not, she has to go. It's not open for discussion. Anyhow, it's not the first time: she tried to resuscitate an elderly woman a few days ago against my explicit instructions. In my new role as director of clinical governance I can't have junior doctors undermining me in that way. Also, I now have a clear responsibility to address the implications of this deviant behaviour,' he said walking away drawing the conversation to a close.

Dr Rossi was left behind in the shadow of the stairwell to wonder how Serenity's moral compass had descended to rock bottom.

Dr Attwood, who had been observing from a distance came over to her. 'Well, how did that go?'

'Predictable enough: he wants to sack her' Rossi said.

'He's taken the bait in that case. It's too easy, a guy like that who is all ego and no principles always lashes out at threats. He just can't play the long game like you Claudia.'

'It's important to get next phase right, it will probably come at the Surgical Division Meeting next week. I'll just go back inside and talk to the children and make sure they behave the way we want,' Rossi said.

Inside the lecture theatre Chris and Ashley had organised the charts into a single pile.

'You look like you might need some of that missing morphine,' Chris said.

'OMG, did you see how mad Stone was over the woman I operated on? Dr Rossi should have told him. Did you hear all the awful things he said could happen to my patient?'

Dr Rossi's return to the room broke the moment, she walked over and stopped in front of them.

'So, guys…' she folded her arms and looked down at the worn carpet as if for guidance. 'I had that chat with Professor Stone about the case the other night. He's a bit pissed, I think it's a bit unreasonable: it's simply because you completed an operation he said couldn't be done. It's all a bit childish really, but we need to be careful. There are few creatures as dangerous in this place as an academic with an aggrieved ego. Even more so now that he has this new job. He's taken it as a personal insult. He also brought up some case of an elderly woman who died after you resuscitated her. He's looking for reasons to screw you over Ashley, so just keep your head down. Watch yourself and I'll chat to you later.'

Chris and Ashley were left alone in the empty echoing lecture theatre. Dr Rossi's words had clearly shaken Ashley.

Chris tried to reassure her, 'It's tough Ashley, this is absurd. You kill an old one and he gets upset, you save a young one, he's upset again.'

Chapter 7: Roundish

Professor Stone's ward rounds came an hour after the team meeting and were always crowded. This morning, in addition to the two nurses in blue scrubs, there were twelve assorted doctors and medical students in the room. The students had oversized white coats bulging with reference material and notebooks. The doctors wore green scrubs, some with sleeves rolled up to flash biceps and extroversion, while some were in white coats with neatly arranged coloured pens in the top pocket declaring their place on the autism spectrum. Just as a bride never wants an attractive bridesmaid to deflect attention from her, Stone liked to populate his ward round entourage with fawning half-wits, sycophants, and enough young and naïve types to make him look good.

Louise Stark was lying on the bed propped up on two white pillows at a 45-degree angle. She was still, silent, and rigid. Her fixed expression betrayed little. Every so often a tiny grimace of discomfort was followed by slight raising of the eyelids and dilation of the pupils, betraying otherwise invisible pain and fear.

It was 48 hours since Professor Stone had operated upon her. Lying in her hospital bed she almost appeared suspended between an intravenous drip above her and anonymous tubes below her. The towering phalanx of white coats around the bed over her, emphasised just how vulnerable she looked: she was surrounded by a pack, of whom she knew little, forced by her circumstances to put herself at their mercy.

When she had developed abdominal pain, her husband, a GP himself, had contacted Professor Stone. He knew Stone socially, mostly through drinking at the bar, a skill at which both of them excelled. Unfortunately, despite being a doctor, the husband had underestimated the risks of judging professional abilities and technical skills, through unverified and uncorroborated tales of surgical heroism in late-night sessions at the bar. His wife was now enduring the consequences of bad judgement on her husband's part and excessive hubris on Stone's part.

Chris rolled his sleeves up a little further and looked on from the back of the crowd contemplating what a great leveller complications were for doctors. He had seen operations go wrong, predictably, reliably and for all types of patients and surgeons. His experience was that the majority of problems weren't because someone had botched it up. All surgeons have an occasional disaster, not of their own making but simply because biological organisms like humans are fickle healers and vulnerable to infection, poor healing, allergies and inexplicable elements. Without the patients co-operating by healing, surgeons were utterly powerless. If the patients didn't heal and develop scar tissue, then no wound would heal and, where bowel, blood vessel or heart valves were sutured, the carefully manufactured repair would simply disintegrate, with calamitous results.

Louise Stark had suffered a truly catastrophic result.

'Well Louise, first of all thankfully we found no evidence of cancer,' said Professor Stone.

Louise couldn't have looked more surprised if Stone had collapsed to the floor. Given that she had been admitted with appendicitis, the team were equally astonished at his pronouncement that she didn't have a disease that nobody had ever thought she had to begin with. The flock of doctors and nurses were sufficiently professional not to betray any emotion or inkling that would undermine Stone. The *omerta* among medics was so ingrained at Serenity Hospital from earliest student days that they all received this news with the blankness and solemnity of poker playing nuns.

Chris drew in a breath as he inwardly acknowledged the sheer audacity of introducing such a distraction into the discussion. Stone had succeeded in disrupting and upending everyone's understanding of the situation to an extent that very little afterwards would make sense either.

'No cancer, that's great, I hadn't thought… but it's good that I don't have that' said Louise.

Professor Stone examined her abdomen with a furrowed look on his brow. He tilted back his head and gave a confident sounding 'Ah.'

He noted the small red scars on either side of her abdomen where he had attempted a laparoscopic or 'keyhole' approach to the operation. He then went on to lift the large pad covering the wound in the center of her abdomen. There was a semi-solid brown liquid oozing through the surgical scar.

Stone gave a small 'mmm,' without betraying any emotion.

Ashley was in the front row: unlike Stone her face contorted on seeing one of her least favorite colors oozing out from under the belly button. Once the bandage was lifted more fluid emerged and a rivulet of brown fluid with flecks of green over spilled from her belly to her left side. It ran onto the white sheet creating a watery stain with the specks of solid matter sieved out sitting on top of the fabric.

At that point, the pungent smell reached out and slapped Ashley across her face. She recoiled and she tried to take a step backwards. She was hemmed in and, as she backed away, her heel landed on the foot of one of the students standing behind her, who was straining to see through the crowd. He became a victim of fashion as her stiletto heel crunched onto his little toe. He yelped and pulled away. The domino effect rippled through the crowd on that side of the bed like a half-hearted Mexican wave. As the student pulled his foot from under Ashley's heel she almost fell and as she grabbed the white coated arm beside her, she unintentionally said 'Oh shit.'

The patient had been scared but silently watching Stone. Mistaking Ashley's trip as a reaction to her abdominal wound, her façade of keeping up a brave face crumbled. Tears welled up in her already red-rimmed eyes, her lips trembled, and she started to shiver.

The distraught woman's abdomen, that could have been a scene in a horror movie, hadn't produced any emotion from Stone. However, he now flashed an irritated look at Ashley.

As he turned back to Louise, Chris tracked his facial expression. The anger that he had flashed at Ashley fell away, almost like a curtain falling. The eyebrows lifted, the forehead furrows relaxed, the head tilted backwards a fraction and the mouth widened. He addressed her directly from the advantage of his height above the bed: 'Not to worry, this is quite common, and it will all settle down: the most important thing is that you don't blame yourself.'

Her bafflement was clear. Up to that point it hadn't even occurred to her to blame anyone, least of all herself. Chris saw how stunned she was and the dawning erroneous realization that she must have done something terrible to have had this misfortune descend upon her.

'So, your immune system is clearly a bit low and you aren't healing well. But we'll just sit tight, and it will all be fine.' Stone airily smiled at the patient and patted her on the head as he turned to leave the room.

Ashley stayed near the back of the procession as it moved to the next room and whispered to Chris. 'What actually happened there'?

Chris edged backwards so they were separated from the group and whispered 'he must have botched the appendix and put a hole in the bowel and now it's leaking out through the wound. That's not good.'

Just as they were entering the next room Jeffrey sidled up to Professor Stone and said 'difficult situation that, of course that happens sometimes with teaching cases: you mentioned at the meeting this morning it was Chris who did the operation wasn't it?

Stone nodded in approval then turned with a grimace to Chris and said, 'Not a great result there, Chris, I hope it settles down or she'll be very upset with you.'

Chris was appalled, for the second time Stone was peddling a lie that he was responsible for this disaster. Even if he had been responsible, which he wasn't, it was a gross breech of the unspoken covenant between Consultant and registrar for Stone to blame him in front of the whole group. From time immemorial, generations of surgeons there had handed down the understanding that teachers and Consultants were ultimately responsible for the care of all of their patients. Errors by surgeons in training were discussed between themselves, or used as educational experiences, but at the end of the day, the Consultant accepted personal responsibility for all outcomes, good or bad. Chris clearly didn't recognize that he had been set up by Stone and Jeffrey. They needed him to be sidelined before the job interviews and this was a bad case outcome that needed a scapegoat to be associated with it.

So public a rebuke, in front of other doctors, nurses and students, was clearly also a tactic from Stone to preserve his own reputation. However, it had not gone unrecognised by Chris that it was Jeffrey who had given Stone the escape clause. He had come to expect that Stone would shaft anyone who was a threat to his reputation or his ego, or even someone within his orbit whose positive light might detract from the Professor's presence in the spotlight. But Jeffrey now obviously had a dog in this fight: for him to ingratiate himself with Stone by offering up Chris was a deliberate assault that wouldn't be forgotten or forgiven.

Ashley and Chris shared a look, clearly the competition for the new job had gone up a notch.

Ashley stepped forward to present the next patient to Professor Stone. Curled up in the bed fixed in the shape of question mark was an elderly woman. Clearly time had eroded Nancy Mason's physical and mental wellbeing and then gradually immobilised her body and mind. As Ashley explained, she was now in a nursing home, poorly responsive, totally dependent and, while she had presented with abdominal swelling the team had decided not to intervene and wanted to sign her off as not for resuscitation. Ashley summarised the situation and looked up to Stone for his assent.

'So, if you agree Professor, we can document the not for resuscitation status and consult palliative care.'

The students were oblivious to the significance of this statement, but the doctors looked at each other and somberly shrugged and inwardly sighed. Declaring someone not for resuscitation is the surgical equivalent of a boxer's trainer throwing in the towel, except this was throwing in the towel on someone's life.

Ashley tried to advance the administrative proposal by opening the chart with the DNR form ready for Stone to sign. After her recent experiences with resuscitation status and elderly women, she was nervous and treading from one foot to the other. She nudged the beige chart further across the bedside table towards Stone as a physical prompt.

She felt uneasy at reducing the final act in this person's life to the filling in of a page in a chart that allowed the doctors to divorce themselves from the cold reality of death. The essential inability to combat and only delay the effects of time and disease did not fit well with her surgical psyche. Although she considered herself to have good judgement, she accepted that most surgeons' enthusiasm for operations as a solution to problems is only matched by that of crack addicts for a smoke, or dumped girlfriends for ice cream. She understood that the nature of surgery with taking calculated risks, dealing with stress, operating for uncertain benefits, being sued and constantly dealing with people requires a level of denial and optimism normally associated only with organised religion.

'I think the best course of action might be to get palliative care involved, and maybe they could start morphine and manage things from here,' she said, trying again to move past this impasse. Palliative, or end of life, care managed patients who were coming near the end. Ashley often felt it was a self-fulfilling prophecy, as those referred to that pathway usually end up getting a massive drug cocktail that would rapidly send a seasoned Hells Angels to a fiery afterlife, never mind a frail 80-year-old.

Stone instinctively disliked being told what to do and was always likely to take a contrarian approach simply for that reason. He sighed and nudged the oversized chart back at Ashley.

'Well, let's just see now, let me just talk to her for a minute,' he said, deciding to ignore the incriminating evidence: the size of the hospital chart is inversely related to the likelihood of good health.

'Nancy, Nancy, can you hear me? You're doing great, I think you are in great shape. We will get you over this,' he said with all the conviction and sincerity of an estate agent trying to sell something recently vacated by crime scene investigators.

Ashley watched the flicker in the patient's eyes as she seemed to react. Chris saw it too and he picked up Ashley's discomfort that another octogenarian was misbehaving in the face of perfectly reasonable medical decision making.

Stone beamed around at everyone: as an actor, he appreciated the audience reaction from Nancy. He decided to take it up a level.

'Nancy, repeat after me, Our Father who art in heaven, can you hear me, you try, Our Father who art in heaven…'

Ashley knew he wasn't religious. She also knew this woman hadn't a chance of any quality of life for her remaining days. Her scientific mind and training were unambiguous in confirming the futility of prayer in improving disease-specific survival rates. On the other hand, even though she didn't have strong religious views, she suspected it might help whether you believed in it or not.

Nancy dug deeply and faintly responded, repeating Stone's words one by one in a dry gravelly voice. The long pauses between each word raised the tension in the room and Chris felt the hairs rising on the back of his neck. During one particularly long uncertain pause, he had time to look surreptitiously at both his watch for the time and the bedside ECG monitor for signs of life. Stone encouraged and berated her through the entire text of the Our Father prayer. It took several minutes, but it seemed like hours to everyone in the room.

As Nancy said 'Ah, ah, amen' he stood up tall and surveyed the audience. He puffed out his chest, tilted his head back and with one eyebrow raised proclaimed,

'Well, now…. maybe she's better than everyone thought.'

The students smiled and nodded at this important life lesson. The nurse who was old enough to be a mother to these children threw her eyes up to heaven. Having been standing impassively behind Stone, she slid in beside him and spoke in a withering monotone,

'Professor, of course you realise she's Jewish.'

Stone shrugged to indicate his disregard for such trifles as the patient's actual religious persuasion. Much like his morals and principles, such things were floating and negotiable. He moved towards the door indicating that he was done here.

They moved to the next room and shuffled around the bed to hear the intern read from the chart. The patient looked middle-aged, a little thin, and his clothes were sagging a little, giving Chris a hint that all might not be well. His experience was that serious weight loss and cancer went hand in hand almost as closely as gun ownership or denim tank tops went with low IQ. The man seemed diffident, almost submissive to him. Chris put that down to how many people in dealing with a crisis adopt a fatalistic position to their progress on the medical conveyor belt that they were inextricably tied onto by their disease.

'As we discussed at this morning's meeting, Mr Connors is 57 and has been diagnosed on his scans and biopsy with a pancreatic tumor with secondary spread to his liver and lung. He is currently well and awaiting a treatment plan,' Ashley said.

'OK, Mr Connors, let me just have a look at all of this,' Stone said as he reached for the patient's notes. He flicked through the laboratory results, the radiology exams, and the blood results. Chris was standing behind him and could see over his shoulder the papers as he rapidly flicked through them. Chris wondered how he could see the detail or absorb the detail in the flurry of pages. Then, as Stone paused and stopped on one particular page Chris noted as a stubby finger traced down the admissions sheet to the insurance status. Stone's stubby finger tapped the page twice and closed the chart.

'Now, Mr Connors the only option you have is surgery. If we take out the tumor in the pancreas you might have a chance. We should transfer you to the private hospital where we have the laser to do this type of surgery' Stone delivered this ultimatum with absolute certainty and confidence.

Mr Connors visibly perked up. 'You mean I have a chance? The others, everyone, said there was nothing that could be done. Will you remove the spread to the liver and the lungs as well'?

'Well, no, that's not possible, but let us deal with the pancreas first and worry about that after,' said Stone in answer to what Chris thought had been a remarkably insightful and key question. Unfortunately, that essential point was just left hanging.

'Well, that's settled: the day after tomorrow, let's get everything set up,' Stone instructed as he turned and moved out of the room.

'OK, who is next' Stone said, looking impatiently at his watch. Chris recognised the pattern, Stone's attention span for people was limited. After 30 minutes he became less polished and briefer, clearly that was about as much time as he could invest in human suffering.

Ashley referred to the printed list: 'In the next room, is Mrs. Vera Roston, 78 years old.'

'Vera, Vera, OK, yes, carry on.'

'Actually, before we go in, Prof you remember she's the woman with lung cancer' she said.

'Oh, yes, yes, I remember her well, just go through the details again and, as a teaching exercise, outline to me what your treatment plan would be in this situation if you don't mind?'

'Yes, Professor. Mrs Roston is 78 with lung cancer which is probably secondary to long term smoking. She actually doesn't have many symptoms with this even though the cancer is locally advanced and incurable. She also has Alzheimer's and poor memory. So, in summary she has incurable cancer combined with Alzheimer's and probably the best treatment is only to control and palliate symptoms if they arise' Ashley said.

Stone nodded deeply a couple of times before responding,

'Yes, good. I agree, that's the correct course of action, have you given her the diagnosis?'

'Actually Prof, you did yesterday: she had a bit of a meltdown. Oh… and she doesn't remember you giving her the diagnosis yesterday either'.

Chris remembered exactly. This unfortunate woman had been repeatedly told her diagnosis, had broken down sobbing on every occasion, which had lasted until the

Alzheimer's kicked back in and she forgot all about it again. She was living in an appalling Groundhog Day, reliving the experience of receiving a new fatal cancer diagnosis every day. He thought that receiving that news once was bad enough but repeating it in a vicious cycle every day was an incomprehensible punishment.

Chris decided to help, much like a puppy helps when a milk container falls and bursts open on the floor. He lapsed into his most professional detached voice: 'Yes, Prof, and actually last week she had the same breakdown with no recollection afterwards of what you had told her. Clinically I think that she might have element of frontal lobe loss of function with her Alzheimer's which makes her disinhibited and overemotional and that why she gets so overwrought: obviously then she doesn't remember, which is why we keep ending up back here. I was thinking perhaps we could maybe not discuss the diagnosis with her anymore.'

'Alright, let's get on with this,' Stone retorted and bustled into the room.

Mrs Roston was sitting in her armchair under a tartan blanket. She had wispy white hair framing a pleasant but somewhat vacant face. Her eyes were surrounded by wrinkles running in all directions, like the lines running from the poles on a globe. The lines deepened with a wave of excitement on seeing the approaching Stone and his entourage.

'Doctor, I've been waiting to hear, tell me what your tests showed?'

Stone slipped both hands into his pockets arched his head backwards.

'Don't do it,' Chris thought to himself, 'just leave her alone'. He watched Stone focus in on the woman but couldn't read whether it was going to be a car crash, or a Sunday drive.

'Now Mrs Roston, you have a shadow on the lung, and we will see about doing something with that for you, Dr Newman you know. He will come back later and explain. Take care now…'

Before he could leave, she reached out her twig-like arm and snagged on Stone's sleeve.

'So, it's nothing serious then Professor, not like cancer or anything.'

'Well, now, you see there are lots of treatments nowadays that we can use for that, so I wouldn't worry about it too much'.

'So, I don't have cancer?'

'Like I was saying, Dr Newman will be back to go over the options.'

She released her grip on his arm, eased back against the pillow and smiled.

'That's great. I was so afraid I had cancer'.

Stone furrowed his brow and placed his hand on her arm. He was clearly exasperated that she couldn't understand what he wasn't telling her.

'Let me put it like this, you do have a tumour'.

'A tumour? Is that a cancer?

'Well, there are lots of sub-types and biologically they all respond differently. We have a study ongoing at present looking at antibody treatments in this setting combined with chemotherapy and it appears to improve disease-free intervals by up to six weeks'.

Mrs Roston gasped and looked at the nurse on the opposite side of the bed.

'Does he mean I have cancer?'

The nurse nodded her head in acknowledgement precipitating a series of gasps, sobs, and ultimately tears. The nurse picked a tissue from the box on the bedside locker, she sat on the edge of the bed put one arm around the patient's shoulders and passed the tissue into the withered hands now clasped in front of her face.

The patient disappeared behind a screen of hands, tissue, hair, and sobs. Professor Stone addressed the group rather than looking at the patient.

'Right, so Nurse Kelly will look after you there and Dr Newman will be back later and that should take care of everything'.

Outside the room the procession was a little slower and more downcast. Stone broke away to speak to Dr Cork, one of the radiologists who was ambling along the corridor delaying the round, with the leisurely, deliberately obstructive pace of his ilk.

Nobody of the team on the ward round felt much like talking: it was as if they were all individually deciding if they would choose euthanasia rather than Alzheimer's if they ever got to that stage.

Stone was engaged with Dr Cork and was holding an imaginary golf club demonstrating a chip shot onto the green.

'So, I landed it onto the green and, you know the eighteenth, with the high bank and it rolled back down. So, I'm left with that putt to win.' he said.

'We have a name for a putt like that' said Dr Cork pointing a finger at Stone. 'It's what we call a Dr Mackey, you know that ED guy?'

'Yeah, I know him, tricky little fellow.'

'Exactly, that's him. So, we call that kind of putt a Dr Mackey, in other words, a nasty little five-footer.'

They both laughed and broke away in different directions as Stone returned to the ward round.

He was still giggling and wiped a tear of laughter from his right eye before he slapped his hands together and spoke.

'Right, who is next?'

Jack Salmon was next, he was a familiar face to all, as he was on his third month in hospital. His face was gaunt and pale, and he looked older than his 48 years. As always his tired and sagging features broke into a smile to welcome them. He was surrounded by a forest of lines, tubes and hanging bags of beige feeding solutions. Jack had repeatedly tried to die over the last few months and only through repeated surgery and heroic painstakingly detailed aftercare had he survived. Ashley had been centrally involved in successfully resuscitating him on two occasions.

He was quite nonchalant about his repeated trips down the dark tunnel with a light at the end that had nearly scorched him on occasion. He had an incurable collagen vascular disease called Marfan's syndrome, which in his case was particularly aggressive and causing his blood vessels to unpredictably get blocked and cause catastrophic complications. He had lost several feet of his small bowel, as well as one of his actual feet due to earlier loss of blood supply.

Ashley was awed at how remarkably cheerful and optimistic he was despite his illness. He also had a mischievous sense of humour and, despite becoming institutionalised after his months of incarceration, he derived pleasure from playing a role in the hospital soap opera.

'Professor, good to see you.' He gave a nod to the entourage he went on 'you've plenty of help with you today. You'll probably be retiring and handing over to one of them soon.'

Stone halted just inside the door and waved across,

'You're looking well Jack, yes, we have the full team today. I won't delay you now, we'll carry on. I'll let young Ashley here come back and check on you later.'

Before Jack could respond in his overly familiar way, which irritated Stone intensely, he turned and was gone.

Ashley was the last one left in the room: she paused to chat, 'Jack, how are things, did you get to try that new wooden leg?

'I'll have you know it's the finest of polycarbonate and graphite, but I like the way you're thinking. If I could get a parrot and a hook for a hand I'll be sorted.'

'I'll be presenting my research and your case notes at the medical conference next week and hopefully we'll get some feedback and ideas as to how to get you out of here.'

'I wanted to talk to you about that, I heard about the old woman you sent walking down the plank the other night. After all that practice on me I thought you would be better at jumpstarting people.'

Ashley suppressed her laughter until she could look over her shoulder and discreetly check nobody was around to hear. 'God almighty Jack don't be saying that… I'm in enough trouble as it is'.

He placed his hand on her arm and, while his face was tired his eyes sparkled brightly, 'you'll be fine, I've seen enough of you trying to save me and the others on this ward on long, cold nights to know you're a better surgeon and person than the lot of them. Take care.'

She remembered what Dr Attwood had told her when she started in surgery '*Only the patients know who the good doctors are*' and all of a sudden she felt at peace with the world. Jack's next sentence abruptly brought her back to ground.

'Ashley, I just need you, to help me, to end it all.'

Chapter 8: Identity

The combined reception area and nurses' station was directly across from the lift. A long cold, clean corridor with multiple rooms on either side stretched away from the reception space. The lift at the end admitted and disgorged those for whom the struggle up the stairs would be too much.

The blank, sterile, featureless walls of the Cancer Screening Institute matched the grim bare expressions of the staff and patients. The white walls, white ceiling, grey and white chequered floor tiles and plain fluorescent light fixtures were uniformly bland. There was a single incongruous flower in a white vase in the window of the waiting room. Its blue colour was almost too vibrant to be alive. In fact it wasn't, the infection control police had decreed that no living thing should enter this space, so the flower itself was lifeless plastic.

The smell of disinfectant and bleach defined the atmosphere as distinctly as the odour of fresh baked bread in a home. If cleanliness was next to godliness then the Cancer Screening Institute was certainly edging its clients in that direction.

The patients and staff all walked in a slow, silent, introspective manner. The ambience merged with the existing anxieties of the patients to create a zombified zone. There was only reality and hard truths in this place where people came to find out if they did or didn't have cancer. In a world of opinions, half-truths, and fake news this was a very binary, black or white place.

Each day at the clinic was specific to a different cancer, every Monday was lung cancer, marked by the smokers congregating under a blue haze at the door outside, maximising their carcinogenic intake before diagnosis. Pink Tuesdays were women with breast pain and very little cancer, marked by a profusion of pink anxiety, complete with friends, families and support groups. Today, Wednesday, consisted largely of elderly men and a scattering of Zimmer frames looking like trucks interspersed with cars on a gridlocked motorway. At today's clinic Ashley was tasked with the hugely unpopular task of running was what the junior doctors referred to as CSI Prostate.

Ashley paused outside the clinic waiting room and took a long slow breath to compose herself. This was the third person today she was going to have to give a cancer diagnosis to. There were three more waiting, plus all the ones with no cancer but a whole lot of complaining about how often they had to pee.

This was always a long day for her: all that talking, trying to be empathetic but with one eye on the clock as she tried to get through all the patients. When giving a cancer diagnosis she felt as if she was giving that person the disease rather than the diagnosis. She always felt personally responsible for causing the crying, desolation and emotional breakdown of decent people whose lives were forever changed in that instant. She grasped the next chart containing its stark facts with both arms across her body like a shield. She tried to use the only available free five seconds that she had to simultaneously calm her own anxiety, relax her tensed shoulders, become aware of herself in that moment and prepare herself mentally and professionally for a difficult encounter. The tiny amount of knowledge she had about mindfulness flickered across her stream of consciousness. *Never mind that, just get it done without causing any more trouble*. She called out for the next patient 'Jody Casey'.

A middle-aged woman stood up and walked the short distance down the corridor to the clinic room followed by someone Ashley took to be her son. She was tall and stylishly dressed: immediately Ashley felt self-conscious of her own deliberately sensible clothes. Ashley walked ahead feeling somewhat confused. She glanced at the sticker on the front of the chart. *Jody could be male or female*. But the man was too young to be the patient. The date of birth fitted better with the woman.

They entered the room and Ashley sat on her side of the table allowing the others to sit opposite.

'My name is Dr Brown, nice to meet you, now, let me get this organised,' she said, opening the chart. She placed the sheet with the biopsy result showing prostate cancer face down to her left. She quickly scanned the referral letter and the previous clinic visits. On the fourth page she found the explanation that resolved her confusion.

Jody picked up on Ashley's raised eyebrows and her *Ah-ha* moment.

'Honey, I'm just here for the all-clear. The guy the last day promised me everything would be fine, so I just need that all-clear and I'm out of here'.

'Ms Casey, is it OK if I call you Jody?' said Ashley.

Jody flicked her head and the fringe of her long blonde hair flicked across her angular face and square jaw in agreement.

'Jody, I'm sorry to say that the biopsy has confirmed you have prostate cancer.' Ashley delivered the devastating news slowly. It was important to her to be clear and precise, not to shy away from the truth or use substituted words. She paused a second to allow the implications of a cancer diagnosis to be absorbed, before launching into her, *its early, its small and we can treat it,* speech.

Jody was looking confused until she was interrupted by the Ariana Grande ringtone coming from her enormous Gucci handbag.

'Just one sec hon,' she said and thrust her immaculate groomed, long red fingernails deep into the bag. She rummaged around, came up with a fist full of cosmetics, dropped them on the desk and reached in again. This time she came up with a gold-encrusted iPhone and, on the third swipe, managed to touch the screen without the fingernail stopping her from making contact.

Ashley recognised the ringtone song as 'Grenade'. She made a mental note that she still had some street cred with her music knowledge. As the phone conversation across the table continued, she had to time to rationalise further. As she listened to a conversation about a guy whom Jody '*couldn't believe he did that',* she began to feel less certain and secure. It dawned on her that she was as about as cool as a transgender woman in her 50's with prostate cancer.

The phone call ended and a colourful blur of hair, eye shadow and lipstick swooped towards Ashley. The effect was almost like a tropical parrot landing on the desk in front of her.

'Now, what were you saying again'?

Ashley clenched her molars, jaw and lips tight enough to crack diamonds. She had a hectic day to negotiate and this interaction wasn't helping. She framed in her own mind what she wanted to say, but decided not to say that, and went back to 'Jody, I'm sorry to say that the biopsy has confirmed you have prostate cancer.'

Ashley looked at Jody's phone, expecting it to ring again.

'No. You guys have made a mistake. I'm here for the all clear. You must have someone else's chart. That's not me, it can't be' said Jody.

'I assure you there is no mistake, but it's early, its small and we can absolutely treat it. So, while you could have done without this, we absolutely can help you and get this under control' said Ashley.

'Girl, you're not listening to me. I can't have that, it's just not possible. You're wrong' said Jody.

'Jody, I know this is a shock, both for you and your son.'

Jody shrieked in a scream that echoed down the outside hall and got the attention of everyone in the waiting room.

'How dare you! Marcus is my husband. You can't get anything right, can you? This is bullshit. I don't have cancer. I definitely do not have a man's cancer. Do you hear me? I identify as a woman, a woman! I don't accept your opinion.'

'I apologise Jody, sorry, and Marcus… I didn't know your relationship. But it's not my opinion, it's the result of the biopsy.'

Elsebeth the clinic nurse, having heard the shrieking, slowly opened the door and edged a bleached blonde wispy head into the room. She performed the movement slowly, like a drunk pretending to be sober as they fumbled open a car door. Ashley saw the movement and was unsure if she was trying to maximise her exposure to the conversation or to minimise her clumsy movements.

'Anything I can help with?' said Elsebeth.

She stepped inside, anxious to partake in what she could see was shaping up to be a real-life soap opera, one that she could share with all the other nurses over her lunch break.

Ashley knew the implications of letting this nursing equivalent of a viral news story into the room: she jumped up and reassured her there was nothing wrong, then shepherded her rapidly back out the door.

The door clicked shut and Ashley returned to her seat at the desk. At least the interruption had given her space to readjust. Marcus had understood what Ashley had said and was now holding Jody's hand in both of his.

'I'm sorry to have upset you and I know that bad news and stress can cause people to be upset and to deny reality. But Jody, there is no mistake, you do have cancer. It has been detected at an early stage and it's something we can absolutely deal with. I can't tell you exactly how this will behave but the majority of people we see have it treated and do just fine.'

In her head Ashley went through the mnemonic she had learned in medical school for dealing with people's responses to bad news. DABDA, denial, anger, bargaining, depression and acceptance were the steps that most people would display in this situation. So far Jody had dealt with denial pretty well, and in a novel way. She'd moved quite quickly into anger. And while Jody's face was hidden by her blonde hair, the tears dripping from her jaw told Ashley that she had rapidly progressed to the depression stage. It seemed that having moved with commendable speed through the first two stages, she had skipped bargaining altogether: so, one more hop and she would be at home base of acceptance.

Ashley slid the ever-present box of tissues across the table in front of Jody. She jerkily pulled three tissues out of the box and used them to mix her black mascara, blue eye shadow and tears on the canvas of her face into an impressionist effect.

'So, I know this is difficult, now that you have accepted this news, the next step is we need to get some scans organised and get you to see the oncologists. I'll organise all of that for you today' said Ashley.

However, Jody wasn't progressing quite as satisfactorily as Ashley had assumed. She stood up and faced Ashley.

'I want to make a complaint.'

'Sure, that's no problem. If you want to do that I can show you how. But is there anything I can help with? Is it about your diagnosis or what we talked about today?'

'It's everything. You are a disgrace, you are a monster going around giving women diseases that they can't possibly have. Where's the hospital manager's office?'

Ashley wasn't sure if Jody was stuck in anger or denial, but either way she clearly wasn't following the prescribed pathway. This wasn't right: she simply couldn't go down a different route from what volume II of Harrisons Principles and Practice of Medicine had laid down. Ashley also felt a flush of anxiety that she was going to be the subject of another complaint.

'Jody, can we deal with this ourselves? To be honest I've had a few issues recently and I would prefer if we can sort this out between us. Let me apologise, can I do anything to make this better. Just let me know whatever, I'll do it'.

But there was no bargaining with Jody, she had made her decision. In resigned acceptance, Ashley started to give her the directions to Mary Gallen's office, just then, in the frosted glass of the door she saw the familiar shape of Dr Attwood pass by.

'Just hang on one minute, I might get a second opinion for you from one of my senior colleagues.'

Dr Attwood stood at the nurse's station nodding his head as he digested the clinical history that Ashley presented to him.

'So, that's the medical background, now the thing is.... she had a bit of a meltdown when I gave her the diagnosis. She just didn't accept that as a Trans woman that she could have prostate cancer and I get that, it's a complicated situation. I might have made things worse then, by mistaking her partner for her son. So that's where we're at, they're both in the room, I said I'd get a second opinion.'

Dr Attwood gave a small smile 'wow, you walked right into a minefield here. No worries, let's go in and have a chat.'

'Ms Casey, my name is Dr Attwood, I'm one of the Consultant Surgeons here. I've heard about your situation. I'm just going to look at your chart here for one minute.' With that he broke eye contact with Jody placed his glasses case on the left side of the table, opened it, removed the glasses and proceeded to clean them. Once satisfied with their appearance he put them on and opened the voluminous chart. He spent some time reading different pages in different sections and appeared utterly engrossed in the files. Ashley stood behind him looking over his shoulder. She avoided looking across the table or catching Jody's stare which although she couldn't see, it felt like a Spanish sun beating down on her head. Ashley felt herself rocking backwards and forwards, she tried to stop. Her left hand began to lift and turn, to show her the time but she managed to stop it. The time on her watch didn't matter anyhow, as time had now slowed to a virtual stop. Every breath she took, to her sounded like a slow wheeze. A pulsation in the side of her head allowed her to feel her heartbeat. It was heaving, but her racing mind had time to consider one or two awkward outcomes to all of this between each beat. She thought if this were a restaurant, the meal should be here by now.

Dr Attwood's voice released her from her mental gymnastics.

He sat up straight in his chair and looked straight at Jody over his glasses. 'It's difficult to deal with bad news and talk about death.'

Jody had been getting ready to interrupt him with a torrent that she'd had time to put together, but his opening line halted her pointing finger suspending in mid-air. 'What, death, she never said I was going to die.'

'And I'm sure you most likely won't, but I'm not talking about your cancer, I'm just talking about breaking bad news. Cancer doesn't kill as many people nowadays.'

'Wait, is this a malignant cancer?'

'Yes, you have an invasive, malignant cancerous tumour. Now that sounds a little frightening and everyone in your situation immediately thinks that they are going to die very soon.'

'Am I?'

'Where did you get that idea from? Now we all know lots of people who have awful stories about someone they know or have heard about someone who had a bad outcome, an untreatable cancer, a medical error, a bad death, terrible chemotherapy or radiotherapy worse than Chernobyl, but you mustn't let any of that weigh on your mind.'

Ashley was no longer in Jody's spotlight, she felt as if she could slip out and nobody would notice. Jody sat immobile with her hands folded in her lap. 'So, what's next?'

'Right. Specifically in your case, you have a small early, non-aggressive cancer that I think we will be able to treat with hormonal medication. Actually, it's an anti-testosterone medication so it won't be an issue with your other medication and I'm sure that will be enough to deal with this.'

'Thank you so much. That's great.'

Dr Attwood then talked a little more, passed some tissues and after a couple of minutes he shook hands with both of them on the way out as if they had known each other for years. He closed the door and sat on the edge of the desk. 'That was a little tricky, but I hope we're back on track now.'

'I'm sorry for dragging you into that. I made a mess of it.'

'Look, these things happen. People just latch onto something and the whole relationship breaks down over nothing. It was a good idea to get me involved, a second person can diffuse the situation. I know it's not politically correct, but sometimes a middle-aged man in a suit with some grey hair fits an expected prototype that people respond differently to, and things get easier.'

'I don't care what stereotype they want if it gets me out of trouble.'

'The other trick, and I know this is underhand, is to distract or frighten them with the bigger picture. Startling someone by mentioning death gets them to focus upon what actually matters, rather than bitching about the small stuff. If you start the discussion by talking about death, things can only get better. Obviously, that approach is only for extreme situations like this one, most people are reasonable, and you don't need to resort to that to get them to see what's important. It's difficult sometimes though because people really are the proverbial box of chocolates.'

'I need to be more guarded in future' she said.

'Don't take too much on yourself. If every patient a doctor has, hates them, she's probably no good, equally if a doctor has no patient that hates them, she's probably no good. People get the medical experience that fits their own personal narrative a lot of the time. The conspiracy theorists in life, get a series of presumed errors and stories they invent about doctors giving someone x amount of time only for them to live three times longer or shorter. The stoic and the dramatists equally get, imagine or invent events that match their own personality's preconceived view of the world.'

'Thanks Dr Attwood, I better keep going with the clinic' said Ashley as she left the room.

She liked Dr Attwood. She let her mind wander to the fact that he was single. No, not with a junior doctor, it would just be unprofessional, but if she got the Consultant job….. She walked to the nurses' station: Chris was there already selecting his next chart.

'Do you go through them in advance and take out the difficult ones? You're supposed to see them in turn,' she said.

‘Absolutely not’ he said as he slipped the chart from his hands into the middle of the pile with the finesse of a card shark.

‘What happened with you and the trans woman just now?’

‘How did you know she was trans?’

‘My radar for these things is really good and I might have seen her chart earlier. I heard them talking to Elsebeth, they really like Attwood, but they’ve gone to Mary Gallen’s office to complain about you: did you use the wrong word or something?’

‘God, I thought we had that sorted. I really don’t know what went wrong. Well, actually, I did say I thought her husband was her son, but things had already gone south by then.’

‘Don’t worry we all have days like that.’

Ashley picked up the next chart and walked to the waiting room to call in the next drama.

Chapter 9: Numbish

The following mornings ward round was being led by Dr Attwood. Chris liked his efficient, business-like style. It was without the drama of a Stone round, in TV terms, more science and education than soap opera. Medical ward rounds always had an element of theatre and ritual. Early in his career Chris had been intrigued by the mystery and solemnity of the process. However now, he was a member of the club and understood the language coded in acronyms and had deciphered the euphemisms used to hide hard facts and avoid difficult discussions with patients.

The mundane routine tasks didn't get his attention anymore. He sought the more interesting interactions and mostly was fascinated by the level of human behaviour a level above the picture that could be drawn from reading only the text of conversations. Patients' unspoken reactions and the ability of the medical system to herd patients obediently in particular pathways enthralled him. He couldn't understand how people on entering hospitals became instantaneously institutionalised, playing their part by behaving and responding to the medical rituals with predictable acceptance.

As a keen gambler he had figured out that 99% of human aches, pains, coughs and insecurities disappear on their own, because they are a normal part of life. One of the sacred secrets being a successful doctor was to claim credit for all the things that go away by themselves.

The key skill he admired was the ability to not kill patients with treatments while they were getting better all by themselves.

He mulled over this near the back of the room and lost himself in the anonymity of the group. There wasn't the large audience that Stone liked on his ward rounds, but there were still four doctors, three students and two nurses in the room. A flash of white porcelain from the front of the crowd showed him that Jeffrey's mouth was in motion. Chris knew how to bear a grudge. He didn't mind competition for the upcoming Consultant job. He did object to Jeffrey adopting dirty tactics, but morally he felt justified to sink to that level if that was what was necessary. He also had a vendetta against Jeffrey over his treatment of Ashley and that needed some loving care and attention.

He hadn't taken Ashley's advice to dispose of methylene blue-laced coffee when they were at the clinic. However, the absence of obvious results in the following days and the impossibility of asking Jeffrey if his pee had turned blue without arousing suspicion, meant that it had been an unsatisfying effort. It had even crossed his mind that maybe having 'III' after your name might make peeing blue normal.

It would have to be psychological warfare; Chris wasn't above some minor vandalism: he just needed to find his enemy's vulnerabilities. Although full of outward bluster and self-confidence, Jeffrey was quite neurotic, with a significant germophobe tendency.

Chris's settled on this as the best avenue to pursue. The next question was how to exploit those weaknesses. Maybe he could give Jeffrey a set of symptoms that he would escalate into a diagnosis. He reached into his voluminous white coat pocket and, displacing syringes, tourniquets and the crumbs of a forgotten flapjack, he found a spray canister of ethyl chloride. He used this local anaesthetic spray on patients before injections or putting in IV lines. It cooled and evaporated on the skin allowing for painless needle insertion. He knew from playing with it during periods of inactivity on-call, that it caused a cold tingling sensation, which if sprayed for long enough would produce a numb patch of skin. As it evaporated, it left no signs and no side effects.

Chris's took the spray canister in his right hand and hid it by folding his arms across his chest. He edged through the crowd as if getting a better look at the patient. Once in the right place he directed a thin jet of the spray from under his folded arms downwards and to his left towards Jeffrey's lower right leg. He maintained his forward gaze until his sharpshooting accuracy was confirmed when Jeffrey shifted slightly from one leg to the other. He stopped spraying and innocently nodded at the dietary advice being given by Dr Attwood to the anxious young woman with a diagnosis of irritable bowel syndrome.

'High protein, low carbohydrate foods are absolutely essential: protein shakes, nuts, absolutely no bread or wheat products'. He reinforced this pronouncement by placing a hand on her forearm and giving her a definitive 'If you take control of your situation, work at this, and stick to it, then after six weeks you'll be fine.'

The advice was delivered with such conviction and certainty that her anxiety visibly relaxed. He seemed to be transfusing confidence into her through that touch on her arm. 'Take any support you can get at home as well. I'm a single parent of two kids as well, so I can appreciate the demands that places on anybody,' Attwood said.

Ashley was in the middle of the procession as it departed the room and advanced snake-like into the next room. She wondered how Attwood knew that about the patient. She was also curious about Dr Attwood: he was so level and unflappable at work she couldn't picture how he had ended up alone with two kids. She liked kids, but she was still single and time was moving on. She wondered what his kids looked like and if adoption would appeal to them.

Chris shuffled along with the group, judged the pace of the medical student between him and Jeffrey and glided into his position as smoothly as a boat arriving at a dock. He had a clear line of fire from his left elbow in front of the medical student and onto Jeffrey's right leg.

The spray again landed perfectly on the back of his right leg. Jeffrey again shifted position, clearly starting to perceive that something wasn't quite right. Chris maintained the spray a little longer, just enough for Jeffrey to clearly identify the sensation: he stopped just before he reached down and brushed his leg. Jeffrey evidently felt nothing: he glanced backward to ensure nothing was brushing against his leg and tuned into the ward round again looking nonplussed.

Dr Attwood was talking to an elderly woman who also had vague abdominal pains. When he had entered the room her lined face smiled and shed twenty years of aging and she put on the expression of someone seeing their tail wagging, bouncing dog at the door.

'Let me be very clear, there is absolutely only one dietary option for your condition, low protein and high fibre carbohydrates. So fresh fruit and whole meal bread in a balanced diet.' Once again, he delivered the summary with the absolute confidence and poise of a contestant on *Who Wants to be a Millionaire*, who knows they have the answer to the million-pound question. The old woman was clearly frail, weak and edging slowly but inexorably towards the end of life. Dr Attwood eyed her up and down and proclaimed: 'You are doing fabulously, I can't believe the improvement since you have been with us'.

He probed further 'Can you feel it yourself? The change is remarkable.'

She raised her pale right hand with its brown patches of aging pigmentation in response and grasped her left biceps. Looking at the outline of her bones draped in loose skin and a thin curtain of muscle Chris felt she wasn't a great candidate for life insurance. But, in response to the penetrating belief of Dr Attwood's warm eyes, the little old woman visibly perked up: her voice went up an octave as she replied, 'I think you're right, I'm feeling great.' The previous pale form in the bed took on a pink hue and, as if a light was coming on, her eyes didn't quite sparkle but they certainly sparked.

Ashley admired Dr Attwood's ability to hypnotise patients, he simply had to dispense advice and they melted in the genuine warmth of his delivery and believed everything he said.

The procession shuffled onwards and into the corridor. Chris managed to land another attempt with the spray onto Jeffrey's leg. He definitely got his attention this time and he shivered, reached down to his right leg and looked around surreptitiously. He was clearly confused and distracted now but was still trying to focus on the ward round.

'Dr Attwood, I have a question: you gave opposite dietary advice to the two women, is it because of the age difference?' Jeffrey asked.

Dr Attwood halted the group in the corridor and brought everyone into an extended circle to address the question at hand: 'Okay, everyone this is an important point, look at who gives dietary advice: nutritionists, dieticians, homoeopathists, coaches, doctors, nurses. If there was a single right answer, we would read it off a list and wouldn't need advice. People love creating a mystery and an industry around all of this, it's quite simple really. Don't eat too much and don't eat what doesn't agree with you. Now you can dress this up in many ways and patients love clear direction. But the content you give them is less relevant than the instruction. Give them a clear plan: they expect and respond to that. Knock yourself out on the specifics, it really doesn't matter. I tend to give them a list that most likely fits their pre-conceptions: they like that.'

The faces on the ward round showed a clear range of responses from bewilderment in the students, to acknowledgement in the experienced doctors culminating in sage nodding from the senior nurse. The responses mirrored the number of years spent dealing with people and the inevitable cynicism that went with that. Seeing that the students didn't understand that there wasn't a rigid rulebook of how to advise people Attwood continued. 'You've all seen how patients latch onto the idea of a strong medicine or an expensive, experimental or a unique one. There's no doubt that they do better if they believe in something, its utterly unscientific and irrational but that's what happens in the real world, so our job is to be positive and help them by how we present things.'

Chris had been focused upon project Jeffrey and hadn't taken any notice of Ashley but now she had stepped alongside Attwood and by pointing the way, directed him towards the next patient. Over the 24 hours since Stone had seen her on his ward round Louise Stark hadn't got any better. Ashley was worried and had arrived at the hospital early to check on her before this morning ward round. Her sunken eyes and weak pulse had elevated Ashley's concern level from nervous to alarmed. Louise wasn't Attwood's patient, but Ashley muttered something about a second opinion in order to get him into the room.

Dr Attwood listened to the history and examined the woman himself. She wasn't as alert or afraid as yesterday. Her pupils were constricted, her eyelids a fraction lower than normal.

'How much morphine has she had today?' he asked.

'Fifteen milligrams,' answered the nurse.

'Well that explains the pupils and the drowsiness, but the fact that she's needed so much worries me that there's more going on.'

He looked at the slightly flushed face and the shallow, slightly rapid breathing. When he lifted her hand it was clammy and heavy. The pulse was just a bit faster and harder to feel than it should have been. The gush of brown fluid, when he lifted the dressing over the abdominal wound, made up his mind even before the smell reached him.

'Louise, can you hear me OK? I think we need to bring you back to the operating theatre and fix this. We need to do it today. I'll speak to Professor Stone. Don't you worry, I'll sort all of this out,' he said.

Once outside he issued the instructions quickly and simply to effect the decision with urgency.

'Do you want a CT scan first?' asked Ashley.

'No, it won't change anything. What we've just seen is classic sepsis, it's subtle and reversible if we act right now. But she's really sick and if you miss that or don't deal with it straight away it's all over. We need to clean out the belly and fix the leak or she may be dead by the end of the day. So, no CT scan: I don't want any delay. Once the round is over, we need to be in the operating theatre.'

Sepsis. Ashley shivered at the concept, an invisible, silent assassin.

Attwood stepped into the middle of the corridor and he waved everyone to gather around. When the huddle formed around Attwood he slowly looked around. 'I want you to remember her for the rest of your careers. Sepsis kills, but it doesn't send an invitation, it just shows up often unexpected and unrecognised. You'll diagnose it partially by looking at the patients, the vital signs may help but the key thing is a sixth sense that somethings just not right. See how she looked just tired, vaguely unwell, it's not an obvious call, but she will die today if we don't fix whatever is probably leaking inside her abdomen. You'll only ever diagnose it in time by subtle signs from the patient and maybe intuition, maybe experience, maybe paranoia of the doctor seeing them.'

He paused to allow that message and Louise Stark's drawn face to imprint upon their surgical souls and then led them along the corridor to the next room. One of the students opened the notes to begin the presentation on their patient. From the back of the group came a loud exclamation 'Multiple Sclerosis, MS it can't be anything else.'

'Say again Jeffrey?' Attwood said.

'I was just wondering if someone had unexplained pins and needles in one leg, would that be a sign of MS?'

'Interesting question, anyone any ideas? Chris?'

'Well multiple sclerosis can cause leg numbness but usually not in isolation: there are other symptoms, visual disturbance and loss of power that usually accompany it.' Sensing an opportunity Chris decided to take it up a level. 'Could also be caused by HIV infection, TB, mini-strokes, actually you know secondary syphilis can do that.'

'Well Chris, that's technically correct. I would point all those things are rarer than Vegans at a Celtic versus Rangers game. But why do you ask Jeffrey?' Attwood said.

'Oh, just a patient I was thinking about,' Jeffrey said.

'OK, well let's move onto the next patient.'

Chris edged away from the ward round and made his way behind the nurses' station to the medicines cabinet. Attwood's question had planted a seed that Chris felt he could nourish and grow into a full-blown psychosomatic illness. He flicked through the small boxes and looked at a couple of labels before he found what he was looking for in a small plastic bottle.

'Excellent, Tropicamide. Good for dilating pupils to see what's behind them. Minor side effect of visual disturbance and blurring. Just right for my hypochondriac friend.'

He dodged the ward round which had meandered down the corridor and went through the double doors out to the doctors' changing rooms. He opened Jeffrey's locker and on the top shelf immediately found the contact lens container. He untwisted the lid on the side marked L and placed the blue cap down on the shelf.

'Ok, just one drop should do' and he placed a drop of Tropicamide in the container, pausing he then added another and then a third. 'Better just to be on the safe side.' He added a fourth drop, and finally 'one for luck.' Happy with his work he paused, the failure of his methylene blue trick was still on his mind. He figured it might be safer just to do the other side as well, so he opened that one too. His conscience intervened at a two-drop dose on this side. He screwed back on the caps, replaced everything where it had been and walked back to join the ward round.

He joined onto the back of the throng and managed to land another spray of the ethyl chloride on Jeffrey leg.

They had just exited Jack Salmon's room and Ashley was discussing his case. 'I'm really excited about this presentation next week. I'll get to present Jack's case, which is really interesting and rare in its own right and we'll get to discuss his case with other doctors from other hospitals. We might be able to get help for him before he gets into even more trouble,' she said.

'Absolutely. That's a great thing to do,' said Attwood. 'I know you've put a lot of work into researching his case and getting this presentation ready. We should just do a dry run before the conference so I can help with the finishing touches. I would just say though that he's got a nasty disease. He's a really nice guy but in the long term,

I'd be guarded about his prognosis. I can see you're close to him: just remember you didn't cause this, all we can do as professionals is try our best.'

Ashley's face flushed and she avoided eye contact as she replied: 'Of course, always, I get that.'

'I know, good. You made the right call getting a second opinion for Louise Stark, sometimes the last person to accept that a patient needs re-operation is the one who did the first operation. Can you and Jeffrey get her ready for surgery and I'll join you there in thirty minutes.'

As the ward round dispersed Ashley walked over to where Chris and Jeffrey were standing. 'Jeffrey, Dr Attwood wants the two of us to get that woman ready for theatre and to assist him with the surgery. I'll get the chart and the bloods done, if you do the consent and the ECG,' she said.

'I just need to put in my contact lenses before the surgery, maybe if you get that stuff done, I'll see you down there' Jeffrey said.

'What? Come on, help me with this… you don't need 30 minutes to put those in? I could remove your cataracts in less time.'

'Yeah, good one. See you later.'

Jeffrey flashed a toothy grin as if that was some sort of compensation and headed off to the locker room.

Ashley turned to Chris: 'can you believe that guy? I've decided that when I finally lose it, I'm going to head-butt his stupid grin and shatter that porcelain like a coffee cup on a concrete floor… What are you so happy about?'

Chris's broad grin was betraying his utter lack of remorse at having doctored Jeffrey's contact lens solution.

'There are none so blind as those with Tropicamide in their eyes,' he said.

'What?

'Nothing, let me help you get that patient ready.'

If wasn't until they were halfway through the operation on Louise that Jeffrey began to realise something was wrong. Dr Attwood had removed a piece of bowel that was leaking have been silently skewered as collateral damage in the appendix operation. He was putting in the last sutures and he asked Jeffrey to cut the ends. Jeffrey reached forwards and closed the scissors in thin air completely missing the threads.

'You OK?' Attwood said.

'Yes, fine, just can't quite see the suture,' Jeffrey said as he made a second attempt to cut and missed again. He closed his left eye and with both hands on the scissors he finally managed to cut the suture.

'We're nearly done here. Do want to get a coffee?' Attwood said.

'Thanks, I will' said a clearly disconcerted Jeffrey. He stepped away from the operating table, then threw his gloves in the bin and his gown into the yellow basket. He walked towards the door squinting alternately through one eye and then the other to test them out. With his right eye closed and looking through the left he managed to walk straight into the theatre swinging door. Walking into the door with a crash caused it to open enough for him to escape but the experiment also confirmed that there was something seriously amiss with the vision in his left eye.

The operation had paused as everyone watched Jeffrey's theatrical exit. Attwood looked across the table at Ashley 'What's going on with him, is he OK?' Attwood said.

‘I’ve no idea,’ she said. Trying to lighten the mood she decided to try and make a joke. ‘Maybe he’s on drugs.’

‘Possible. It’s always something to factor in with doctors.’

‘No, no.... that’s not what I meant, absolutely not, I was only joking’ Ashley said.

‘Anyhow, this woman will be much better now. Clearly it was unrecognised perforation of the bowel during the appendectomy, but now that we have fixed that she should do fine. She might have a rough couple of days after all the infection we washed out of there though. Can you finish off here and I’ll just check on Jeffrey.’

Ashley used a stapler to close the abdominal wound with a neat row of metallic clips. Whatever was going on with Jeffrey didn’t matter as much to her as the fact that she had got Louise Stark her operation. Like Attwood had said, if they hadn’t fixed it, she could have died by the end of the day. She felt a warm feeling after Attwoods praise, but how Stone would feel about her interfering with one of his patients she would just have to see.

Chapter 10: Triathlon

He looked tired, skulking home in the dawn half-light. Apart from a white tip on his tail, he was completely black in colour. He presumably had been on a night out of feline partying. Chris watched him over the top of his foot which was extended and resting on the low wall outside his apartment block. He changed legs and extended the other leg bending forward until he felt the tension and then a burning sensation in the back of his thigh.

It's too early, how did I get talked into running at this time of the morning.

He was just too competitive: at work, at college, at filling the bags in the supermarket before the teller could calculate the cost of his shopping. When Ashley had said she would be running in the morning he hadn't been able to resist and had suggested they go together. He fancied himself as a sportsman: while he hadn't played sports at college, he did watch a lot on TV. He figured he must have absorbed some fitness and talent by osmosis. He had managed to run a marathon at one stage, but while he used it as a topic of conversation, he never went into irrelevant details of the finishing time. The first half had been okay, but in the second half, his strategy of relying on self-confidence rather than training had come unstuck. He had finished but did so alongside the people in full gorilla suits. It was such a searing, awful, never again moment, on a level only comparable to an experience he'd had once with Southern Comfort whisky.

He bent over, reached with both arms and touched the air reasonably close to his toes. Next, he stretched his arms out and finally satisfied with the appearance of his reflection in the glass door of the apartment, he was ready.

Ashley appeared in the distance running with a steady pace. He studied her motion, she glided with very little vertical movement and an efficiency that concerned him. Coming to a stop she pressed a button on the Garmin device on her wrist.

'Good to go? How about 10k at a 5 min per k pace?' she said airily.

'Sounds fine, let's go.' Chris had no idea if that was fine or not. His mind worked in miles not kilometres, but it was important not to show weakness.

They set off at a pace that seemed just about bearable. The red sandstone buildings on the Hyndland road were a cold crimson in the early morning light. He had to concentrate on his stride length, staying centred, breathing deeply and not falling over. He got into a rhythm which felt economical, but he was too pressurised to converse with ease.

By contrast, Ashley was breathing easily and chatting at will. 'So, you know how so many middle-aged people are running nowadays? Dr Rossi has a theory about that… you know she's a runner?

'Ya.'

'Well, she thinks that everyone is running because, with Facebook, CCTV and activity tracking the world has become like a small town where everyone knows everyone and knows what they are doing all the time. So, it's impossible to have an affair in a small town without everyone finding out. Buying a car for a mid-life crisis is out with the recession. Therefore, they are all running rather than having affairs or buying cars. What you think?'

'Ya… makes… sense'.

'Do you think any of the Serenity Consultants are involved in affairs?' Not getting any response she looked sideways at him. 'You doing OK?'

Chris was far from OK, but he doggedly kept going. They were past Byres road, now off the street and into the Botanical Gardens, beating out a steady tempo on the path. He was glad of her conversation: it was distracting him from the discomfort. He also knew that if he had been on his own he wouldn't have been able to keep this pace. They overtook a woman dragging, rather than walking her reluctant little white dog. Like Chris, the small curly haired puppy clearly wasn't a morning creature and intermittently sat down and had to be pulled along on the leash to keep him moving. Chris empathised with the puppy, he was on an invisible leash that Ashley had unconsciously tied to his ego and she was gradually strangling him with it.

She kept chatting away, Chris found it harder to listen and take in as he became more and more stressed. She had kept her running shape, still seemed light, almost as if a little following wind would be sufficient to propel her along. His breath came in short gasps, his head was bobbing with each step and his limbs no longer swung with ease. Instead they had to be dragged through each movement.

'How… far?'

'You mean how far have we done or left to go?' she replied.

'Yeah.'

His brain was now sufficiently deprived of oxygen that he couldn't manage the simple sums of working out the difference between distance travelled or left to do. He just wanted it to end. His legs were heavy, and his chest heaving and burning.

'Must be near… there,' he offered hopefully.

'That's 5.5 k, just over halfway.'

His head sank a little further, but he kept grinding it out, without any flash or style, forcing it out one step at a time.

He tried to focus on the finish and the knowledge that the pain would end at that fixed point. The long straight stretch of the Great Western Road with its gradual climb into the distance was now his north face of Everest.

Eventually they reached the hospital forecourt. Ashley's Garmin beeped, signifying the end and she loped to a stop. Chris, following a few paces behind, stopped immediately, placed his hands behind his head and tried to slow his panting.

'I'm going to change and have a shower. See you for rounds at seven?' she said.

Chris nodded. Once she was out of sight he sank to the ground and lay on his back.

Inside, Ashley stopped at a vending machine to get a drink. She sat on a bench drinking a bottle of water, taking a moment to herself feeling pleased with her morning's work and the spanking she had delivered.

Dr Rossi came around the corner sparkling from the light reflecting off her designer sunglasses on her blonde head and large diamond earrings. Ashley wondered what she would do if, after operating on ten people during the day, one of those earrings was missing. Would she open them all up again and look for it? And what if it wasn't found until the tenth patient?

As Dr Rossi stopped to talk and Ashley saw her reflection in the sunglasses, she was suddenly aware of her running gear, her favourite but grubby Nike trainers and the light coating of dust her sweat had absorbed in the park, giving her a bad fake tan look.

'Ashley, I just saw Chris on the ground outside, was that your work?'

'Yeah, no… we just did a 10k'.

'Good work, have you got a race coming up?'

'No, just clearing the head.'

'Good. Anyhow I've just been at a meeting with administration to discuss the fallout from the resuscitation of that elderly woman. There's a formal complaint we will have to deal with. Professor Stone is making a big deal about it which makes it a bit tricky. I know you feel bad about it, but don't worry, I'll help to get it all sorted. I do think Chris should have done better to back you up, I'll talk to him later.'

'Thanks, I really appreciate the support' Ashley said.

'You know, with the running, it's no coincidence that surgeons do well at endurance sports. The key skill is the ability to endure pain for long periods. Having the personality type that can endure long periods of discomfort in training and put up with all those hours of suffering is what determines success. I've always thought that it's a perfect parallel with surgical training. All that competition to get to medical school, the years of slog there and then years of slavery as a junior doctor… You see what I mean?'

Ashley had never considered herself a sadomasochist. She was hard working, competitive, and enthusiastic she saw those as healthy, normal traits. Her default position on everything in life was to try hard, aim to help and get along with people: it was an automatic response for her. She just didn't see herself reflected in Dr Rossi's description of the disturbed psychopath taking enjoyment in pain.

'Well, I never looked at it like that… That's interesting. I always looked at sport as more of an internal competition, to improve myself, to go faster. Like, trying to improve my times and get fitter.'

'Yeah, but to get there you have to have a mental ability, maybe above the average, depending on how successful you are, to absorb pain and discomfort. No?'

'I guess, I just think running is good for my mind. The exercise and the buzz after a run just clears my head.'

'What I'm really trying to say to you Ashley is that, like Chris you are both products of this hospital. Sometimes if you get this medical Stockholm syndrome, you put up with the conflict, the bickering, the best and worst of humanity and sometimes you just can't appreciate what's normal anymore. In fact, in a strange way, people come to enjoy it. That buzz you get after a run: that's endorphin and hormone release by the body, almost like an internal pharmacy doling out painkillers. Have you noticed how elite athletes, with their skinny bodies and pinched faces, look just like junkies? Try taking away their exercise: they go nuts, just like a drug addict when they go cold turkey.'

Ashley was certainly feeling the discomfort now. Not that she thought Dr Rossi was wrong. It was worse than that: she was probably right.

'I'm not saying this as a negative thing, it's great that you are focused and driven. It's great to see, just be careful: if you get into an internal competition where you're competing against yourself all the time, then it is guaranteed one of the losers will be you. Focus on what's important: we need to get you into a Consultant job here in good shape for the long haul. Mind yourself, I'll see you in theatre later.'

Chris had recovered sufficiently after his run to enter the hospital through the front door rather than as a patient through the ER. He made his way towards the locker room and, seeing Ashley outside still on the bench with her head down looking at the floor called out to her,

'Hey, Ashley, didn't mean to go so hard with you on the run.'

She looked up at him.

'No problem, maybe further tomorrow?'

Immediately changing the topic in order to avoid even acknowledging Ashley's appalling suggestion, he said: 'Were you talking to Dr Rossi, you know she does triathlons? I have a clinical question for you, how do you know if someone does triathlons?'

'I guess, they're fit, lean and maybe a little psychopathic?' said Ashley.

'No, you don't need to know whether or not someone does triathlons: they will invariably tell you.'

'Actually, you're right, is that part of the psychopath thing?'

'What's with you and the psychopath thing today? I heard a story about Dr Rossi. You know how triathletes hydrate with loads of fluid before a race. So, then they're in the wetsuits and waiting for the start and then they are in the water swimming the course. So inevitably lots of them need to pee and because they want a fast time they don't want to wait and queue for a toilet so they just pee while swimming in their wetsuits.'

'That's good to know, I'll never buy a second-hand wetsuit, or swim behind one of them again.'

'No, but it gets better. One of the pharmacists who does triathlons told me this. Dr Rossi is such a Type A personality and so competitive that at the start of one triathlon she didn't wait until they were in the water. She was standing on the beach at the start with a bunch of others and not waiting until she was in the water, so in case it interfered with her swimming she peed into her wetsuit. Which was fine, it all just filled up the space inside, until it reached the shoulders and started coming down the sleeves. The guy I know who was behind her saw it dripping out of both sleeves just as the race started.' Said Chris.

Ashley looked at him suspiciously. 'Do you actually believe that?'

'That's what I heard. You know her, what do you think?'

Ashley didn't know what to think. She wasn't sure if she should be disgusted, or maybe in awe of that competitive zeal, or maybe just a little more frightened of her from now on.

'I don't know, but anyhow how about tomorrow, or maybe a swim?' Ashley said with an additional steely gaze.

Chris laughed off her suggestion and retreated around the corner towards the showers. When he reached the locker room, Jeffrey was in front of a mirror with a contact lens on the tip of a finger. Chris looked at the open container with the L on the blue lid and felt a twinge of guilt.

'Jeffrey, if someone was the victim of a prank and you found out about it, you'd tell them, wouldn't you?'

'No way, people get what they deserve. I wouldn't interfere.'

'But even if it would frighten them, or even medically affect them?'

'Not a chance, I'd just sit back and let it roll.'

'What if it was me?' asked Chris.

‘Especially not if it was you. I saw you and Ashley did some kind of hare and tortoise run this morning. You know which one you are, don’t you?’

‘Yes, I see. Talk to you later.’ Chris walked away, leaving Jeffrey to fix his contaminated contact lenses and marvelled at the power of karma.

Chapter 11: Perils

Jeffrey had left the locker room and picked up his usual double expresso macchiato, but by the time he was climbing up the back stairs he had also gotten double vision.

He was worried now. He had decided he had multiple sclerosis and on top of everything else that diagnosis would disqualify him from obtaining a Consultant job. Professor Stone fixing the interview wasn't going to help if he failed the medical. Seeing Dr Rossi ascending the stairs he stopped and waited for her.

The echo in the stairwell made his trembling voice a little shriller and more anxious 'So for the last couple of days I've had numbness in my leg. Now with the blurring of vision I'm even more convinced. I really think I have MS,' he said.

Dr Rossi nodded slowly. She had been making her way to the operating theatre when Jeffrey had stopped her. She was expecting a petulant outburst, possibly a replay of the latest playground squabble with the other children. This was much more interesting. She wondered whether he was cracking under the pressure of surgical training: maybe a little bit of Munchausen syndrome. She'd seen lots of hypochondriac doctors. They took a few symptoms, mixed them together in a brain only suited to soaking up information and produced a fruit cake.

'Another thing… last week my urine turned blue for two days.'

Rossi unintentionally gave him the special look doctors sometimes give patients, where the left eyebrow is raised and the head inclined forwards. It translates as '*Mad as a small mental hospital'*.

Stone being his mentor meant that she had a jaundiced view about him to begin with. But now that she looked at him again, she could see there was something wrong: his head did look asymmetrical. It was the eyes: the pupils were different sizes. She was opinionated, strong-willed and belligerent at times, but she was an astute enough clinician not to let her prejudices cloud her judgement. Maybe there was something wrong with him.

'Well, it's probably nothing but I think you're right: it might do no harm to get an MRI scan of your brain and a lumbar puncture to make sure you don't have MS. I don't know about the urine thing… porphyria is unlikely. You remember the movie '*The Madness of King George'*, that's what he had.'

Seeing his bulging eyes, she instantly regretted making the suggestion that he might actually have a genuine disease. 'Anyhow, leave it with me, I'll get back to you later.'

Jeffrey sighed with relief: sharing his fears and having a plan calmed his nerves. Somehow the thought of having a disease to go with his symptoms was a relief. Dr Rossi wasn't the most empathetic person, but she got things done. He stood on the landing and became aware of a tapping noise in his head. He thought it was his heartbeat, or the second hand of a clock but then he realised it was Dr Rossi's high heels rapidly ascending the stairs in her usual manner.

Rossi knew Jeffrey was a hypochondriac, but those were significant symptoms that needed investigation. What she couldn't understand was the eyes. Possibly a brain tumour, or maybe trauma… MS was possible, or what illegal drugs could cause unequal pupil sizes?

Chris wasn't on her list of possible causes. He had showered and drunk two bottles of water after his run but was exhausted now and shrouded in brain fog. He was slumped onto the nurses' station desk, with his head resting on his folded arms. He was dozing despite the four coffees he had in an attempt to get a caffeine lift. He wasn't in a deep sleep. It wasn't that the stimulant effect of the caffeine was countering his tiredness, but the discomfort of a litre of fluid now resting in his bladder was effectively combating full unconsciousness. A series of loud cracking noises suddenly made him sit up.

'Christ almighty, gunshots,' he mumbled and quickly looked around for the back door. As the fog in his brain cleared, he focused on the noises. They were coming closer, but they were too repetitive and exact to be gunshots, they were almost like a machine press hammering out a regular rhythm. He eased forward and looked down the corridor at the advancing Dr Rossi with her stiletto heels drumming out a staccato beat on the tiled floor.

She always scared him and he had known her long enough to see that she was in DEFCON 5 mode at this point. Chris didn't know about her early morning meeting about the deadish episode, or her interaction with Jeffrey. He was sharp enough though to see that something was clearly bothering her. He sensed trouble when he saw the angle of her face and saw that if she walked into a wall, the first point to meet it would be her chin and not her nose.

Although, given that determined steely walk and stormy expression, either her nose or chin would fracture any wall they encountered today. She was wearing her customary shiny pearl necklace, today it reminded him more of a belt of machine gun bullets around the neck of a Marine. To succeed in a testosterone-fuelled world as a female surgeon, she had had to be smarter, work harder, cut faster and outdrink anyone else in the herd of junior doctors vying like wildebeest climbing a riverbank to become a Consultant. She was hard-core, Marine Corps and she had just landed on Chris's beach.

She slammed both hands down on the desk in front of him and fixed him with a stare holding him in position as rigidly as if she had him pinned under one of her stiletto heels. He nervously swallowed, knowing escape was impossible. What with his fear and the coffee sloshing around in his bilges, if he was ever going to wet himself it was going to be now.

'Deadish?' With a single word she held him suspended in mid-air, gasping for a response to an unanswerable question.

'Well, the thing about that was… the patient, she was, you know dead. But then she wasn't for a while and then she was again, so, I, actually we, Dr Brown was there…'

She tightened her lips, waiting to see if Chris pursued that line of defence to implicate Ashley, but Chris realised his error and tried to backtrack.

'Obviously, we both were there and together so, and it wasn't great, but it's all sorted now, and nobody died, oh… except the patient, but that's what we wanted. No, I mean that's not what anyone wanted. I didn't kill her!' Chris knew he was babbling incoherently, but she frightened him, he really needed to pee and he wasn't certain he hadn't killed the elderly patient now.

'Chris, when that resuscitation went wrong you should have been out there with Ashley. I would have hoped you could have seen the need for a mature, professional intervention, or at the very least some support in talking down the situation.'

'I know, I accept that wasn't good. I mean, I was trying with sign language….' said Chris.

'I've just had an hour in administration dealing with the fallout from the complaint about that comment. I really don't lose any sleep over 95-year-olds dying. I do care about you guys making this institution look like a scene in a bad horror movie. Now we have to endure an after-action review of this case with Professor Stone in his chief of clinical governance role. Do you know how much I object to losing an hour of my life to a meeting with Stone and Mary Gallen pontificating and posturing about stuff that doesn't matter unless they can escalate it into something?'

She began to de-escalate the array of weaponry in her facial expressions. As the head began to drop forward and some of the contours on her face went from below the horizontal to marginally above, he sensed he might not be in so much trouble.

'You've got to understand that it's not what happened that matters: it's how people perceive things. If they can use a situation and twist the truth and take things out of context then they have ammunition to fire at us. You need to be so careful when you're working in a snake pit' said Rossi.

'We were just trying our best, it was all a bit confused.'

'Chris, it's like this, you and Ashley, I've known you both for years. It's not that the woman was going to live: of course she was going to die. It's about how you talk to people, improvise, be quick on your feet, and at least pretend to be in control and competent. This job is more about managing the process, managing the people, choreographing and controlling the situation than doing big operations.'

Chris nodded in acknowledgement. His discomfort about the whole situation was magnified because, as she had pointed out, she had known him for years. He had always respected her skill, tensile steel personality, and empathetic professional demeanour. She was one of the people who had supported him and encouraged him to choose surgery as a career.

She paused, giving Chris time to absorb what she was saying and then continued. 'Look at Stone, we all know he's at best an average surgeon. Maybe not even that good: but he has a huge practice, the referring docs respect him, the patients love him and he's up to his neck in every administrative committee, political fundraiser and charity function in a hundred-mile radius. They can't see that his surgical technique is about as precise as a hurricane. But he controls the narrative. The flashy suits, the pastel dicky bow ties, the confident speech… if you look and sound the part you can get away with murder, literally in his case.

He's a showman, an actor and its bloody effective at getting everyone to believe he's a superstar.'

Chris was taken aback; it wasn't usual for Consultants to be so frank with registrars.

'So, what I'm saying to you is wise up: you need to learn to create the same aura that he has. Just maybe be a better surgeon, that helps too, if you have less disasters to explain away.'

'But why do you support him and work here with all of that going on in the background?'

'Simple, he's useful. In any department it's useful to have a schmoozer to do all that stuff. He goes to all the meetings, gets the funding to staff and equip the place. He absolutely loves the spotlight and performs really well. Sure, it feathers his ego and he excludes anyone else from being involved, but why would any of us want to constantly live in that fake world anyhow?'

'Ok, but I'm such a minor player in this, and so is Ashley: why is he out to get us?'

'Chris, people who are only out for themselves, without principles or moral standards, will always go with the quick fix. They don't have a view of the bigger picture beyond instant response to a threat by attack. He feels exposed by the lack of notes in the chart for the deadish thing, plus you witnessed the Louise Stark catastrophe. Now you will serve nicely as a scapegoat to remove any blame and hide the fact that he can't operate his way out of a paper bag. There's also this job coming up, and everything that happens now might influence who's successful in that interview. You understand he doesn't see the appointment of a new colleague as an open competition, he sees it as a favour he controls and can bequeath. It's about power, if he controls appointments, he expects blind loyalty forever in return.'

Dr Rossi noted Chris shifting uncomfortably. She read this as him being unsure and uncomfortable with all this grown-up talk.

'Look Chris, I'm sorry to have to say all of this to you. So, we need to manage this situation and I just want you guys not to mess up.'

Chris felt an overwhelming sense of achievement that Dr Rossi considered him a prospective colleague, someone who could step up to the plate and be trusted to use their surgical skill and judgement to look after people. It was what he had worked towards for years. He had invested the majority of his adult life in long hospital shifts and a grinding sequence of study, exams, qualifications, research, more exams and all while treating and operating on the thousands of patients that an apprenticeship in surgery requires. To have this recognised by his teacher and mentor was a vindication of his life's work. It just had never fully occurred to him that there was a parallel universe of political intrigue and scheming that also needed to be worked in order to succeed.

'So look, you and Ashley just need to keep a low profile, do your jobs well, and mind the patients. Just remember, *primum non nocere: first do no harm*. I'm going to simplify this for you, stop killing people. No more PR disasters. Got it'?

'Absolutely Dr Rossi, and thanks for your faith in me' said Chris as he quickly stood up and walked down the corridor.

Meanwhile Dr Rossi walked back along the corridor and spotting Ashley in the treatment room, she clipped over to her.

'Ashley, if you wouldn't mind just booking an MRI brain and a lumbar puncture for Jeffrey this afternoon. I hope it's nothing, but he does have good symptoms for MS.'

'No problem, I'll get that organised. Should I do the puncture?'

'No, maybe call me and I'll do it with you this afternoon.'

Ashley immediately returned to the computer and began to book the radiology tests. It felt different booking tests for someone she knew. She grimaced as she entered the clinical details. She needed to put in the possible causes so that the doctors reading the scan would know what to look for. As she typed out 'possible brain tumour, or query multiple sclerosis', they seemed like scarier diseases when they could affect a real person. Chris reappeared around the corner looking much relieved.

'Why the worried face?' he asked Ashley.

'Dr Rossi thinks Jeffrey might have MS. He has numbness in his leg and blurring of vision. Sounds a bit like it' said Ashley.

'Probably since he put in his contact lenses this morning?'

'What? I don't know, what difference does that make, that won't cause leg numbness.'

'That's priceless,' said Chris, delighted with his theatrical production.

'No Chris, it's not, it's absolutely not. I have to organise an MRI and a lumbar puncture for him.'

'Oh shit. She's taking it that wat too seriously. Maybe they should wait a while. Alright, I'll go and talk to him, don't do anything. Or say anything. I'll sort it out,' said Chris and started heading away to find Jeffrey.

'What do you mean? But Dr Rossi told me to, I have to!' shouted Ashley at his back. He didn't turn around but waved his hand in a gesture that left Ashley none the wiser.

By the time Chris walked into the changing room he had organised his thoughts. He would tell Jeffrey to relax, that he was working too hard. Give it 24 hours and if the symptoms went away then he would know it was nothing. Given that Chris had been dispensing the symptoms, he was fairly certain they would disappear now that he had to stop before things escalated any further. Unable to find him in the changing room, he did at least find an inviting couch where he stretched out full-length waiting for Jeffrey to show up.

While Chris dreamed about crossing marathon finishing lines, Ashley was working diligently. She went to the radiology department and found Dr Cork the radiologist at his desk in a darkened room. Ashley sighed internally, everyone else in the world looks at computer screens in daylight but radiologist do it in the dark. It was part of the drama they tried to create around a speciality that should have long since have been replaced by computers. It astonished Ashley that they had perpetuated the concept that humans could read a computer image better than a machine, it was the equivalent of running a bank on a big paper ledger with tellers, rather than using an IT system. Apart from creating drama, Ashley found one of the key paradoxes of radiology, to be that they spent most of their working day trying to stop scans being done. As a surgeon all she wanted to do was operate, she couldn't understand why after choosing radiology all these nerds wanted to do was take the ball away and go home.

Ashley explained the need for Jeffrey's MRI and Dr Cork asked cursory questions that only served to betray how little he knew about multiple sclerosis. Ashley patiently and pleasantly answered the pointless interrogation in order to get the scan done. He eventually agreed to do it and Ashley left, looking forward to the day when radiologists would be consigned to history in the way of chimney sweeps, barrel makers, CDs and cherry Coke.

The result unsurprisingly, was normal. Armed with a normal scan she marched on and arranged the lumbar puncture test. She assembled all the necessary equipment in the treatment room on the ward. Once she had Jeffrey on the trolley, she phoned Dr Rossi and had everything ready to go when she arrived.

Dr Rossi adjusted her gloves and turned to Jeffrey who was lying on his side, on the trolley in the foetal position facing away from her. Ashley, ever the professional had forced him to put on a sky-blue hospital gown, which was open at the back. She slipped the crisp white sheet down to the level of his hips and, once she had a satisfactory 90-degree angle between the sheet and the trolley, stood back.

'Now Jeffrey, just bring up your knees to your chest and I'm just going to clean your lower back with some antiseptic' said Dr Rossi. 'Just some local anaesthetic now' as she stabbed him with the small needle and injected the clear solution. His piercing shriek in response to the local anaesthetic, was a little disproportionate she thought. It didn't augur well for what was to come.

She lowered her head and steadied herself for what was shaping up to be a difficult experience for both of them. *Probably worse for Jeffrey though,* she thought, *although I'd feel better if he didn't whine like a stuck brake pad.* The purpose of the lumbar puncture was to get a sample, to test, of the fluid around the spinal cord. Getting the slender, but six-inch long needle through his skin and muscle, onwards between the vertebral bones, through the lining of the spinal cord and into the space where the fluid would be, resembled drilling for oil with thin knitting needles in the small of his back.

Ashley stood behind Dr Rossi watching the process. She couldn't bring herself to feel that Jeffrey was getting what karma dictated he deserved. She was incapable of schadenfreude, but she just didn't feel sorry for him. She watched as Dr Rossi picked up the six-inch needle. She slowly punctured through the skin, then she prodded through the grisly steak of muscle. The firm scrape of needle on ivory told her she was inching between the vertebral bones. After a couple of further scrapes as she plunged the needle in and out, it eventually found a gap in Jeffrey spinal bones, and she edged the needle forward into the fluid surrounding the spinal cord. As Dr Rossi was patiently skewering Jeffrey onto her needle he bellowed vigorously. The shouts echoed down the corridor and even into the changing room where they briefly awoke Chris, who momentarily wondered what all the noise was about before he slipped back into a peaceful sleep.

Chapter 12: Sorryish

The following morning saw Chris and Ashley in the hospital boardroom. They had been instructed to attend at 8am to meet the family of the late Mary Kennedy.

'This is a fine table for this size room' Chris said.

He was sitting with Ashley on their side of the fine table, while the three middle-aged siblings, two men and a woman, were on the other. They were sitting rigidly upright, soberly dressed, almost as if they were coming from their mother's funeral. Chris's mouth was dry and he just couldn't get comfortable in his chair. It wasn't the chair that was the problem though: it was being in a meeting about how he and Ashley had contributed to these people's mother needing a funeral in the first place that was unsettling him.

The woman replied: 'Yes, looks like cherry wood.'

'Yes, cherry, definitely,' Chris said. They had been alone for ten agonising minutes with the family, waiting for Professor Stone and Mary Gallen to arrive. If only the pleasurable moments in life could last as long as those ten minutes felt to Chris. He had utterly exhausted his repertoire of small talk and was now shifting in his chair, acutely aware of the darkening stares from across the room. The table had exhausted its contribution as a distraction. Chris briefly considered discussing the weather, but knew that would have been a wretched attempt to drag out the inevitable.

'I know I said we should wait for the others before we start, but maybe I could just chat to you about what happened with your mother.'

'Absolutely, that's why we're here' replied the son who Chris had met on the night of her death.

'First, can I just say I'm sorry for your loss and I know what happened at the time of her death made things worse and I just want to personally apologise to you for that. The bottom line is that we didn't know her background medical history, we didn't know she wasn't supposed to be resuscitated in the event of a cardiac arrest. We just got an emergency call and did what we felt was right. I'm not justifying it, that's just what happened. I'm sorry, we shouldn't have resuscitated her, and I can only apologise for that.' Chris said.

'What about the deadish thing your colleague here said?' the son said.

Ashley inclined forward not varying her gaze and looking directed at him she began to speak. ‘I’m also deeply sorry. I got flummoxed with the situation, I was distracted and it just all came out wrong. We now know that the tests and scans taken during your mother’s admission showed she was critically ill with heart disease that wasn’t curable. She had a massive heart attack that night: it wasn’t preventable, she was going to die irrespective of what we did or didn’t do and that’s just the nature of these things sometimes. We made the situation worse by resuscitating her when we should have stepped back and left her to die in dignity and I can only apologise for that, I can’t change what happened.’

Separating her intertwined fingers, the daughter released her hands and laid them flat on the table in front of her. The blotches of purple alternating with white on her fingers quickly began to fade but were a clear sign of her tension.

‘It’s just we wouldn’t want to see this happen to anyone else,’ she said.

‘I would say personally, I’ve learnt from it, and we have changed the policy so that anyone who is not for resuscitation now has a different colored wristband to avoid this confusion in the future' Chris said.

The son was now sitting forward: he said 'I guess we didn't know how sick she was and I appreciate your apology and explanation, so I guess we can move on and I'm glad that maybe the new wristband thing might help others.'

Chris felt emotional, recognising the dignity of the family who had lost a parent but could see the big picture. He felt he should respond but knew that his voice might betray his emotions. A loud bang against the door caused everyone to turn to see who had tried to walk through the door without using the handle. On his second attempt Stone wrestled with the handle and, after successfully defeating it, he burst into the room.

Just behind Stone came Mary Gallen holding her administrator head high in the air.

Everyone took their places opposite the family, except the Professor who opted for the seat at the head of the table. Chris took mental note of his separating himself from the potential cannon fodder he was presenting to the family. Although, at the same time, he wondered if he was getting paranoid: maybe Stone was just posturing and it didn't mean anything.

Ashley previously calm manner now dissolved as she blurted out 'I've just apologized for killing their mother.' It was a stress reaction, an inability to divorce professional from personal life. Doctors who were living, breathing and drowning every day in a sea of human misery often cracked up and felt they were responsible for all the suffering in the world.

Stone immediately took the role of chairman 'Well thanks for that Dr Brown. I think everyone knows each other, I want to thank you all for coming to clear the air. Firstly, as professor of surgery, chairman on the department and head of clinical governance I'm happy to address any questions you might have. We run a highly successful program with the best international results. Obviously if anyone was to feel unhappy or thought there were issues with any patient's care then perhaps, I can clear up any misinterpretations.'

Mary swelled up in her chair on his left and addressed the family. 'Now we are not here to ascribe blame: as you know we have an open disclosure a no-blame culture in Serenity. Dr Brown you seem to have acknowledged just now, that her death was all your fault? You don't mind if I just record this meeting just so there won't be any misunderstanding afterwards.' Without waiting for a response, she placed a recording dictaphone in the center of the cherry table.

Stone glanced at Chris with irritation, it was clear that Chris's face had betrayed his belief that this wasn't what an apology sounded like. Chris felt he needed to get back to the point he had been at with the family before Stone had come in to discuss his own importance and virtues.

'Professor we've already had a chat and I've apologised for what happened to their mother,' Chris said.

'Well, that's great: if anyone felt upset, then clearly Dr Newman should be sorry that you feel like that,' said Stone.

'It's not a question of how we feel about the situation, it is about the facts of how my mother's death was managed' said the son sharply, his previous acceptance now dissolving rapidly. He went on, 'If you think this institution is so great, how did our mother get put through CPR that she had specifically said she never wanted?'

'If I can help there,' interjected Mary 'we have hospital policies and procedures covering all of these areas, I can provide them for you. The hospital has no liability and no responsibility in this matter.'

'I'm finding it hard to understand this: we came here as a family because we were upset at our mother's death. You record the meeting and in legalese tell us you have no responsibility and your policies are fine. So how was my mother resuscitated against her will?' asked the son.

'No need to be shouting or getting aggressive with the nurses now,' said Stone.

'What the hell do you mean by that?' said the son who up to that point, had neither been shouting nor aggressive.

Ashley had been watching this car crash unfold with horror, it felt like the worst family Christmas day row ever. She wanted to put her head in her hands or preferably slide under the table and escape. If only she'd had time to read the chart the whole deadish episode might never have happened and she wouldn't have had to be here.

In the silent standoff between Stone and the son, Ashley quietly spoke, 'Like Dr Newman I personally just want to say how sorry I am about what happened, no policy or explanation will change the distress of that night and I'm just sorry.'

'So, Dr Newman and Dr Brown have both apologised,' said Stone. 'Ms Galen as hospital manager, has outlined the hospital policies that were in place: they may, or may not have been followed by these two doctors. In any event that is their responsibility alone. I wasn't there, I had nothing to do with it. I will therefore request the hospital administration to set up an inquiry into these two doctors and take whatever action up to and including sacking them. I can assure you the inquiry won't be found lacking in pursuing the matter and taking disciplinary action.'

The son stood up rigidly and signified the end of the meeting with a terse: 'Fine, we will look forward to the report.'

Mary stood up and addressed a final offering to the family.

'In the meanwhile, I'll ensure Dr Brown attends a patient support group and gets some education in anger management and retraining in unconscious bias.'

She followed the family out leaving Professor Stone and a shell-shocked Chris and Ashley.

'Anger management, I never did, I never said anything, why is she even saying that?' said Ashley, simmering at Mary finding her guilty of a crime nobody had even accused her of, and suggesting she needed retraining in some kind of bias she had never even heard of. She hadn't even the good grace to wait for the investigation report before passing sentence.

Professor Stone looked at their ashen faces and with an expansive, dismissive wave he said 'Well, that could have gone a little better.'

Chris almost choked, *could have gone better?*

'This will all pass away: Chris you're a smart guy, you will figure this out and it will be fine. Ashley, you're a great girl, I'm sure you will be fine dealing with the investigation and some patient education sessions. I just came up with it on the spot and I think it will be the best way for you guys to sort this all out.'

Stone stood up and readjusted his appearance by buttoning his suit jacket. He brushed down the cloth with the same rough backhanded swipes that Chris recognised from operating with him. He couldn't decide if the swipes were to shoo away his fat gut that he'd never noticed before, or perhaps it was a type of shaman ritual to ward off the evil spirits.

From his reclining position Professor Stone edged forward and, with his arms extended onto the table surface, he said 'Can I just say, that I agree with everything that everyone said here today. Ashley did her best and we have to work within the rules of open disclosure. It is, as always, a question of good judgement in these matters. So don't worry Ashley I have your back, you understand?'

Chris felt his heart race: he had first-hand experience of Professor Stone having his back with Louise Stark. He hadn't needed stitches, but he knew how it felt to be deliberately stabbed on that occasion.

'Oh, thanks Professor, that's great to know,' said Ashley.

Chris despaired; Ashley was giving Stone the big Labrador eyes. It had completely gone over her head that what he had said was a threat.

'I'll just get a coffee and I'll be back with Mary for the next two complaints in a couple of minutes. I guess they don't directly involve you Chris, but you can stay if you want' said Stone as he left the room.

'Chris, what the hell just happened there, Stone was there on the ward when that woman died. What does an inquiry mean? I think we're in serious trouble,' said Ashley, with her face hidden in a forest of fingers.

'Well, it looks pretty simple to me, Stone was there, but he walked away when he saw it was going downhill. Now they are saying it's all down to us, he wants to sacrifice us to prevent him or the hospital getting any criticism. This didn't need to happen, they're reasonable people, I had it under control, until he came in with his ego and that witch recording the conversation,' Chris said.

'I feel sick, why would he do that to us? OK we made a mistake, but he could have had a tiny bit of empathy for the family, some support for us and put this behind us. He basically came in and told them how great he was, that the hospital had a policy, falsely accused the guy of being aggressive and disowned us. We better talk to Attwood, we need help.'

'Yeah, Attwood is good, but if this is going to be a knife fight, I'd rather have Rossi. She's tough, I heard she did her own colonoscopy.'

'That family were so nice, it's a shame it all turned so unpleasant. I can't believe I have two more to deal with today. How on earth do I get myself into these situations? I'm not a bad person, it does seem unfair, but it's not their fault.'

Chris admired Ashley's ability on occasions to soak up difficult encounters and move on, he was incapable of forgiving and forgetting so easily.

'I'm not so sure Ashley, you missed the bit where the daughter said she just didn't want this to happen to anyone else. Anyone who's been doing this for any length of time knows that that statement is a complete cliché. It's usually planted by lawyers.'

'You don't really believe that do you?'

'Tell me, every time, every single time you see someone take out a lawsuit, aren't the words "*I just don't want this to happen to anyone else*", front and center? It's planted there by lawyers to justify their appalling profiteering from peoples' injuries. They use that phrase to set themselves up as some sort of messiahs, who have come to save the world through their good works. Their good works obviously being getting paid shedloads of money.'

'Ah no, I don't believe that. You are born cynical. What did make you this way?'

'Mock me all you like, but it's true. I bet the next two complaints which, as the insightful Professor pointed out, are just yours, they will go away if they're offered money. All that moral indignation and guff about preventing others being affected goes up in a puff of smoke when they light the first cigar with the winnings. Medical litigation is no different from playing the lottery, they're coming in here scratching a few cards to see if there is any cash underneath. It's just another way of making some money in life. I'm not cynical about it, it's just a fact.'

'No… some people are just more sensitive and complaints actually help to improve the service anyhow in the long term.'

'You know what's actually interesting here is something completely different. After all the stuff you've been through in the last while, all the encounters with unpleasant patients and malevolent staff, have you learnt nothing from all of that? You've been working hard, trying your best to help people and look where it's gotten you: in a room for a half day dealing with bullshit complaints. I've got to say I admire your ability not to look facts in the face and to soak up all of this abuse from everyone. You're like a medical punch bag where everyone can let out their frustrations, a bit like Twitter.'

Ashley didn't get a chance to reply before Professor Stone and Mary re-entered the room. Mary was guiding Dorothy Parks in and showed her to her chair. This gave Ashley time to compose herself as she knew from experience that Dorothy maneuvering herself into any chair was comparable to an eighteen-wheel truck reversing down a supermarket aisle. On this occasion, at least, Ashley knew she hadn't done anything wrong. Her operation on Dorothy's hernia had been successful, there were no complications, and she hadn't left the burger between the folds of flab on her abdomen. She had a duty to discuss the risks of obesity with her patient. Chris had a point: Dorothy really didn't have grounds for a complaint and Ashley resolved to be strong.

Mary began proceedings. 'So, Dorothy, we've had a chance to talk when I met you in my office, but maybe you can tell us your story.'

'Yes, Dr Brown was grossly negligent and botched my surgery. Thankfully I'm a survivor of hernia surgery, but it has been very traumatic.' Dorothy said with all the sincerity of someone who had recently consulted a lawyer.

'That's terrible Dorothy, I'm a nurse myself you know, and I understand these things. Maybe you can give us a little more detail,' said Mary.

The '*I'm a nurse myself comment'* had resonated with Chris and Ashley. In the context of hospital politics, being an ex-nurse gave Mary the ability to express medical opinions on any area whatsoever under discussion. It was a comment they had heard frequently before from nurses when they were patients themselves, patients' relatives or as opinionated bystanders. No good ever came from it.

'Yes, the treatment I had, it fell below the standards to be expected of a similarly qualified practitioner' Dorothy quoted, looking at everyone around the table to make sure they understood her legal advisors definition of negligence.

Nurses in Serenity Hospital fell into two groups, the selfless, caring, compassionate and utterly professional group, who stayed in direct contact in patient care, and the group that hated people in general and especially sick people. This latter group inevitably gravitated to management, and away from caring for and about people, as soon as possible in their careers. Many were simply so bullying and unpleasant that was easier to promote them to a desk job than suffer them on the wards where they had to interact with people. Mary lived in the world of greasy pole-climbing ex-nurses in management. Serenity was no different from any other organization, in that the ambitious, aggressive and narcissistic were grotesquely overrepresented in the management structures.

Mary Gallen trafficked off the goodwill justifiably accorded to nurses. As the living embodiment of Florence Nightingale, she represented all that was good in the world while all others, especially doctors, were made from puppy dogs' tails.

'Dorothy, clearly, you've had a lot of complications and you've had a terrible time. Did you have a wound problem and did someone say something about your weight? Possibly you can tell us about all of that?'

From Chris's point of view, Mary had just stepped into the role of lead prosecutor and had accepted the assertion that Dorothy had had a complication of the surgery. That she wasn't on their side as hospital manager was bad enough, but accepting as fact that there were complications without any evidence simply confirmed his view that everyone was out to get them.

By contrast Ashley thought it was good that Mary was being empathetic and allowing Dorothy to share her story. Chris saw her widening her eyes and dropping her blonde head: she was going full Labrador puppy again. She only needed to stick her tongue out and wag her tail to complete the picture. He shook his head in despair.

'Yes, it's been awful. I could have died. I was perfectly well before I came to hospital, then I had all these complications after the surgery. Dr Brown accused me of leaving that burger on the wound to cause an infection and said I was fat. It's appalling for a doctor to treat a patient like that,' said Dorothy.

'Yes, I know' said Mary writing down the facts.

'Oh yes, another thing, I just don't want another patient to go through what I went through,' said Dorothy.

The paper coffee cup crumpled under the force of the pressure of Chris's violent grip. As it was half full, the liquid shot upwards and ejected the lid into the air. It all happened as if in slow motion, like the launch of a space rocket and everyone was tuned in as the coffee splashed back to earth on the table in front of Chris followed by the black lid gently landing with a click.

Once Chris had mopped up his cynicism from the table, the discussion resumed.

'Dorothy, I'd like to apologise for what happened and I accept full responsibility for the complications' said Ashley.

'Perhaps, on Ashley's behalf, if I might just make a couple of points' Chris said.

Mary's raised eyebrows clearly indicated any points for the defense were to be viewed in the same way as adult birthday cards with the age on them.

'Dorothy, when you say you were completely well before you came to hospital, surely you must have had some problem that required you to come here?' Chris said.

'Of course, I had a strangulated hernia.'

'Yes, that's a painful nasty thing to have, so you weren't completely well then when you came to hospital.'

'Well, yes apart from that.'

'Sure, perfectly well apart from that painful, potentially life-threatening illness which could have killed you?'

'Yes.'

'But Dr Brown operated, fixed the hernia, got rid of your pain and saved your life.'

'Well, yes, but that's doesn't matter, that's her job. It's what she said about the burger and me being fat and the complications I had.'

'I understand, she saved your life, and you are angry with her for that, but when you say complications, there actually weren't any. However the burger got in there, it certainly wasn't Dr Brown's fault and ethically doctors should talk to their patients about their weight to improve their long-term wellbeing. Think about it like this, if you were in a restaurant and a sommelier recommended a bottle of wine, you wouldn't take offence, you'd probably take the advice?'

'I prefer beer with Chinese food, but maybe.'

'Right, so if a sommelier offering advice is ok, then how could a doctor's advice on healthy eating be offensive?'

Dorothy didn't have an immediate response, which allowed Mary in: 'I would just like to thank Dorothy for coming in today and as she said we just want to prevent this from happening to anyone else.'

Stone pushed his coffee cup to the side to make room for a story. 'Well, can I just tell you now, that I remember operating on a man one Christmas Eve who had a huge hernia, the size of a small horse! He was huge, we're talking a front row rugby player, and he really let himself go. We needed a hoist to get him up onto the two operating tables we had put side by side to accommodate him. So, it took me four hours to do: I had to remove half his colon, a whack of the stomach and the spleen. But I fixed it and I got home just in time to put the Christmas presents under the tree.'

'Wow, did he survive?' asked Ashley.

Stone gave her a lingering look to see if she was being sarcastic about Dorothy's survivor of surgery comment. Ashley's sincere blue eyes truthfully told him she didn't play that game. 'I've no idea, the point is that I've seen a lot of these cases over the years and I'd like to thank Dorothy for sharing her experience with us today.'

Dorothy didn't quite grasp the relevance of the story. Chris did, it was a Stone special, another episode which might, or might not, have been true, where he came in as the all-powerful surgeon arriving like a superhero on his white horse to save the day. It was staged for Christmas Eve, so as part of the fiction he could pretend he contributed more than anyone else to the emergency roster.

Mary was smart enough to realise she wasn't going to be able to make much progress with Dorothy so, having decided she had heard enough evidence, she thanked her for her time and escorted her out of the room.

Things didn't get any easier for Ashley when Jody Casey and her strong jaw line next entered the room and began to explain how she too didn't want this to happen to anyone else.

Chapter 13: Committee Meeting

Dr Attwood looked at his team and compared it to the opposition. Around the table with him, were Professor Stone and Dr Rossi, in addition to the four Consultant Anaesthetists and four Emergency Room Consultants present: this constituted the Surgical Division of Serenity Hospital. On his team at this meeting, he had Rossi at quarterback. He could rely on two of the anaesthetists, and maybe, two of the Emergency Room doctors. They were known as ER docs because they all secretly wanted to be like actors from that show. That left Stone, two anaesthetists and two ER doctors on the opposing side. Six to five in his favour, he had made sure the ones he needed would turn up. Going to any meeting, without having the bases loaded as much as possible, would be such an amateur mistake.

Apart from Rossi, none of them looked particularly fit, but this was a mental rather than a physical battle. Like any game, experience, ability and match fitness were key.

He compared the faces around the table: mostly he was struck by the wrinkles and furrows. Some were age-related, but most of these facial contortions just mirrored a harrowed state of mind. Grey thinning hair combined with erratic hairs on earlobes and emerging from nostrils marked the silverbacks, apart from Dr Rossi. Her earlobes aged with expanding diamonds.

Attwood looked at them and reflected on the maxim that every political career ends in failure. Whether or not it's true for the greasy pole of political life, it's a certainty for surgeons. Age, with its gradual deterioration of physical skills, eyesight and stamina, denies surgeons the option of a prolonged career. It's only the most belligerent, impotent bull elephants that stomp around their surgical watering holes into old age. However, the unwillingness of type A personalities to walk away, from the career that defines their very core, at the right time is a toxic mix. He remembered being with the previous Professor when he had been tasked to do more and more of the operations as his mentor's skill and eyesight had deteriorated. He had learned to walk and talk to the Professors right side as his left sided deafness pushed him to the other side. It was pattern he'd seen repeated in aging surgeons, where the space created by loss of skill and eyesight wasn't filled with any insight.

In this room he needed to understand the interactions, personalities and motivations of the individuals to win today's game. Looking at Stone, he figured the years of robust exchanges with colleagues must invariably have left a host of disgruntled colleagues and minions biding their time to extract revenge. The scars wouldn't be visible on the surface but over a career some of these colleagues and minions would have ascended into management and administrative roles. They would then be perfectly positioned to engineer the final act, the fall of the alpha male. He appreciated the delicious irony of the school dimwits ascending into management posts and finally extracting revenge on the honour's students, forty years after the last wedgie.

Dr Attwood had been chairing the meeting and the exchanges so far had been constructive, and almost friendly. That in itself was a warning sign, it was too friendly, almost contrived. He and Rossi had anticipated a backlash. They knew the pattern well after years of working with Stone. He had a predictable response to challenges or threats. He also knew how to fix a meeting. First he would do the corridor discussions, undermining an individual, then he would set them up by making a big deal of any spurious problems. At every opportunity there would be constant negative commentary and references to things that were very worrying, but he couldn't discuss. Using these building blocks of minor events that were exaggerated and distorted combined with vague serious allegations a disturbing background impression would be created. Finally, when the temperature had risen sufficiently, he would weigh in acting as a detached elder statesman and suggest an administrative intervention or process. This process, while seeming to be a fair, neutral exercise, would have a predetermined outcome. His intervention, under the guise of wise leadership, would be about as open to reason and compromise as a guillotine blade in descent. Attwood knew that Ashley had been the subject of the corridor character assassination, and that the next phase might come today. He casually looked down at the agenda.

'That's everything on the list, any other business we need to address today?'

One of the ER Consultants, Dr Mackey, shuffled his wiry frame forward in his chair and focused intently on his white polystyrene cup of coffee, while he ran a hand through his sparsely populated scalp. He was recently appointed to the hospital. He had worked with Stone as a junior doctor, but beyond that the others knew little of him. He almost apologetically began to speak.

'Well, now that we're here I might just raise an issue'.

Attwood leaned back in his chair. With his left hand resting on the side of his face, he was externally impassive. However, internally he was rapidly reviewing his playbook on Dr Mackey. Certainly a Stone supporter, didn't come across as a strong personality. He didn't have any skin in the game and would have no need to get involved unless he was coached by Stone.

'It's just a problem were having with one of the registrars.'

OK, so you're the messenger boy, Attwood thought to himself. He anticipated this would be a character assassination. It was the natural order of things that the tentacles of Stone's extensive preparation for the coronation of Jeffrey extended to slandering the competition. Attwood shuffled the possibilities in his mind and started preparing a checklist to tackle whatever was coming.

'Dr Brown is being somewhat difficult with our doctors. She expects too much to be done before she sees patients for us. We are too busy to be doing all this work for her: she should just see patients directly when we ask,' said Dr Mackey.

'OK, Dr Lacky, just tell me a bit more, what specifically is the issue?' Attwood said, deliberately using the wrong name and giving himself a little time to process the accusations and respond. He also wanted more detail in order to find holes he could attack and undermine. He flicked a glance at Dr Rossi and saw her with the cold, narrow, unfeeling eyes of a traffic warden who has already written the ticket fixed upon the Dr Mackey.

Rossi had zero tolerance for fools or anyone who didn't meet her high standards for patient care. That covered quite a lot of people in the hospital, but she was especially intolerant of ER doctors, not in a lactose-intolerant way, more like the way of Celtic and Rangers. To her they didn't justify the title of doctor: they were like traffic police, who simply pointed patients in the direction of the doctor who could actually do something to help them.

'Actually, it's Dr Mackey, not Lacky. Anyhow, she expects blood tests and X-rays to be done and notes written, and the results to be back before she will see referrals. We do the initial assessment and then refer to the service that can deal with the problem. It's not our job to be doing all of these other things' said the ER doc.

'I see, so she's asking too much, expecting you guys to have done all the tests and made a diagnosis before you refer them on,' Attwood said.

'Exactly, we don't need to be doing all that.'

Attwood and Rossi had years of running meetings to play off and championship levels. Rossi was familiar with Attwood's wrong name ploy. It was a simple distraction technique. Rossi liked it as a tactic: not only did it make people appear unsettled, it frequently did so when people were already in a stressful position, to an extent that they babbled or lost their train of thought. It was obvious that Dr Mackey either was unsettled or didn't have much substance to him to begin with. Either way, he was now distracted. Attwood passed him on to Rossi in a choreographed move.

'So, Dr Mackey, I'm confused… maybe you can help me on this,' she said. 'If you haven't done the tests and X-rays and don't have a diagnosis, how do you know it's even a surgical problem before you call her as the surgeon? Without basic blood tests and investigations, you might be at risk of missing what's wrong with the patients.

For example, you might not recognise someone with say, unexpected ectopic pregnancy or a heart attack mimicking belly pain.'

She had melted the death stare and replaced it with a confused puppy dog look instead. Attwood, who was well used to double speak in meetings, appreciated the delivery. As doctor, whatever his name, was floundering. Attwood could see he wasn't up against a strong player. The team manager might be a tougher nut to crack but for the moment a good cop, good cop strategy was best. He decided that fake concern about patient safety, a tried and tested strategy, was the way to apply a stranglehold.

'Dr Rossi raises some issues there that are obviously a worry as they mean that patients might not access the right service. Now that you've brought it up, I would have some concerns about some recent risk issues that were identified coming from the ER department. As you know we have a risk register in the hospital that captures all the notified errors and near misses,' he said.

Attwood picked up a voluminous red folder which had index tabs neatly organised and different coloured post-it notes highlighting specific pages. The ED doc was sitting back away from the table with a concerned look. He wasn't worried about explaining how to spell his name anymore.

Everyone in the room was now captivated with Attwood's large red folder. There was an air of anticipation, and uncertainty. In the same way as when the school principal came into the classroom looking for someone, until the name was read out, nobody was relaxed or certain they were entirely guilt-free.

Dr Mackey had simply been given instructions to drop some casual slander and it now appeared Attwood had a dossier on his department.

'We're getting a little side-tracked here. I just wanted to raise some concerns about Dr Brown, it's not a big deal, and I just thought I'd mention it. We can just keep it among ourselves and keep an eye on it.' He wanted to move on and clearly wished he hadn't got into this. His worried expression declared that probing under the bonnet of his Department was likely to unearth some real rather than metaphorical skeletons.

'Here we go,' Attwood said cheerily shuffling a selection of pages on the table in front of him.

‘Let’s start with the simple ones, in the last month three people with previous appendectomy have been referred to surgery to have their appendix out. This one is good, in putting in a needle into chest to remove fluid one of your guys somehow put the needle into the heart almost killing that man. Here’s a brain haemorrhage your guys misdiagnosed as a migraine. This is a leaking aneurysm your guys thought had a kidney stone…’

Rossi who knew the game plan of good cop – good cop now intervened in a fake defence.

‘Thanks for that Will, we all have stories we can tell. The individual disasters don’t matter, but the key point is that it’s all about patient safety. I guess maybe Dr Brown, in asking for a higher standard, might be a good thing from a quality culture perspective’.

Before the ashen-faced Dr Mackey could respond, defend or draw breath, Attwood drew this round to a close. ‘So, I guess if Dr Brown has a flaw it’s being a perfectionist and working too hard herself. I think in terms of the organisation and patient care that’s probably a good thing. What do you think Dr Mackey?’ He felt a little guilty about simply reworking his standard advice for interview questions about a candidate’s weaknesses.

Dr Mackey wasn't a heavyweight in this sport and he stumbled and muttered a few platitudes before Stone dispensed with his glove puppet and weighed in himself.

'In my opinion, there are serious issues at stake here. It's simply not good enough that Dr Brown behaves like this, she's endangering the reputation of the hospital and our teaching program. The risk to the University of us losing out on foreign student financial contributions would be huge. We need to take action.'

Attwood needed to shift his focus now: with Dr Mackey he had been able to confuse and undermine. Stone was too good an actor to outperform, however while he was good on the stage, he was hopeless on facts.

'Sorry Professor, you mentioned students, income and reputation there: it would be good if you could give me some examples. Perhaps specific incidents that might support what you have said, as obviously there has been nothing said or discussed here or elsewhere that supports your contention that she had endangered any of those things.'

'Fine if you want to go down that route, we can do that. It's all the things we discussed here today, it's the resuscitation of the woman against her will, it's the complaint that she's transphobic, it's the complications that the Stark woman had after her appendectomy. She removed a cancer that she shouldn't have, the list goes on. The bottom line is that everyone accepts there's a problem here. I'm not even going to get into the issues around the missing morphine' Stone said.

'Well, the first thing is that narrative, that everyone knows there is a problem, is simply not the case. She's a fine doctor and a solid individual and I object to this unfair characterisation. I'm happy to deal with your other points individually, nothing we discussed today is an issue, the resuscitation was over-enthusiastic but no more than that and she didn't operate on the Stark woman. Actually, I think she was your patient Professor. Removing the cancer saved that other woman's life and, in any event, it was done under the direction of Dr Rossi' Attwood said.

Rossi, who was across the table from both Stone and Attwood, had been following intently. The stakes had now increased considerably. Stone was unloading every scrap of dirt from vague complaints to complete fabrications. He was after Ashley in a major way, the familiar rising red flush on his jowls and the fleck of spit in the corner of his mouth were the physiological evidence of it. She recognised Stone's rising irritation and the need to tread carefully. It was a fine line to achieve what they wanted without risking an overreaction. 'Perhaps I'll have a talk to her, put a plan in place and I can report back to the committee' she said.

Stone was having none of it, he had an entirely red head as the flush had extended to envelop his scalp. This was what Rossi and Attwood knew from previous experience as *condition Mars*, where his head appeared to have been replaced by the red planet. This was a volatile phase and, as if to emphasise that, he banged his fist on the table.

'I'm the Professor of Surgery and I'm not having this, I want her dismissed here and now. I don't want to hear anything else, just get rid of her. Now!' Stone said.

The room went silent. It was clear to everyone that the outburst from Stone was disproportionate and grossly unfair. The looks and lack of support told him he had lost the support of the dressing room on this one. Even his sycophants looked to the ground avoiding his gaze and any indication that they would back him on this issue.

Attwood immediately sensed weakness and saw it was too important a moment to let this advantage slip.

'Professor, if I could refer you to the standing orders of this committee section 5.1: any issues with regards to disciplinary issues involving staff must be listed in advance as an agenda item and be carried by a majority vote. As this issue isn't on the agenda we can't have a vote today. Are you proposing a motion for the next meeting?'

Stone's head hadn't gone so far out of orbit that he couldn't see he could lose a vote and that the indignity of that would be insufferable.

'Fine, well what I can do as Director of Clinical Governance is to initiate an independent disciplinary investigation into Dr Brown, which on completion will dismiss her from the training program,' he said.

'Would it be worth waiting for the outcome of that independent investigation before deciding that it's going to dismiss Dr Brown?' said Rossi. She deadpan delivery drove another dagger into Stone's back.

This dagger obviously penetrated far enough to hit a nerve; Stones planetary head was now adorned with two bulging orbiting moons in the form of eyes that threatened to spin away as fiery comets.

Attwood weighed in again with a one-two punch: 'Professor, there's a saying that goes, in any argument, when the facts are against you, argue the rules. When the rules are against you, argue the facts. When the facts and the rules are against you, bang the table and shout like hell. I don't think you have the facts or the rules with you on this one.'

It was a telling blow: after a lifetime as top dog Stone abruptly, unexpectedly was looking at the end of his moral leadership. And he probably knew it wouldn't stop there. Once he lost the invisible elements of control, he might as well walk around in a clown suit. If that happened and people no longer feared his power he had too many enemies to survive long.

'What do you mean by that? I've had enough of this, I'll deal with her directly through the hospital administration. I will have my investigation and she will be dealt with,' said he said elevating his bulk, his blood pressure, his anger and his ego out of the chair and out of the room.

This wasn't how departmental meetings usually went and the silence betrayed embarrassment and unease in the room. They, one by one, slowly got up, stretched a little and shuffled away. Eventually Rossi and Attwood were left alone at the table, which was littered with coffee cups and paper, the only visible detritus of the mighty combat that had just unfolded.

'That was good, he's behaving exactly as we predicted. We just need the next part to fall into place and we'll be rid of him for good,' Attwood said.

'He's very predictable. I think we're on track. But that was intense: we just need to be careful of the registrars getting caught up in this, especially Ashley. Just as well you knew about the meeting standing orders, or else he would have fired her there and then,' Rossi said.

Attwood leaned back and placed both hands behind his head, inhaling deeply, but finding little comfort from the air as it was so full of bad karma and evil auras. 'Yeah, about that, Stone likes to pontificate, but he never bothers to RTFM.'

'RTFM?'

'Read The Fucking Manual.'

Rossi looked at him in surprise: 'You made that up, about needing a vote to dismiss Ashley?'

'Yup.'

She laughed and some of the tension from the meeting dissipated. She was impressed by Attwood's sheer audacity, not to mention the skill in knowing that Stone firstly wouldn't know the rules and secondly wouldn't admit his ignorance of that fact. It had been a beautiful finesse play.

'Hang on: that risk register you quoted to put off the ED guy, don't tell me you invented that as well, is that folder you were taking things from even a risk register?' she said.

Attwood held up his hands in mock surrender. 'Whoa, hold on a minute, who do you think I am? I may have misread, or misspoken, or misremembered the committee rules. But we definitely have a risk register in the hospital. It's actually an online database. I only said we have one, I didn't say those examples came from it. This folder is actually my tax receipts.'

Rossi liked to think that she had a wicked twinge rather than an evil streak, but she couldn't help but admire the duplicity and mischievousness of Attwood's game. She shook with laughter, as she jerked forward and backward Attwood could hear what he thought were her pearls ratting together. Or maybe it was her joints after all those triathlons.

Chapter 14: Soccer Mom

'I'm not saying they are all evil, self-obsessed, disease-ridden burdens on their families, but look at that one' said Chris.

Ashley looked at the one he was pointing at. To be fair to Chris, the uncontrolled dribble from this one's nose must represent a serious public health issue.

Once they had located Ashley's sister Jill at the side of the soccer pitch they took their places along the white side line near the goal. Soccer for the under-ten age group was clearly a serious business. The brightly coloured team shirts were matched with white shorts and socks, the only variation being fresh patches of green grass stains or brown mud depending upon the preferences of the player. All colours except the banned blue and green ones, were represented on the field. The internecine Glaswegian warfare between Rangers and Celtics was a little too real for infants. That degree of aggression had been reserved over many generations, for those Scottish teenagers deployed overseas in the colonial British army. There was no military precision in this game. Only the goalies had any fixed position on the field. The remainder of the twenty children milled around in a mass of flailing arms, legs and bodies.

It appeared that a caterpillar composed of segments of children was encircling the ball which was rarely seen. Occasional segments were thrown clear, to land on the seat of their previously sparking white shorts, before they re-joined the fray. From the centre of the mass came some shouts, cries and an occasional whack that might have been a foot making contact with the ball or a soft head.

Suddenly the ball shot out of the side pursued by a blonde ponytail attached to a small girl. The ball was actually under control and heading directly towards the goal in a straight line. The outstretched ponytail carried in its wake a galloping brigade of small children. The pursuers formed a single mass throwing up behind them a cloud of dust, sweat, snot and asthma medication.

'That's your friend Dr Rossi's daughter, Isobel, she's really good,' Jill said.

'Wow, she really can move,' said Ashley, clearly impressed.

'Shoot, shoot. Don't let the keeper get you,' screamed Chris at the child approaching at speed.

The goalkeeper had been focused upon scratching an especially tricky area on the top of his head. He now re-joined the game and began to trundle towards the approaching Isobel. She delicately nudged the ball forward and it maintained direction and speed. As she closed on the goal, she was distracted by Chris shouting at her to shoot and, when she looked back towards the goal she was confronted by a long white sock with a boot on the end. The goalkeeper had launched a karate kick which now landed with a dull thump onto Isobel's belly. She came to an abrupt halt and fell over. The crowd collectively groaned and bent forwards in sympathy.

A woman emerged from the crowd and walked over to a flattened Isobel. She was wearing an oversized grey sweatshirt, sweatpants and a red baseball hat.

'Is that Dr Rossi' Ashley gasped. 'I've never seen her without high heels. She's smaller than I thought.'

'It's probably just as well, because that goalie might just get away with blunt trauma rather than a stab wound from her stilettos when she's done with him' Chris said rubbing his hands in anticipation.

'What are you guys talking about, I meet her all the time at these games, she's a sweetheart,' Jill said.

Ashley watched Dr Rossi approaching the two kids on the ground, afraid at what might be coming. Chris watched with the anticipation of a pay per view subscriber to a cage fighting bout.

Dr Rossi reached the boy first and scooped him up, then patted the top of his itchy head and directed him back to his goal with an encouraging, 'Well done, good save.'

Then she reached down, grasped a hand and pulled Isobel upright again. She wrapped her arm around the little shoulder and steered her towards the side line.

'Well done, that was a great try. You ok?'

'He kicked me, that's not fair. You need to tell his dad.'

'I'm sure it was an accident, he's a good kid and everyone's OK. Have a drink of water and get back out there.'

Dr Rossi walked over to Ashley and Chris. She was brushing her hands together. Chris had seen her patting the goalie on the head and he instantly got that itch on top of his head that always appeared when he thought about scabies.

'Hi guys, nice to see you. Isn't it a lovely day for this, I have a picnic basket if you guys would like some drinks and sandwiches after the game,' she said.

'That sounds lovely Claudia,' Jill said, 'but these two are going out for dinner later and I'm like you, taxi-driving children and I've got to pick up the boys when we are finished here.'

'Your daughter's a great little player,' Ashley said.

'Thanks, she loves these games: she really likes to win as you can see' Rossi said with a mix of maternal pride and caution.

'I thought that goalie might have been in trouble after that tackle,' Chris said.

'Not at all, they're just kids playing. Actually, he's Bill Attwood's son Josh. Nice to see you guys.'

She bounced across the middle of the pitch as the swarm congregated around the ball in the far-left hand corner of the pitch.

'I heard Attwood was single, is he divorced with custody or what?' Chris asked.

'Chris, you don't know?' answered Ashley.

'Know what?' he answered.

'Know what?' said Jill.

'Stop! I can't believe you guys don't know this story' said Ashley.

'Well no, tell me' said Chris.

'Ok, just come over here for a sec away from everyone. So, as I understand it, he was married with two small kids, she was in a road traffic collision and she was brought into Serenity. He was the Consultant surgeon on call and he rang Professor Stone to come in and take over. Stone brought her to theatre, but she died on the operating table' Ashley said.

Silence descended as they stood in the sunlight listening to children at play and remembered that sad things could still be happening in the world.

Chris found that situation too awful to think about and he chased way in a different direction, 'I never pictured Dr Rossi as a chilled soccer mom. I thought she would be as tough as she is at work.'

'I think you guys exaggerate everything. I see her lots with the kids and I just can't picture her as the person you're depicting,' Jill said.

When the final whistle went, a small girl ran off the field and jumped twice her height to hug Ashley around the neck. When Ashley had safely returned her to ground, she put both hands on her shoulders and looked her up and down.

'Well Sarah, if it isn't the best goddaughter in the world. Look at you, you're growing like a weed. You had a great game,' she said.

Chris liked kids and this small blonde, blue eyed girl seemed fun. Something about her eyes grabbed his attention. He looked again, the blue eyes, then it struck him. He'd forgotten to change the drugged fluid in Jeffrey's contact lens fluid. He'd definitely get around to changing that tomorrow.

Ashley chatted all the way back to the carpark to Sarah. Not having had the time to buy her something nice, she simply slipped her some notes from her wallet. This served the dual purpose of easing Ashley's conscience and reinforcing her role as the coolest aunt.

They said their goodbyes and Chris and Ashley walked towards the town centre and back to the world of single people.

'I don't know. What about Dr Rossi's soft side today? She's like a different person altogether outside work' Chris said.

'You're right, I don't think I'm so different at work as I am outside. Do you think I need to change that? If I put on an act, or pretended to be someone else at work would I cope better?'

The conversation was veering towards topics that Chris avoided like the last maroon wrapped chocolates left in the box. 'I think you should drop the vegetarian thing.'

Chapter 15: Trauma

A rivulet of cold sweat trickled slowly down the centre of Ashley's back under her surgical gown: it seemed to take almost a minute to run its course. She shivered, not from cold, but terror as the patient's warm blood soaking through the front of her gown spread across her abdomen and dripped onto her shoes. Her feet were soaked, and every time she shuffled her feet the soles of her shoes stuck momentarily to the pool of clotting blood on the floor.

'This isn't good,' she bluntly told a wide-eyed Chris, who was assisting across the other side of the table on the patient's left side.

'Just keep trying, Attwood's literally two minutes from getting here,' answered Chris steadily. He was trying to be calm, but his voice was an octave above normal, betraying his inner panic.

The unfortunate kid on the table had been brought straight from the ER to the operating theatre after arriving from the scene of a car crash. He was clearly about to die from bleeding into his abdomen and protocol had dictated that he be brought to the operating theatre for immediate surgery. It had been fifteen minutes since he had arrived at the hospital, and now he was lying unconscious, anaesthetised on an operating table with an incision the full length of his abdomen. The next 15 minutes would tell if he was to live or die.

Ashley had begun the operation as soon as he had been anaesthetised. The monitors and alarms were bleeping constantly. Every parameter that was being measured was dangerously out of normal range, a fact that was emphasised by a cacophony of flat bleeps and pings.

The anaesthetists and nurses were calm, but busy, darting around getting kit and talking in terse brief messages containing the minimum of information so as to get things done rapidly.

Ashley pushed large cotton pads into the abdomen trying to compress the bleeding area and control it with pressure. The blood lapping over the sides of the wound and onto the floor showed how ineffectual her efforts were.

Dr Attwood appeared at her side, gloved and gowned. She hadn't noticed him entering the room.

'OK, Ashley, I'll just step in here for a minute' he said.

He quickly scanned the monitors with their grim numbers. He looked at the blood all down the front of

Ashley's gown and expanding pool of maroon clotting blood on the floor. Moving to the abdomen he packed another couple of pads into the cavity which was now like a laundry bag stuffed to the brim. But still the blood seeped over the edge.

'Right, that's not going to work. I'm going to open the left chest and clamp the aorta'.

Ashley nodded, pressure wasn't working, so the next step was to get into the chest and clamp the blood supply off before it got to the abdomen. Much like a stopcock for the plumbing in a house, controlling the aorta could stop blood getting to the leak. Getting to it was the problem.

Attwood took a scalpel and looked at the incision which ran the full length down the centre of the abdomen. Placing the blade in the top of the wound in the midline just below the ribs, he cut at forty-five degrees across the left side of the chest, across in front of the heart and diagonally up until he was just below the armpit.

The lack of bleeding from this wound worried Ashley, no blood meant the tank was almost empty. That wasn't good at all. Attwood moved rapidly, deepening and extending the incision. He placed the steel retractor between the ribs and turned the ratchet. The metallic clicking sound masked the cracking noise of spreading ribs. The pink spongy lung appeared through the hole in the chest, just obscuring the rapidly beating heart in the centre. Attwood pushed the lung back and reached deep into the cavity.

'Now, I need the large DeBakey Aortic clamp,' he said.

The nurse passed the large instrument, which resembled a large curved scissors but with two flat blades rather than a sharp edge: they were designed to pinch blood vessels and occlude flow. Attwood deftly slipped a blade each side to the blood vessel and gently squeezed it closed with a click.

'OK, done' he turned to the anaesthetist 'how's he doing?'

'Not good, I'm not getting a pulse, he has no cardiac output'.

'Damn it' said Attwood 'I'm just going to try open cardiac massage'.

He reached both hands through the wound and placed one in front of the heart and one behind. Cupping the heart he began rhythmically squeezing the heart to try and restore circulation.

As he felt the flaccid, empty heart and lack of resistance when he squeezed, he turned to the anaesthetist again and said,

'It's empty, get as much blood as you can in with the rapid infuser.'

Although she was standing beside Attwood, Ashley felt detached. It was almost like this was a TV program. She could no more influence events here than change the script of a show she was watching. She felt powerless and increasingly panicked. This was unreal: *don't let this poor kid die, it can't happen.*

But it did happen.

Attwood called it. He slipped off his surgical gown, binned it and turned back to address the room.

'Thanks everyone, we did everything that could be done. He was just too badly injured to survive, but well done, everything we needed was here and the response was as good as it could have been. I'll go and talk to the family.'

There was no effort to distract or play down the situation: nothing could be said. Even the stock coping mechanisms of doctors to use black humour, or instantly discuss the next patient just didn't happen.

Attwood departed as the nurses started to remove the drapes and monitors from the body. Ashley watched as she took off her own gown, now heavy and saturated in blood. As the drapes were removed from the lower half of the body she saw green grass stains on the kid's right knee.

Grass stains on her knees had been the embodiment of her childhood. Seeing them she could smell the meadow, hear kids laughing and feel the heat of the sun. In this context it was so heartbreakingly awful that she had to walk out of the operating theatre. She slowly walked down the long empty corridor, feeling utterly empty and deflated. In the distance she saw Attwood at the reception desk standing with two parents and two siblings. They were sobbing and shaking, their worlds forever utterly changed. Ashley ducked out down a side stairs, she couldn't face that scene and was thankful Attwood had chosen not to subject her to that experience.

She took one step down and then sat heavily on the cold step. Chris followed behind her and stood silently.

‘I love surgery, but I’m not sure I can do this anymore. I just couldn’t face that ever again. That was just so awful. It’s so unspeakably terrible, I don’t think I can do this job or put myself where Attwood is now. Could I be the Consultant responsible for dealing with this? That poor kid, those poor people. I’ll accept defeat and transfer to radiology or dermatology anything easier than this….’

Chris shared a look of those who had soldiered together, and said what they both were thinking, ‘A drink?’

‘Yeah……. did I tell you Jack Salmon asked me to help him end his life?’

Chapter 16: Bar

The Aragon Bar had a long counter and matching bar stools of dark mahogany colour. The shelves behind the bar were cluttered with bottles containing autumnal colours of aged whiskeys. Being so far north it started to get dark at three in the afternoon, but the bar maintained a permanent twilight level of light and a smell of wood polish that was conducive to a drink at any hour.

They sat in silence over three drinks each. Only then had they relaxed enough to talk.

'Do you think you have a drink problem,' Ashley said.

'Absolutely not, no way,' replied Chris.

'You do drink a lot, me too: more recently maybe. But you always have beers at home and you're here at every opportunity. Seriously now, do you think you might have a problem?'

'No, I'm telling you, genuinely: yeah, I drink a bit, maybe a lot, but I don't have a problem.'

'So, you drink a lot, but you don't have a problem. So, what's the definition of an alcoholic then, someone who drinks more than you do?'

'That much would probably get you over the line, but in addition, someone I don't like, who drinks the same amount as me would also be an alcoholic.'

Ashley nodded, satisfied with a definition of alcoholism that excluded both of them. She raised her beer glass and poured the remaining half through her lips. Her Adam's apple bobbed up and down three times as she swallowed, before it floated back down below her shirt collar.

'Ashley, you ok? You know how we were talking earlier, our job isn't easy, if things are getting hard at work, if you need to talk, I just want you always to know you can always buy a dog.'

Some of the beer Ashley was absorbing now exited from both nostrils in an uncoordinated snort of laughter. Her convulsive reaction was only partially to Chris's joke, it was also fuelled horror of him possibly offering to be her counsellor. The only thing worse would be if he made a pass at her, she looked over the bar for the black hawthorn club that Patrick kept for alcoholics who crossed the line into amateur dramatics.

There was very little contrast between the darkness of the bar and the windows showing the evening gloom descending. Ashley and Chris wrapped themselves in the comfort of dark obscurity and were revived in the bar's resuscitation fluid. As in all bars near large hospitals, the large room was sprinkled with individuals and small groups engaged in post-mortem discussions of '*what if*' and '*you won't believe*' scenarios. The educational value of ensuring mistakes were learned from was partnered with the social advantages of shared suffering.

The door swung violently open and Chris glanced over his shoulder expecting from the nature of the entrance that it was going to be an extrovert.

Ashley looked around and even in the dimly lit bar she couldn't mistake the figure. It wasn't the shape or size that gave him away but the dazzling ivory he flashed in lieu of teeth. In the half light of the bar, he advanced with what appeared to be a moustache sized neon sign in the middle of his face.

'Guys,' he shouted with the same gusto as he had opened the door. The grin was even bigger than normal and

Chris almost felt like he was caught in the high beam headlights of an oncoming vehicle. Dr Jeffrey Cavendish III didn't do subtle.

'Ashley, Chris, I thought you might be here. Bad luck with that case today by the way.' Not getting much of a response didn't stop him from continuing on. 'The whole hospital has been talking about your deadish episode and the investigation, it's gone totally viral. I don't know how everyone got to hear about it, the nurses, everyone. In fairness, you guys knocked it out of the park: you did CPR on a 95-year-old who was CTD with a fixed Q sign'.

Chris visibly winced. 'Why do you feel the need to talk like that in a bar, we all know you're a doctor.'

Jeffrey constantly used the code of acronyms and jargon. It was a code that allowed him, as one of the initiated, to converse at a level above mere mortals. He took it to extreme levels, CPR being Cardiopulmonary resuscitation and CTD being, circling the drain. The fixed Q sign was a level above the O sign, which was typically displayed by an elderly or critically ill individual. The O sign refers to unconscious individual with a completely relaxed and sagging jaw creating an open mouth resembling a capital 'O'. This typically wasn't a good sign, possibly indicating overdose of opiates, brain failure or imminent death from a variety of causes. It is also associated with fathers lying back in an armchair after a large Sunday dinner, so it's a hard sign to accurately interpret. However, the' Q' sign is never good. This is where an 'O' sign is complemented by the tongue protruding at an angle to create a 'Q'.

Ashley wasn't sure how to respond to this assault of acronyms. Of all the registrars, she had never warmed to Jeffrey. She had worked, scrimped, saved and dragged herself through college, medical school and surgical training to gain her place as a registrar. Jeffrey, in comparison, was a product of a long family line which had genetically determined both his medical career and his freckles, and he had done equally little work to acquire either of these accomplishments.

'Yeah, tough day at the office, you want a drink?' she asked, hoping he had other plans.

'You bet, beer for me,' he replied, Ashley looked over the bar counter and saw Patrick the barman had been observing from a discreet distance. Without her uttering a word he raised an eyebrow and lowered a beer glass under the tap. He returned, placing three condensation wrapped glasses in front of them.

'Ok, I grant you that it wasn't cool, but it wasn't that bad' Chris said.

'Come on. You resuscitated a woman who was do not resuscitate, she was 95 years old and then when you recognised your mistake, you put a pillow over her head to end it' Jeffrey said.

'Look, first, there was no pillow involved, where did you get this shit. We didn't know about the do not resuscitate order and, by the way, she didn't look 95: she was so pickled with 30 years of HRT that she would have passed for one of your girlfriends.' Chris was hoping that attack was the best form of defence.

Jeffrey shrugged off the insult, though his lack of much conviction suggested that there was a whiff of truth in the allegation. He tried to engage Ashley in the conversation. She had both hands wrapped around her tall glass and tried to ignore him. All she wanted to do was climb into the glass and wallow in a bath of ethanol-fumed oblivion. She knocked back the drink, nodded at Patrick to order another round and turned to Jeffrey.

'Sorry, I missed what you were saying, my attention span isn't any longer than a malpractice lawyer examining their conscience,' Ashley said.

Jeffrey moved in between Chris and Ashley at the bar and occupied the vacant barstool between them. Ashley shuffled her chair back a little to win herself some space. Jeffrey raised the glass to his mouth: when it touched his porcelain teeth it clinked like toasting champagne glasses.

'Jeffrey, did you get the lumbar puncture result?' asked Ashley, switching abruptly into serious doctor mode.

'Yeah, normal. No MS, I'm good to go,' Jeffrey said.

'But is everything OK, are you back to normal? What about the numbness in the leg and the problems with your sight?' Ashley asked.

'The leg is perfect, absolutely back to normal. Actually, my vision isn't quite right on the left, it's still a little blurred'.

Chris nodded at this and after taking a drink, he turned towards Jeffrey and said: 'You should probably change your contact lens solution more frequently.'

'Why? What difference does that make to anything? You aren't really much of a doctor, are you? Most vision loss is caused by neurological problems or raised pressure in the eye, it has nothing to do with contact lenses or solutions' Jeffrey said.

'Suit yourself' Chris said as he turned back to face the bar and dosed himself again. He calculated it was probably his fifth drink. Just enough to have filled his bladder and to numb the common-sense area of his brain sufficiently to facilitate some deeply inappropriate behaviour.

Jeffrey leaned heavily onto the bar and turned away from Chris to face Ashley on his right side.

'Ashley, I'm not complaining, but you obviously did something wrong with the lumbar puncture. That was excruciatingly painful. Did you forget the local anaesthetic, or give me the wrong dose? I thought you might have used too big a needle or something. But definitely something wasn't right. I have a really high pain threshold you know.'

'Jeffrey, fuck right off. Your ability to tolerate pain is as good as my ability to breathe underwater. I don't necessarily like you, but I would never do anything like that.'

As she looked indignantly at Jeffrey a voice came from behind him: ‘I would’ Chris said standing up.

Jeffrey ignored him and sipped white foam from his beer. ‘If I wasn’t such a nice guy I’d probably sue you and Rossi for assault or something. There’s no way that should have hurt so much.’

‘Seriously though, what do you think caused all your symptoms? If the leg numbness is gone, that was probably muscular, the eye thing might just be strain… do you get migraines?’ Ashley said.

‘No. I don’t know what caused all of that, but it is coming and going, so I guess it’s nothing. But anyhow back to you, what’s all this stuff about an investigation?’

‘Let’s not go there, I’m not sure what’s happening, I hope Rossi and Attwood can make it go away.’

‘Actually, I’ve gotten that tingling on the outside of my left leg again just now. It feels a bit different tonight, warm and kind-of damp’ Jeffrey said. He reached down to his left where Chris was standing beside him. As his fingers reached his thigh, he abruptly withdrew his hand from where it had passed through a jet of warm fluid.

‘What the hell’ he said as he jumped up and skittled his metallic barstool across the tiled floor. Chris was retaking his seat after readjusting his zip and was finishing his drink by the time the clattering subsided.

The bar went silent as everyone turned to stare at Jeffrey. He stood like a cowboy, legs wide apart, and arms by his side, palms facing forward with an open-mouthed look of horror. He took another step backwards and the metal barstool took another jangling revolution across the cold tiled floor.

‘What are you all looking at me for, did nobody see what happened? ‘Jeffrey shouted. The bar patrons looked at the loud, belligerent man with the damp patch extending from the side of his leg towards his groin and they began to laugh. He pointed at Chris: ‘Did you just pee on my leg?’

‘Jeffrey, you’ve not been well, the weakness, the sight loss and now, you’re hallucinating. You should go home and lie down for a while,’ Chris said.

Jeffrey wrapped his damp fingers into a clenched fist and advanced toward Chris.

The vibration and bang from the knock of wood on wood, when Patrick smacked his hawthorn club on the bar brought Jeffrey to a stop. He pointed the truncheon in Jeffrey's direction, in an advisory capacity he said, 'Buddy, I think you've had enough, maybe you should call it a night'.

'What the hell, I've barely had the top of one beer… what about this guy, what are you going to do about him? I can't believe he did that,' Jeffrey said.

'I didn't see nothing. Buddy, you can walk out, or I can jump over this bar and throw you out.' The bang of the door as Jeffrey exited neatly book-ended his visit.

The barman took Jeffrey's full glass off the counter and wiped the drops that had jumped overboard when he had hit the counter. He was laughing and walking away he looked back at Chris, 'One of these times someone's going to deck you when pull that trick.'

'Sometimes with you, I just don't know what to think. You've done that before? That was crazy. You don't think he's going to tell someone in the hospital' Ashley said.

'Not a chance, he's never going to tell a story when he looks bad. Forget about it.'

'I'm done here, I'm going home to get some sleep before the room starts to spin. You done here?' Ashley said.

'No, I might just hang on a while, see you tomorrow.'

As Ashley got up to leave Chris walked over to the table where two nurses he knew were drinking. Despite the rolling barstools and drama he had filed away the fact that they had laughed the loudest at the earlier performance. He sat down to see if could convert that appreciation into adulation.

Chapter 19 Drunkish

Chris didn't make it home. At 8am, a hint of cherry, some autumn fruit elements and a strong waft of red wine tannins were the main elements that he could taste in the exhaled air inside his surgical mask. The previous night's alcohol residue was now stale and overpowering, rendering his already tired brain almost fully intoxicated once more.

There was no doubt about it: this was a hangover of spectacular proportions; he was as sick as a small hospital. No, worse than that, this was a hangover worthy of a world-leading, academic, university teaching hospital. This wasn't a minor ailment, or a two aspirin headache: this was a disease crying out for treatment by the best that cutting edge human medical science could mobilise. This even put man-flu down the list of critical illnesses.

He should have left the bar at the same time as Ashley the night before. The stubble on his chin rubbed against the facemask like sandpaper. He hadn't felt he was able, or indeed safe, to shave himself even if he could have found a razor in that unfamiliar bathroom an hour earlier. He felt somewhat less than prepared for a full day in the operating theatre. It felt like his recurring childhood nightmare of arriving in the exam hall with no work done, but worse. Maybe arriving at the start of a marathon with no training and two stone overweight. Yes, that was more like it, but if he arrived at a marathon like that, at least he would be the only one to die: here and now, his precarious condition might end up with the operating list becoming exhibit A in the murder trial of a serial killer.

He eyed up the small round stool on wheels that he needed to use for the first operation. With slow deliberate movements he hitched up his surgical gown and eased himself down onto the stool delighted that it didn't shoot away from under him. The process was slow and inelegant, resembling a geriatric placing themselves on the throne, but it was infinitely better than landing on the floor. How did I manage to drive to work this morning in this condition, he wondered and on that topic how the hell did I get home last night.

That particular post-mortem consideration would have to wait until later though. The anaesthetist at the head of the table and the nurses shuffling around the theatre, were oblivious to his suffering. He inched his stool forward until he was positioned between the patient's legs which were suspended in mid-air in stirrups. The legs were enveloped in the green surgical drapes which covered the patient like long pillowcases. Haemorrhoids weren't his favourite operation at the best of times, even less so now, as he surveyed the pudgy white parts of the man lying on the operating table.

The smell of sweat and worse was relieved when the nurse handed the bowl of sweet-smelling alcoholic surgical preparation solution into Chris's shaky grasp. She swung into routine with an offer of 'swab for preparation?' He accepted the swab and reluctantly lowered the bowl, with its soothing alcoholic fumes, away from his face then dipped the swab in it and started to wash off the patient's skin. Splashing the liquid liberally around certainly cleaned the patient and he went at his task with gusto. He was also benefiting from inhaling the evaporating fumes of the liquid. He splashed it over the patient's legs and buttocks which were resting on the edge of the operating table. It mattered little to him as the solution drenched the patient, the table and a puddle developed on the floor. The sweet restorative inhaled fumes gave him some relief and he felt for the first time that he might survive the day.

'Single drape with an opening?' asked the scrub nurse. 'Perfect' he replied and took the five-foot-square green surgical sheet then placed it completely over the patient with the central small opening over the area of interest for his knife.

'Right, diathermy please' Chris asked and took the electrical cautery instrument. He pressed the yellow button to check it was working: he heard the buzz from the connected machine and proceeded to put the point of the instrument on the base what he selected to be the juiciest haemorrhoid. He pressed the button again and was rewarded with a spark and hiss as the electrical current from the instrument began to burn and cut through the skin. Unfortunately, what Chris had failed to notice was that his earlier generosity with the alcoholic preparation fluid had resulted in a pool of the highly flammable liquid under the patient's buttocks on the operating table. Normally the fluid simply evaporated away but the deluge had swamped the operating field. The mist of evaporating alcohol suddenly caught fire from the spark of the diathermy and with a blue whoosh the pool of alcohol and the patient caught fire. For a split-second Chris gasped as the parts of the patient exposed in the circular opening in the drapes was enveloped in the blue flame resembling a hairy pink Christmas pudding doused in ignited brandy. He leapt from the stool and flung his body over the patient and the opening in the drapes, smothering and putting out the flames.

The scrub nurse was doing an excellent impression of a wide-eyed statue. Chris couldn't see her mouth with the blue surgical mask, but it probably resembled the opening to the Channel tunnel. The anaesthetist at the top of the table, who was looking at his phone and the circulating nurse filling in the computer data, hadn't even noticed anything out of order. Chris stepped back from the patient and surveyed the damage.

'That was a bit spectacular,' he said to fill the void. A quick inspection revealed that while the patient's nether regions were singed free of hair, apart from a sunburn-like, mild pink tinge they had both escaped without injury. 'We'll just add a Brazilian wax to the bill… OK, let's carry on.' He reached out with his right hand for the diathermy without looking at the scrub nurse. If she reacted or baulked, he was toast, burnt toast. He waited in angst, this could go two ways, an incident report, a safety inspection, and an open disclosure with the hospital lawyers, followed by a lawsuit to blacken his reputation or everyone could just gloss over it and move on. *Christ, if they breathalysed him this morning he could end up in jail.*

The slap of the diathermy being passed into his hand told him it was move on. He needed to resume the operation, go through the usual steps, make the usual requests and make the usual inappropriate jokes associated with sphincter surgery. He was stone cold sober now. He had almost barbequed a patient: he had successfully glossed it over with the scrub nurse and if he could just maintain a semblance of normality now, he might just get away with it.

'You're going to use diathermy for this?' said Ashley who somehow had been transplanted into the room and was now looking over his shoulder.

'You're like a cat I used to have. He would just appear out of nowhere and meow at me for something,' said Chris. 'Yeah, I think they get less pain when you burn it rather than just cutting.' He didn't know when she had just entered the room, or if she had witnessed the piles flambé. It did help that her conversation was a diversion so he could pretend the near incineration of this patient's posterior was a normal daily occurrence of no consequence.

'Obviously it's up to you, I think the other way is better, do you give local anaesthetic at the start or the finish?' said Ashley.

'Either.'

'I see.'

'What about antibiotics?'

'Yes.'

'But which ones, how much, for how long?'

'Well, for routine procedures like this I just go with whatever is written on the drug company pen I'm using' said Chris speaking more to the room to emphasise that everything was routine and there was nothing to see here.

'Mmm, it's probably a routine procedure, only as long as it's being done on somebody else, I guess.'

Chris pinched one of the haemorrhoids in a forceps and pulled the bulging purple swelling downward into view and used the diathermy to cut and burn away the tissue around the base. The thin mist of smoke and the sizzling of high voltage on skin which accompanied Chris at work wafted its way around the operating theatre and into the nostrils conjuring up visions of an oily barbecue. When he had reduced the haemorrhoid to the shape of a purple capped mushroom, with a thin partially cremated stalk attaching itself to the patient he asked for a stitch to tie around the base. As he held out his hand for the stitch he turned to Ashley and said, 'That looks really nice now, much less bleeding than if you use a scalpel.'

'Yeah, mmm' said Ashley looking sideways in clear disagreement at Chris's carefully crafted mushroom.

'What, what's wrong with this, it's perfect?'

'Well, if I was doing it, and I'm not saying what you're doing is wrong. I would use the scalpel and suture the whole thing rather than having that burnt tissue. I know it will scab over and heal fine, but I just prefer the other way.'

Chris's heart rate had come back to normal after his earlier fright, but now he felt it rising again. He always felt uneasy when Ashley took up the kind of position that, if their genders were reversed, might be seen as mansplaining. Like needing to ask for directions when driving, there were certain things that were socially unacceptable. In a moment of clarity, he realised she wasn't benignly trying to be helpful: she was messing with his head. She was in feline mode again, playfully swiping at a mouse using paws loaded with claws.

Chris had about reached his limit with both haemorrhoids and Ashley's back seat driving, but he had a solution for both. 'You do make some very good points. I'll tell you what: there are two more haemorrhoids next up on today's list, you do both of those your way and we will compare outcomes when we see them back.'

Chris finished up and exited the operating theatre. Taking off his mask he took an extravagant breath in relief that he had gotten away with coming close to incinerating a patient. He vividly remembered the man's comment in the clinic that his haemorrhoids were so painful that every time he went, it was like a blast of a flamethrower. How ironic that turned out to be, might be funny to tell him the story. However, on balance Chris decided that sometimes people are better off not knowing things, because they would just sue him. His smirk was immediately extinguished by the icy glare of a waiting Mary Gallen in the corridor.

'Dr Newman, there are two police officers waiting at the door to see you, I'll walk you over to them' she said.

Chris was suddenly very awake and very sober. *How had they arrived so quickly, who told them?* He couldn't run as Mary was ready to escort him across. If he could construct a reason to go back into theatre to do something with his patient he might get away. But before he could articulate a coherent response, Mary was guiding him by the arm towards the exit. He couldn't think: his chest felt like there was a rabbit leaping around where his heart should be. If he didn't get his thoughts together quickly this could be the end of his career. Forget about the upcoming job interview, it could all be over today. It might even be jail if they charged him with operating while under the influence of alcohol. If the patient had a burn he could be looking at assault with grievous bodily harm. This situation demanded dramatic immediate action.

He'd have to fake an epileptic fit. He'd even wet himself to make it believable. They might still check his blood alcohol levels, but if he could just delay things, that might be coming down anyhow.

'Erm, what do they want to talk to me about?' he asked Mary, as he walked along measuring out the halfway point where he would drop to the floor and start jerking and peeing.

'The missing morphine' she said.

'Oh, the cops want to talk to me about the missing drugs… Is that all?' he said, mentally cancelling the fake seizure.

She scolded him in her most schoolteacher voice: 'The police are speaking to all the relevant doctors. Can you not see how serious this is?'

Chris could easily think of some far more serious crimes.

They walked together around the corner to the entrance of the theatre reception area. When they turned into the wide corridor they heard loud voices and what sounded like a scuffle in progress. Two large police officers in neon jackets were clearly in conflict with a doctor in green scrubs who was brandishing his ID badge at them. The doctor's face was hidden by the oversized heads with tight haircuts surrounding him. He had his back to the wall, with one cop directly in front of him, close enough to identify what flavour of toothpaste he'd used that morning. The second cop was just to the side but close enough to land a blow with the long flashlight he was longingly fondling on his belt.

'Look, see my name badge, can you read? Dr Jeffrey Cavendish III. I can assure you I am in no way impaired, how dare you suggest such a thing.'

Chris stared in disbelief, this was great to watch, so long as he remained a spectator. He willed Jeffrey on to get argumentative, maybe to ask the cop if he knew who he was, or who he was going to contact to complain.

'Son, you just walked sideways down the corridor and into a trolley and fell onto it right in front of us. Why are your pupils so dilated? I've been a police officer for twenty years and I know when someone's on drugs.'

Chris grimaced and resolved to definitely get around to changing the liquid in Jeffrey contact lens container today.

'Well, thanks for your expert medical opinion officer but I am not on drugs. I just have a temporary problem with my vision in the mornings. I wouldn't even have any idea where to get drugs. I'm not going to let this go, you'll regret this.'

The second cop moved closer. 'Doctor, you seem to be getting very upset about something.'

The first cop inched even closer to Jeffrey's face: 'You telling me you don't know where to get drugs. You, a guy working in a hospital full of drugs, where you give them out all day, every day, don't have a clue where to get your fix?'

The second cop's hand moved from his flashlight to his handcuffs.

'Not a clue where you'd get drugs huh? In a hospital with missing morphine? Stumbling round the place, eyes like two espressos in shot glasses, high as a street corner in San Francisco. Turn around and put your hands behind your back.'

Jeffrey tried to pull away and raised his arms only to find himself being pirouetted like a female tango dancer by his policeman partner. In a flourish he ended up face to the wall, with his wrists handcuffed behind him. The cops took an arm each and propelled him down the corridor towards the exit. He screamed and shouted with as much enthusiasm as when he had been subjected to the lumbar puncture.

Just before they disappeared out of sight, Chris heard a desperate squawk of 'do you know who I am?' He turned to Mary who had been standing like a telephone pole.

'Will I go and help him, or does the hospital have a lawyer?' Chris asked.

Mary didn't answer immediately. As she processed what had just happened, Ashley arrived beside them.

'What's all the fuss about?' she asked.

'Jeffrey has just been arrested on suspicion of drug use: I think I should go to the station and help him, or maybe the hospital will send someone?' Chris looked at Mary for support.

'No, it's not an issue for us. I always suspected him. There was something I just wasn't ever very happy about with Dr Jeffrey Cavendish III. I can't believe Professor Stone ever thought he was a suitable candidate for a Consultant post. Well, this will certainly put an end to that' Mary said.

'I really don't think so… there could be other explanations… lots of things could have caused a misunderstanding,' Chris said.

'Absolutely not. You heard the police officer, he was high, stumbling around. I had noticed those dilated pupils, but I didn't want to say anything. Clearly he's taken the missing morphine.'

'I would just point out that morphine causes markedly constricted pupils, the complete opposite of what you are describing,' Ashley said.

However, Mary had settled on a position now: she scowled at Ashley. 'That's not particularly helpful or relevant right now Dr Brown.'

Chapter 18: ER Pit

The following morning there was a giddy anticipation when everyone gathered for the morning ward rounds. The hospital was a small village and gossip moved fast. The ups and downs of recovering patients like Louise Stark and her appendix or Joy Dean and her colon cancer were small matters. The deadish investigation was a good story, but Jeffrey being arrested for suspected drug use was as keenly discussed as the latest soap opera drama on Coronation Street.

Jeffrey presented the first patient to Professor Stone. 'Jack Salmon who was admitted two months ago has had some issues. As you know Dr Brown presented his case at the conference and the advice was that we should try high dose steroids, so we have been doing that. He previously occluded some arteries in his abdomen and lower limbs, unfortunately, yesterday he knocked off his left carotid artery. He now has a stroke with loss of speech and complete loss of power on the right side of his body. We have done a scan and the vessel is not amenable to repair. His level of consciousness has been fluctuating and his blood pressure has also been low, so not good overall,' said Jeffrey.

'Hm..., did the steroids cause the stroke?' asked Stone.

'Well, I don't know. Ashley, you were looking after this?' said Jeffrey.

'Well, it's not a recognized complication of the treatment, but can happen in patients like Jack who have Marfan's syndrome. But I don't know for certain, maybe...'

Stone looked at Jack for the first time. Normally Jack would have been engaged in friendly banter at this stage, but now robbed of his voice he was silent and immobile in the bed. His appearance had aged thirty years overnight. 'Alright, let's move along, there isn't anything further to do here.'

'What about a Neurosurgical Consult?' asked Ashley.

Stone patted her on the shoulder, 'I'm afraid you're going to have to look at the autopsy report to figure out what's going on here' He misinterpreted the gasps of the medical students as wonder and bustled away to the next room.

Ashley waited back and stood on Jack's left side. She held his good hand and felt a weak response. Whatever life there was in his limbs his eyes had very little. The spark of impishness was gone and he seemed at peace, almost to have accepted his fate. She hadn't acted on his request to help him die, now she couldn't even talk to him about it.'

After the ward round Mary Gallen appearance on the floor was unusual and a statement in itself. She stood with a folder open, issuing orders to all the staff when Chris and Ashley arrived.

'Dr Brown I'm going to allocate you to the Emergency Room this morning. Dr Newman you will be in the operating theatre'.

Ashley wasn't happy with the allocation. The unpopular Emergency Room 'Pit' was where anyone could come to get their urgent medical needs catered for. Rather than being a bland clinical area, this was where the full range of humanity gathered. It could range from the disproportionately distressed with a simple paper cut, to the disabled, drunk, drugged or dying. It was less like a doctor's waiting room than a watering hole of all shades of humanity. 'But, I thought Dr Cavendish was covering there today, I have patients on the floor to follow up on,' she said.

'Well, he may be returning to work later, now that we have had him tested with a negative drug test. But I'm still not happy about all of this and I will be meeting him today with Professor Stone. In the meantime, you will just have to cover both areas.' Mary closed her folder to indicate the discussion was over.

Ashley didn't have any options and simply walked away towards the Emergency Room, kicking the floor with her runners with each step. She had given up wearing white coats and the Versace no longer came to the hospital. She now habitually wore creased green scrubs.

The large open plan area had 20 numbered, blue curtained, cubicles around the edges. The central administrative desk was where nurses, doctors and students gathered around computers and telephones, studiously avoiding eye contact with the patients, relatives and random pedestrians milling around the space.

Ashley's job today was to act as ringmaster and decide who was sick and why, who was crazy, and, if she was lucky, who she could operate upon. The intensity of the pit often created friction because of the high number of patients and the simmering tensions of those waiting. Ashley had once thrived in the cut and thrust of this frontline. Today she no longer felt the enthusiasm she once had. Rather than tingling with anticipation at solving people's problems, she felt weighed down by those same problems, as if she was absorbing the pain, suffering and general madness into her own life by osmosis.

'Mindfulness' she thought to herself again, 'let's try that again: OK, focus, deep breath, I love this place, just repeat that in my head all day and I'll be just fine.'

'Right, who's first?' she said to the ER registrar.

He motioned her over to the desk at the nurses' station and she stood beside him at the computer to look at an X-ray. The four medical students followed obediently like sheep in a flock gathering behind them.

'So, cubicle 4, this is a 45-year-old man, this is his abdominal X-ray and there appears to be just there, down in the pelvis, what he tells me is a golf ball in the colon, probably just in the upper rectum'.

The silence was broken by one of the medical students who helpfully offered her considered opinion: 'I wonder how he swallowed that.'

Ashley thought it was the wittiest comment she had heard in ages, and so quick. She bit her lip and concentrated on the x-ray until she was sure she wouldn't launch into an unprofessional bout of laughter. She wondered why the other students weren't giggling behind her. She looked around and realised that the opinion had been given in complete naivety and not in jest.

'Eh, well, no, perhaps how it got there… I don't think that's the main issue right now, let's focus on how we can get it out?' she said.

The students nodded seriously then huddled together and conferred with all the sincerity of a group at the United Nations solving the worlds more critical problems. The student who couldn't tell the difference between an orifice and a hors d'oeuvre summarised the conclusion.

'He needs to go to the operating theatre, have a general anaesthetic and through an incision across the lower abdomen we can locate the foreign body in the colon then open that up, and remove it,' she said.

Ashley was somewhat taken aback at a sensible reply.

'That's actually a very reasonable option, it avoids the risk of perforation by trying to remove it using a scope. You do have a big wound, a slow recovery, a risk of infection from opening the colon. But not a bad option,' she replied.

'However, I've got probably 30 people to see today, and I don't have time for this' and with that Ashley walked around to the cubicle picking up a pair of blue gloves as she went. With a clenched jaw she put on the gloves with a snapping sound like a handgun being cocked. She disappeared behind the screen. There was a brief mumbled conversation that the students couldn't make out and then silence for a full minute.

Then a sharp scream reverberated around the ER. The background mumble of voices and conversations all across the department stopped and an eerie silence descended. From behind the curtain came a sharp cracking noise followed by a series of less intense cracks as a golf ball rolled out from under the cubicle curtains and across the floor of the department. Its meandering path was watched by many eyes as intently as predators at the watering hole following a fawn's progress.

Ashley appeared from behind the curtain and peeled off her left glove and threw it into a bin. She then raised her right hand and with her left hand reached under the cuff of the glove and deliberately, slowly removed that glove. Before the cuff inverted and the rest of the glove disappeared from view, the ER doc noted the residual tufts of short curly hair between the fingers.

'I didn't know you were left-handed' he said.

'Yeah, no not really, I try to use both to improve my ambidexterity for when I might need it in surgery. So I make myself brush my hair and my teeth left-handed, things like that to help. Sorry I just need to wash my hands for a sec.'

Nobody picked up the Golf ball. The students stared at it and listened to Ashley's subsequent conversation, so banal and out of context with the preceding drama. They weren't sure if they had witnessed a good teaching point, or an assault that should probably be notified to the police. The casual chat between Ashley and the ER doc, who were now discussing how to tie a surgical knot with one hand made them think this was normal. Much like the scent of intestinal gas in a crowded elevator, everyone ignored it, but they all knew it wasn't quite right.

'OK, who is next,' Ashley said moving on from her ambidexterity chat.

'This is a good one' said the ER doc as he led Ashley and her students into cubicle 5. He pulled back the blue curtain with the flourish of a circus ringmaster about to reveal the tiger in a cage. Behind the bars of the cot sides on the bed was a man lying face down, his upturned stubble covered face scowling at the audience. His face down position wasn't entirely voluntary as both hands were handcuffed to the cot sides at the level of his head. The tank top revealed an interesting topography of tattoos across shoulders that undulated with muscle. Ashley was particularly taken by one on his upper arm, that had a head that looked like a werewolf, but the animals coat was curly almost woolly.

As she tried to figure out what species this might be, the ER doc spoke to the man. 'I'm just going to show the surgeon, your wound.' Again, with the theatrics he whipped the white sheet off the patient revealing his bare lower half. There were four wounds in a line one on the outside of the right buttock, one on the inside and then when the bullet passed through the space it obviously had entered the left buttock before exiting on the outside of the left buttock. 'So, drug deal gone wrong, single bullet four wound....'

'Hey man, I never saw that guy before I wasn't dealing I wasn't doing nothing, he just shot me.'

'Ok, sorry alleged drug deal. No other injuries.' Said the ER doc.

'Right, can we step outside' said Ashley and led the crowd back to the desk. 'I don't think he needs anything from me. There's no organ damage, why don't you just stitch him up and let him go?'

'But it's so cool, gunshots, drug deals, four wounds from one bullet' he grinned at the medical students who unlike Ashley were suitably impressed.

'This isn't some sort of entertainment. I'm too busy for this, you're like that drug dealers tattoo, a sheep in wolf's clothing' said Ashley.

'You mean a wolf in sheep's clothing' he said.

'No. Who's next?'

The student missed the next part as they, along with everyone else in the department, watched the golfer leaving cubicle 4. He nonchalantly strolled out the exit, clearly relieved, perhaps even a satisfied customer, but also very much wanting to put the experience behind him.

'At least he won't want to complain and have to tell someone how he ended up here,' Ashley said inadvertently vocalising a thought that should have been silent.

'Sorry, did you say something?' replied the ER doc.

'No, keep going, I'm listening' Ashley was a little taken aback at how she felt. She wondered if she had begun to absorb some of Chris's cynicism, but it felt good. Another voice had joined the conversations in her head and she liked it.

He had deep brown eyes that followed Ashley as she entered the cubicle. His hair was matted but it was an obviously friendly face. He wagged his tail when she came near the trolley on which was sprawled a large man, barely contained in his tank top. On the man's head was a large bandage like a lopsided turban covering one of his ears. The circular patch of maroon blood on the downslope of the turban and on that side of his head did, in fairness, give a strong clinical clue to the possible site of an injury. On first impressions, Ashley sniffed at the not unpleasant aroma of whiskey and did a quick count of his visible tattoos on the bulging arms and tanned legs with partial images of creatures that were peeking from exposed areas of abdomen and armpits.

Applying her personal formula that an individual's IQ is inversely related to the number of tattoos they display; she made some harsh judgements about the patient. Her withering social categorisation wasn't undermined by the friends flanking his bed. The patchwork of shorts and t-shirts where every single garment was fashionably lacerated and frayed, while every piece of footwear was, in direct contrast, branded, just out of the box, shiny, and even blinding with bling. Their uniform appearance also included partly bleached hair, which was accompanied by large silvery, hooped earrings, large enough in circumference for Ashley to fancy they would match the handcuffs that often went together well with this ensemble.

'OK, I appreciate this is the front line, but please, why is there a dog in here?' Ashley said to the nurse.

'It's complicated, I'll let Rod here explain,' replied Jane the ER nurse, flicking her head towards the man wearing the bloodied turban. Her ponytail flicked in the opposite direction and for a split second she was like a gun dog, with her head forward, nose pointing at Rod and in perfect alignment with the ponytail stretching out vertically behind her. Jane was the stereotypical unperturbable, blue scrub wearing ER nurse. She had the steely expression of a nightclub bouncer, coiled like a spring and ready to beat heads together.

Rod levered his large frame up on his right elbow and pointing at the dog he said: 'Let me tell you about that dog, he's Rocky by the way.' He spoke with a strong Glasgow accent where words were meshed together and sometimes separated with hissing noises. It was a form of speech that was difficult to follow unless slowed down and punctuated by a blood alcohol level that also made legs slow and unreliable. 'My uncle, who was married to my mother's sister, he lived across the road from me. He just loved dogs, horses too, most all animals, liked to gamble most of all. He had dogs all his life, just like all my family, hers too.' He pointed to one of flanking Amazonians. 'Now those dogs…'

Rod meandering failure to answer the question wasn't helping to undo Ashley's stereotype of him.

'I'm sorry to interrupt but I'm really busy here, maybe just tell me what happened to you?' she said taking a step forward to inspect the bandage: from close up, she inadvertently inhaled the overpowering whiskey mist.

Taking a positive spin, she figured that at least all that alcohol in the air should kill any germs coming off him.

'It's OK, those dogs were pit bulls, but he's more a smooth hound. No good for guarding, but a good tracker,' said Rod.

'I tell you what, let me just have a look under here,' Ashley said, as she was still unaware of the mechanism of injury, and had decided that conversation with Rod was unlikely to be productive. She decided to approach the consultation more like a veterinary one and simply to look at the wound and try and figure it out from there.

She unwound the turban and after the first loop she patted her patient on the head and said: 'Good boy, just one minute and I'll have this thing off you'.

Satisfied that there was no growling and she hadn't been bitten, she continued with a circular motion: each freed loop revealed an ever-enlarging pool of blood on the underlying layer. Finally, she got to the last loop and with it she wiped away a jelly like congealed clot of blood from the side of his head. Underneath she could see the earhole flush with the skull but no ear. In its place was the oozing raw outline of the tissue where an ear should have been attached. She paused to admire the sharp-edged clean cut.

Although she found it hard to envision a situation in which she would be allowed to amputate an ear if she ever did, she would want the edges to be this sharp and level with the surrounding skin.

Intrigued, she decided to revert back to trying to get Rod to use words.

'How did you do this?'

'I didn't, it's like I was telling you'.

'No way, the dog did it?'

'No, Rocky, never. I was in a bar fight, I said something about my mother's sister and she went off, got a knife, came up behind me, cut off my ear and said that would stop me hearing any more trash talk about her'.

'Did she not mean to say it would stop you saying things about her?'

'Don't know.'

'Is she the one married to your uncle with the dogs?'

'Yeah, how'd you know that?

'It really doesn't matter, what's important now is that we get the ear and see if we can suture it back in place and try to save it.' Ashley looked expectantly, hoping to identify the responsible adult in the room.

From the group of people, a man with a handlebar moustache and biker denim jacket spoke up. 'That's what Rod's been trying to tell you, you're just not listening. Rocky was in the bar too.'

'The dog? How do you mean?'

'We were looking at the ear on the ground: nobody wanted to pick it up and before any of us could do anything with the ear, the dog ran across the bar and swallowed it whole.'

'Oh, that's a shame,' Ashley said.

Jane nodded slowed and pursed her lips: even in the dystopian world of inner-city ER nursing, having the dog eat a body part deserved some kudos for being off the scale of normal human experiences.

'No, no, you don't get it, that's why we brought him, we figured you could like, operate on Rocky, get the ear and, like… transplant it?'

Ashley paused briefly and looked down at Rocky. As a surgeon, her first instinct and love was to operate. *Could I, maybe if we*, she rapidly went through a checklist of operating theatres scheduling, friendly anaesthetists, what drugs work on dogs, the inevitable meltdown from the infection control people if they found out. The infection control team were the medical equivalent of government revenue auditors: introverted, socially awkward, utterly humourless but potentially problematic, Ashley didn't want to attract their ire. She had previously endured a severe dressing down for wearing the wrong kind of shoe in the operating theatre. They would be apoplectic if they found a dog peeing on the anaesthetic machine. On the other hand, it would be funny to see their response. Reluctantly, after calculating that the fallout from operating on a dog in Serenity Hospital's shiny human operating theatre would not be counterbalanced by the operative satisfaction of retrieving an ear from a greedy pooch's belly she decided against it.

'Absolutely not, I've never heard anything so preposterous, I'm sorry, there's nothing to be done, I can't anaesthetise, operate on and extract a mangled ear from the acid filled stomach of a dog. We'll just tidy up the wound and it's all over'.

The man rocked his moustache from side to side in contemplation and reaching into his inside pocket he said, 'What if I made it so you didn't need to anaesthetise the dog?'

Equally appalled and terrified, she backed away.

'I just see, they need me, over there, at the nurses' desk. Excuse me, someone will be back soon.'

At the nurses' desk Ashley leaned heavily against the counter for support. A black cloud was swirling around her peripheral vision and she felt as if she were descending 50 feet underwater, unable to breath and watching the light fading above. Her moment was interrupted by the biker jacket appearing at her side. She quickly surfaced and looked him in the eyes,

'Please don't kill the dog, it won't help. It's over, the ear is gone, it's not salvageable'.

'I get it, not going to work, I won't touch him, fine. Forget about it.' Looking left and right to ensure they weren't being overheard he whispered at Ashley. 'Listen, let's say what if I could get you an ear?' he offered helpfully.

'Where, how, no who… actually it doesn't matter. No way, we are not going there.' She looked at him briefly and knew he would inevitably relieve some third party of the wrong ear. 'That's, really, thanks, an exceedingly kind, I suppose, offer. I'm afraid it's all over, there isn't anything we can do. I appreciate your help, and I'm sure Rod does as well.'

He accepted that and walked away, Ashley shook her head and smiled to herself. Just where was that guy thinking he could get an ear, who was the ear donor going to be, was it going to be an involuntary ear donation? It wasn't as fatal a transaction for the donor as a heart transplant, but it was never going to be pretty, or legal or explicable.

Ashley gazed from the desk across to the waiting room and the mass of people milling around with their multi-coloured clothes and faces. Some quiet, some tetchy, some high, some laughing with friends. People were so different and amazingly unpredictable. At one level she was envious and regretted that a lifetime of study, work and long hours had denied her the exotic experiences and high and low emotions that other life choices might have given her. Given her current difficulties with the hospital, she was feeling insecure: she wondered briefly if she could have lived a different, richer existence. Maybe she could still do that now? On the other hand, she didn't ever think she could ever get someone another ear.

Chapter 19: Countermeasures

Chris closed his eyes and pictured himself in Sicily. If he was in the Mafia, he would have a hilltop villa, a walled garden, a pool and all that went with it. He could even smell the parched, rolling hills dotted with lush green olive groves. His mouth watered as he lifted an imaginary glass of cold, gold-tinged, white wine. Opening his eyes again he looked at the three people sitting around the table with him, Attwood would be the boss, Rossi some kind of scary female assassin, Ashley he wasn't sure… maybe she had been cast in the wrong movie, like that woman in *Godfather III*.

'Chris are you with me,' Attwood said.

'Yes, Don…, err, sorry, Dr Attwood,' said Chris.

Attwood was sitting across the table from Chis and Ashley, Rossi sat on his right. She was silent, sitting back, eyes and mouth narrowed, arms folded, just watching and waiting.

'Firstly, you need to recognise what outcome constitutes success: revenge or inflicting an injury on Stone is not what we are trying to achieve,' said Attwood. 'No matter how satisfying those things would be, they won't disrupt or derail his attempts to sack Ashley. We want to protect you and Ashley, your positions and careers. If there is injury and revenge as collateral damage, fine, but that is not the ultimate objective. He's willing to throw you guys under the bus to save him any embarrassment over the deadish thing. Actually, sorry is it the other one, the one you saved. It doesn't matter, it's not a one-off thing, he's been a problem on lots of levels for years, and he has to go. Claudia, what do you think?'

Dr Rossi remained impassive, but just when the length of the pause was becoming unsettling, she leaned forwards and placed her hands on the table. 'We all need to realize this is a coup d'état. We are going to overthrow the emperor. Unfortunately, violence and weapons aren't in the rules of this game, so that's out. It's also not a legal process, so forget evidence, fair play and what's morally right, that's for whinging losers.'

Attwood wryly smiled. 'Okay, that's taken away both of the two main avenues open to civilised and uncivilised society. What's left?'

'There's a way to do this: it takes planning, time and some careful manipulation of people and information.

Don't look for evidence or procedure, this is going to be about perception, manipulation of reality and creating our narrative. There is no point in the usual repertoire of accusing him of bullying, misogyny, racism, homophobia or any of that: they've all been overused so much as to be meaningless. Everyone knows that when you play one of those cards it's a front for some grievance or another. However, Stone is vulnerable on lots of levels, so let's just go through that checklist. First, patient safety: that's a great card to play to take someone down. Let's get Chris to log a patient safety alert about the Stark woman's appendectomy, claim the complication was due to a malfunctioning stapler.'

'But how does equipment failure get Stone into trouble' said Chris.

'It's simple. You, in apparently wide-eyed, puppy dog innocence, naively log it as equipment failure. That triggers a hospital safety review. Then the hospital blames the manufacturers in an attempt to avoid liability. Then the multinational company providing a faulty piece of equipment is in trouble and possibly liable. Either way, both the hospital and the manufacturing company will throw everything at it to divert the blame to someone else.

Neither of them want to be blamed, so they will use all their contacts, lawyers, and every trick in the book to deflect liability. Stone then gets caught in a pincer movement between the two of them and their sets of lawyers. The hospital knows a multinational medical equipment supplier will have deep pockets, fat lawyers and too much skin in the game to roll over and accept their product might be at fault, so they won't want to take them on. The usual response then will be the for the hospital to launch an investigation, but the terms of reference and the person doing the investigation will be engineered so as to find the surgeon who did the operation to blame and not the hospital or the corporate supplier. Even if the investigation weren't rigged, which it will be, anyone looking objectively at what Stone did in that case couldn't but come to the conclusion he was dangerously incompetent and should be suspended on patient safety grounds,' said Rossi.

'Beautiful, Claudia, simple but lethal. One risk with that is that he will claim again that Chris did the operation. We can deal with that by showing he personally claimed the insurance payment for doing the operation, which would be fraud if he didn't do the operation himself. So that allows us to set him up for insurance fraud if he tries to implicate Chris in that shit show. What next?' Dr Attwood said.

'Well, the next big category that's always useful in these situations is to follow the money. That charity that he's involved with gets money from the public, from drug companies, from everywhere. It's channelled through a university account, he sits on the board of the charity, receives all the money, and spends a lot of it on his own personal expenses. We just need to show personal spending from charity funds. So, what do we do? Remember that charity golf outing last month? I bet you didn't pay for the dinner or drinks afterwards, correct?'

'Not a penny,' Attwood said.

'Perfect, so what you do is you write a cheque to the university accountant explaining that it's your share for the dinner and drinks, after the golf. I know him, obsessive-compulsive, very straight, awful company at dinner, but perfect for this job. He's not on the inside track with the charity, but once you offer to pay, he'll start to ask questions about an account he has no oversight of. Once he sees no-one else has paid, he will smell a rat and realise the charity needs to be audited. Then the whole financial house of cards will come tumbling down. Just to be sure that trigger gets pulled, an anonymous complaint by a "whistle blower" to the charities regulator and the Revenue Inspectors for tax purposes should do the job.'

'I know that guy, fifties, balding. He always has that serious, anxious look, like he's in some kind of pain,' Attwood said.

'Exactly. That's him. You're right, he always has that pained expression, I always wondered if it's chronic haemorrhoids. Anyhow that's the second phase. The third prong of attack is his social life. He often drives home after drinking; we could tip off the cops and get him arrested for that. Crude but effective.'

'What about his personal life? Anything good to mine there, anything going on with Mary Gallen?' Attwood said.

'I don't think so. He likes to act as if he's a player, but I think it's an act: he's all cough and no spit.' She paused to think for a few moments before continuing: 'We can still dump him in trouble with administration and nursing. I'll tell Nurse Mary, his best friend that I heard he was bragging about cheating on his wife with someone else. I'll just say it's a random nurse whose name I didn't get. If they're not having an affair then there's a good chance Mary will be offended that he is having one, with someone other than her. If they are involved with each other, even better if she thinks he's been bragging about it. It's a win, win either way.'

Ashley had sat quietly listening with increasing horror. She felt hollow inside: she knew Attwood and Rossi were excellent professional surgeons, she hadn't realised they could be such cold, ruthless, character assassins. It suddenly dawned on her that getting to the top in surgery might not depend on technical skill and empathy, as much as sheer dogged determination and harshness.

Chris had no such qualms: he was smiling broadly and revelling in the subterfuge. He leaned back, feeling as satisfied as the kid in the group who just got picked first for the football team. Being on the inside track gave him a sense of belonging.

Attwood was running this conspiracy the same way he ran any business meeting. 'Next, the job interview. Stone, Mary Gallen, myself and an external Consultant will be on the interview board. Mary's chairing it and is obviously under the influence of the Professor. We should just think of her as stoned?'

He glossed over the blank looks and continued 'She will only vote in the event of a tie. She's sufficiently wary of Jeffrey to be neutral at best when it comes to the vote. The key will be who appoints the external interview board member. That request will come to me as chair of the division, so I'll pick an appropriate person and get to them in advance.'

'Right, so we have a plan. Remember the hospital safety and complaints systems are really just communist like state control mechanisms to turn everyone into informers and snitches. So let's use that to our advantage, log every spurious, invented and imagined event on the reporting systems to create a fake high risk incident trail that leads directly back to Stone. When the heat comes on, they on reflex will look up the complaint and risk register uncover our handiwork and it will be another nail in his virtual coffin' Rossi said.

'Good, that's enough to be going on with. So, Chris, you lodge the safety alert about the stapler used in the botched appendix. Otherwise you two guys just need to keep a low profile and stay out of trouble. Stone and his minions are probably having a similar conversation right now about us. If you give him any ammunition we will have a more difficult fight on our hands,' said Attwood.

'You send the cheque to the accountant,' said Rossi, 'and I'll speak to Mary Gallen. It will take a week or two for things to happen and we'll have to adjust and respond depending on the kickback. Be under no illusions about this, we are now on a war footing. This will get nastier, don't give the other side any openings, don't step on any landmines and most importantly, get the narrative out at every opportunity that we want delivered to everyone in the hospital.'

Attwood leaned across the table and tapped on it with his index finger to beat home his message: 'In every conversation get the topic around to Stone. Then the mantra is that Stone is of course a great colleague. It's just he's been having a lot of complications. Once we get that narrative moving, you can add that he's had a lot of lawsuits recently, maybe he's getting on a bit and might be unsafe. You've heard that there have been rumours of financial irregularities with the charity and the university that might be weighing on him. Finally, maybe he would be better to step away from clinical practice and move into a purely teaching job in the university.'

'OK, everyone clear about all of that?' added Rossi. 'Good. There are some other things we can do from the top shelf of skulduggery… I won't go into that so you guys can honestly deny everything if you end up at a small table with a cop in a bad jacket drinking coffee from a paper cup.'

Once Ashley and Chris had left Dr Attwood voiced a lingering concern. 'Claudia, are you sure we have this under control. Do you think Chis and Ashley suspect what's going on?'

'No, they haven't a clue. I think they'll be OK. I'm all set with everything else.'

'How much morphine have you gotten?' he asked.

'Plenty.'

Chapter 22: Splenectomy

She had been here before: the warm blood soaking through the front of her surgical gown felt uncomfortably wet and warm. It was déjà vu all over again, but the last time the kid had died. In the crowded operating theatre, with everyone engrossed in their own tasks she felt very alone. Ashley's throat felt constricted, her breathing shallow, and she was nauseated and empty. Children bleeding out and hanging on the edge of life scared her beyond anything else.

In front of her Brian's skinny teenage body was covered in green surgical drapes, elevated and tied onto IV drip stands at the head of the table as though they were curtains on a stage. In the centre of the stage was a rectangular opening exposing Brian's abdomen. Ashley had just made a large incision right down the centre of the abdomen and once she had opened it up the blood had sloshed out like a wave lapping over the edge of a pool. She was standing tightly against the operating table with both her hands inside Brian's abdomen trying to scoop out the clots and see what was trying to kill him. She and Brian were engaged in mortal combat against death itself.

On one side were Brian and Ashley, and on the other was a stupid fall which in some undiscovered way was causing the bleed. They were fighting the consequence of a banal everyday occurrence, and the cruelty of fate which had pitched a child from a carefree bicycle ride into the arms of the grim reaper in a heartbeat. This operation was a race, she was chasing death, and he had a head start.

Ashley withdrew her arms from the abdomen, she was cradling within her two hands more clot and semi-congealed maroon blood than she could hold. Smaller dark clots fell back into the abdomen as her hands slowly retracted and little streams of brighter red blood ran between her gloved fingers over the patient and onto the floor. She threw the contents of her grasp into the kidney dish where it landed with a slap like a wet towel hitting a tiled floor.

Get a fucking grip on this or he's dead, Ashley shot a glance at the screen and saw that his blood pressure was tanking, and his heart rate was so fast that the ECG trace was blurred into one broad line with the individual beats no longer discernible. *I can't do this, I'm going to kill this kid.*

She couldn't betray her fear to the others in the room but by tensing every muscle she could control herself and fix her gaze upon the monitor. By doing this she managed to speak without giving away her inner turmoil.

'If someone could give Dr Attwood another call, we could do with him now.'

One of the nurses went to the phone to make the call again.

Ashley looked at the blood-stained drapes, the pool of blood at her feet, and the opening to the abdomen with pink coils of intestine swimming in blood and clots. She felt light-headed: *how did I ever get into a situation where I could be in charge of something so awful.* But she was and this was going to end soon if she didn't do something. Should she try that Stone twist technique, but that clearly didn't work. Open the chest, like Attwood had tried with the last one? That was a big step… maybe try to compress the bleeding like she had seen tried the last time. 'OK, large packs, at least ten, pass them to me quickly now.'

The nurse passed the unrolled large cotton packs. They were the size and shape of a fat hand towel. She worked quickly pushing each one as far and as firmly as she could into the abdomen starting in the upper left and working her way clockwise around the abdomen until it was stuffed as tight as a pillowcase full of laundry.

She turned to the anaesthetist, who was partially hidden behind the green drapes. Unusually, he wasn't playing *Candy Crush* on his iPhone. Today he was playing for real, adjusting monitors, giving drugs, and compressing bags of blood to force the flow more quickly through the IV lines.

'I've tried abdominal packing: hopefully the pressure will compress and stop wherever the blood is coming from, until you guys catch up with all the blood loss' she said as he nodded and reached for another unit of blood.

The operating theatre became remarkably quiet for a place where an extraordinary human drama was playing out. Each member of the team acted in choreography without the need to shout, dramatise or act as if they were auditioning for a role in *Greys Anatomy*. Only the monitors, alarms and sensors betrayed the stark truth. As he lost blood volume Brian's heart was having to push what was left twice as fast as normal to keep everything alive. The ECG was showing the tempo of Queen's 'Don't Stop Me Now', 180 beats per minute. If he were a runner that would be zone 5, a flat-out sprint. Ashley knew it couldn't be sustained for long: that level of strain wasn't compatible with life. How long he could manage it depended upon God or Ashley.

The tone of the heart rate monitor normally resembled a high-pitched ping. As Brian's oxygen concentration dropped, the sound program automatically changed, as an alarm, to a flat ding. To surgeons, the combination of the low pitch and high rate was the equivalent of playing the theme from *Jaws* when the shark is around. Just as in the movie, that sound means that death is in the close vicinity.

Ashley had played her only card by packing and compressing the bleeding. She listened to the rate and the pitch of the monitors in silence, hoping for a change. At least the swabs had cleaned up the blood and if there was bleeding underneath, it was no longer visible or lapping over the side of Brian's abdomen. Like a hunter listening and watching for signs, Ashley picked up on the subtle change in tone to a higher pitch and a slowing of the rate from Queen to something more like Elton John. *Thank God he's stabilising.* Getting control hadn't required a skilful dexterous movement, it was essentially a mental exercise to work out that deployment of a holding technique was the right move.

'OK, happy to for me to have a look again'.

The anaesthetist squeezed the last few drops of blood from the bag through the IV line and turned to look at his monitors. 'Yeah, good, heart rate down, pressure better, I've filled him up pretty well. He should be OK to have another look.'

Ashley turned back towards the patient. She rehearsed the steps in her mind. *Get everything set up to control bleeding, start in the quadrant furthest away from where you think the bleeding is coming from, remove them one at a time. When you get to the last one have the suction ready to take away the blood and a suture mounted ready to stitch and a clamp to pinch an artery.*

The scrub nurse across the table looked expectantly at Ashley.

'OK, let's get two suction tubings set up here, and more packs in case we need them, I want a number 2 Vicryl suture in the needle holder left there. Leave the large artery clip there, where I can easily get it in a hurry. Right let's go, and did you get Dr Attwood that time?'

'Yes, he's on his way.'

Like coaxing the first garment out of the washing machine Ashley slowly teased and pulled at the swab in the lower right side of Brian's abdomen. It slowly emerged from the abdomen and to Ashley's satisfaction it was still largely white, just a few specks of blood. The next one came from the lower left side. Then the upper right side.

'Good, good, now we're down to the last two over the spleen and no signs of active bleeding, so I think it's going to be under here.'

The second last swab was soaked with blood, but Ashley was relieved to see no flowing active bleeding. Reaching up into the upper left side of Brian's abdomen just below the diaphragm, Ashley pinched at the last swab. On the back of her left hand, she could feel the heaving of his heart in the chest. This swab was clearly plugging the hole where all the bleeding had come from. She knew that once she lifted this one out, the blood would start to hose out again. She placed the suction below the swab ready to suck away the blood before it pooled and obscured her view. She pulled the swab out with her left hand and immediately saw the gush of blood rising up and hissing like a jet from a garden hose.

Shit, bleeding that you can hear is never good.

A warm jet of blood played across her hand as though it was coming from a shower head. She could see the dark hole in the bruised, lacerated purple spleen. With each heartbeat the jet of blood rose higher and then fell back again.

The spleen was lying just within her reach, it was about the shape and size of a mango lying just below the chest cavity. She slapped the palm of her left hand onto the convex surface of the spleen. From between her fingers came a much-reduced ooze of blood.

In life, as in sport, there are times when there is a tiny almost imperceptive shift in momentum and things begin to move in a different direction. Ashley felt that shift: it wasn't over, but she had the smallest advantage: some control over the situation which had eluded her until now. If it were a game of football the wind had just edged the ball towards the posts.

'OK, keep going with the blood transfusion, I'm getting on top of this. Can I have a large artery forceps?' Her left hand compressed and squeezed the spleen. She inched her fingertips up over it like a rock climber seeking the edge. The tips of her index, middle and ring fingers felt a void and by flexing just the very tips of her fingers she got a grip on the back of the spleen. It was already being pushed forward by the large clot behind and when she exerted traction the spleen peeled away slightly from its attachments and started to fall down into the middle of the abdomen right into the centre of Ashley's incision.

Still compressing it with her left hand, she reached her right hand around and underneath the spleen. She teased around behind it blindly until her fingers felt the cord of the artery and vein that fed the spleen. If she could tie off those vessels that served as an umbilical cord to the spleen it would stop the bleeding and she would be able to safely remove it.

This was the technically difficult bit: the final sprint, the summit of Everest, the one small step for man. But any misstep would mean the child would plunge over the abyss. With an infusion of confidence brought on by identifying the source of the bleeding, Ashley was feeling mentally stronger.

She could feel, but not see the cord of blood vessels: they were hidden behind the spleen and obscured with blood and clot. She made a mental note of where it was, visualised putting the artery clip across it, like using pliers. She withdrew her right hand without shifting her focus and placed her palm upwards toward the scrub nurse. 'Artery clip.'

The familiar and comfortable slap of the instrument began the choreography. She opened and closed the instrument with opposing pressure from the palm and fingers of her right hand. With the jaws of the instrument half open she began a sweeping movement from above the patient, into her field of vision, into the abdomen and then out of sight behind the spleen. She felt resistance where she had visualised it should be when she was about to close the instrument. With a slow squeeze she closed the instrument and felt the right amount of pressure that should be there if it was placed correctly across the blood vessels. Leaving it in place she reached for a scissors and slid it along on top of the closed artery clip. She felt the scissors slide into place around the tissue and she slowly closed the blades together. As they closed she felt a satisfying crunch and instantly the tension was released. The spleen flopped forwards and Ashley lifted it out of the abdomen then placed it into the nurse's hands. In the space left behind, she was now able to see the artery clip moving with the patient's pulse. She quickly took a suture and tied off the blood vessels. Scanning the abdomen and seeing there was no longer any blood, she sighed with relief and began to close the abdomen. As she reached for the suture she spotted Dr Attwood watching through the glass panel on the door.

How long has he been there?

It seemed a long time ago that Ashley had been frantic for him to arrive and bail her out.

Was he there the whole time watching?

She felt torn between two conflicting visions. Firstly, she was proud he had trusted her and allowed her to carry on and finish the case. Alternatively, she felt like the kid learning to cycle when the parent, after promising to hold on, lets go.

When everything was over, she walked out to find Dr Attwood. He was seated alone in the operating theatre coffee room. 'Ashley, I was hoping you would come in, sit down and let me get you a coffee.'

'Thanks,' she said as she sat at the small round table.

Dr Attwood left the paper coffee cup in front of her. The wooden table was old and stained with a generation of coffee consumed over stories of victories and defeats.

'You did great in there. So much of what we do is leadership, not shouting from a pulpit, but by your actions guiding the team and giving everything a strong spine that allows the system to work. It's about being sensible, calm and using all the tricks that you've acquired in your surgical toolbox over the years. Well done,' he said.

'I was really scared there. You know, over the last while I have been sort of losing my way, since we lost that kid on the operating table: then all the investigations and trouble I got into with Professor Stone and those patients complaining. It's all been a bit much, I wasn't sure I could do this job.'

'I know, but how did you feel coming out of that operating theatre just now? You did something great there. They won't remember who you are in a few months, they'll barely remember he had an operation in five years. But you've given him and his family back his life for whatever he wants to do with it. The odd patient might remember you forever: the same number will sue you and hate you forever. But on balance we do good, we do our best and that's enough. I'd be happy to have you as the surgeon for anyone I know.'

'Thanks. I just don't know. if that had gone wrong, I'd never get over it. Even if I did everything right and he still died, I'd have to deal with Mary Gallen poking her nose in, maybe Professor Stone using it as a reason to undermine me so Jeffrey could get the Consultant job. That's before we even get to a coroner's inquest, a civil lawsuit, a medical council complaint and my picture all over the internet. We all know good people who have been through all that when they did nothing wrong.'

It was a logic Attwood couldn't find a flaw in. He just shrugged in acceptance of the cruel realities of the job.

'Maybe……. it's not the time to ask and you don't have to answer, but can I ask what happened to your wife: how did she die?'

'That's alright…' He hesitated. 'Look terrible things just happen sometimes. It was just a car crash, nobody did anything wrong, nothing could be done here to change the outcome. It's awful and it always will be. But that's history, you need to go and talk to that kid's family, I saw them outside, all terrified, waiting to hear what happened.' After Ashley left, Attwood looked at the table and remembered the night he had been sitting here when

Stone came to give him the bad news after operating on his wife.

He felt a burning sensation in this throat and wondered if Ashley might have done better.

Chapter 23: Twelve steps

Ashley stomped down the stairs with a scowl on her face, fists so tightly clenched that her knuckles were white. The thump of each step echoed in the stairwell as she trudged down. The indignity of having to attend a patient support group meeting in order to improve her empathy with patients was a low point in her career. The adrenaline of the successful splenectomy operation the day before was now long gone. She was back to feeling edgy, restless and just vaguely not herself. She looked again at the e-mail on her phone. '*You will attend mandatory training in patient empathy*' The nerve of Mary Gallen, to instruct her to go for empathy training, fleetingly she considered outright disobedience, but that just wasn't her either.

Ashley's view of the world however had begun to change. Now that her naivety had been beaten out of her, she had decided that to be a successful surgeon, she needed to be like a Special Forces soldier. When faced with a cancer or a terrorist people needed somebody with the same personality traits to deal with either scenario. They didn't need to be empathetic, or touchy feely, you didn't even need to like them, but you sure as hell wanted them to be tough, decisive, skilled and able to aggressively neutralise the threat to your life. She had never been the most popular or extroverted person at school or college, but she had always been tough, hardworking and determined. She couldn't change her own personality, so maybe it was time to change the rules, so that they fitted her perceived strengths rather than vice versa.

'Empathy… I care about stuff. Why do these pen-pushers think some box ticking exercise will change who I am.'

She arrived at the basement level meeting rooms. She looked around at the four doors around the landing and contemptuously thought: 'If this actually mattered, it would be on the top floor where the manager's offices are not down in this dungeon'.

Finding the 'Dealing with Bereavement Class' was harder than she had expected. There were no signs on the doors and two rooms were in use. She looked through the strip of glass on one of the doors and saw a group of about ten people sitting in a circle looking downcast and avoiding eye contact. One of the group, clearly distressed, was speaking from his chair on the far side of the circle.

'Great, the therapy doesn't seem to be having much effect on this lot,' she sighed and slowly pushed open the door. She eased herself into a chair just at the edge of the circle.

The speaker was a thin middle-aged man, wearing blue jeans and a loose sweatshirt. His thinning brown hair was brushed in a comb over. The attempt to hide his bald patch was undone by his slumped, forlorn posture which exposed the top of his head for inspection. Ashley eyed him up in the cold dispassionate way that doctors sometimes do, while attempting to make a snap diagnosis. She looked for nicotine stains, tattoos, tremors, pallor or jaundice. She eyed up his veins as potential conduits for intravenous lines with a searching gaze perhaps more appropriate to a lioness eying up a zebra. Seeing nothing that piqued her interest, she moved on with the consoling thought that if she ever needed to operate on him, then opening and getting access to the belly of a thin guy like him was so much easier than the whale seated to his left. Only then did she briefly tune into what the guy was saying.

'I tried to get away from that stuff by going drinking, I went for a bender that lasted a week. I somehow ended up in Belgium when I came around…'

Ashley lowered her head and investigated her iPhone. Surely, they could see she was a doctor in her scrubs who was just passing the time here. She obviously needed to look at her phone to ensure her patients weren't dying while she endured this forced re-education. She deleted Mary Gallen's e-mail and scrolled through the others.

.'…I spent thousands, partied with lots of absolute wasters. It was just a tragic rollercoaster.'

An older grey-haired woman who was facilitating the discussion intervened in a motherly way apparently trying to ease the discussion away from the man's discomfort.

'That's a scenario that speaks to all of us: an incident, an excuse, a rationalisation that allows us to descend into an episode of drinking and fallout like you have told us about. Does anyone else have similar experiences to share?'

The man on Ashley's left spoke up. 'I once got arrested driving a ride-on lawnmower down a motorway because I wanted to buy alcohol. I was four times over the legal limit for driving so I lost my license and my job'.

Ashley looked up from her Phone, everyone was nodding towards the man. The mother figure caught

Ashley's eye before she could return to the enveloping safety of her iPhone refuge.

'What about you doctor, would you like to share any of your experiences?'

Ashley froze: public speaking or group therapy was as appealing to her as being dropped onto the catwalk in Paris Fashion Week surrounded by supermodels. Her plan had been to hide at the back and simply tick the box of having attended the meeting. Now her hand was being forced. She mentally tried to take the temperature of the room. Maybe she should dive in and try to put her normal shyness to one side. If anything, the recent conflicts in her head had made her a little disinhibited. The group seemed to be on a theme of drinking, probably to deal with bereavement. She hadn't many sad or wild stories to tell, but she had one which resembled the snippets of conversation so far, so she decided to go all out with that.

'Well, I'm new to all of this but there was one time I got so wasted on a night out, with my friend Chris, that, when we couldn't get a taxi, he decided to drive his car home about 4am. Obviously that was crazy, but he was swimming in Southern Comfort whisky fumes, so it made perfect sense. So anyhow, the two of us drove off and we came to a roundabout: we were laughing and giggling so much that he missed the exit. What to do? He slammed on the brakes and decided to reverse backwards around the roundabout, to the exit that we had missed. It was the middle of the night with nobody around and it seemed a reasonably logical choice given the state he was in. But next thing there was a huge bang: somebody else's car had run into the back of ours. So, really, really, not good. We got out to go to the other car and found a guy humming ABBA's "Dancing Queen" at the wheel. He was clearly 10 times drunker that then we were. I kind of thought *"this is great, he's so drunk that we won't get into trouble*". But just as we're figuring out what to do with the guy, the next thing a cop car just happens to come onto the roundabout, sees the crashed cars and puts on the blue lights'.

Ashley looked around the circle and wondered why they weren't getting into the spirit of the story, nobody seemed to get the humour of this predicament. The circle of faces was serious, nodding and quizzical. She decided to up the ante. After taking a breath to conquer her own imminent laughter, she launched into the lead up to the punch line, 'So, this tall, serious looking cop, eases himself out of the driver's seat, takes an age to adjust his hat as he looks over the scene. He slowly walks over to us assessing everything like a picture book as he walks. He sees the drunk guy at the wheel singing to himself, with his car impaled on the back of ours. So, by the time he gets as far as us, he has in his own mind investigated, adjudicated and sentenced the drunk guy. He doesn't even ask us what happened: he simply grabs the drunk guy by the arm, hauls him out of the car and, with some skill, maneuvers this staggering, inebriated drunk guy back to his car and pours him into the back seat'.

Ashley threw her head back, laughed and, misinterpreting the concerned expressions of her audience as rapt attention, she ploughed on. She now had some momentum to her story and was getting into her own version of role playing. Surely this would demonstrate just how empathetic and normal she actually was.

'So, the cop is talking to the guy in the back of the car while we're standing there sweating, wondering how this is going to play out. Eventually the cop walks back up to us and taking his hat off he scratches his head and says, 'That's a shame you guys got hit by that drunk: you know he's so wasted, he thinks you were reversing backwards around the roundabout. Still your car should be drivable so you guys can head away: here's my card call me tomorrow and I'll send you a copy of my report for your insurance.'

Ashley leaned backwards in her chair shaking with laughter and exclaimed: 'Isn't that just brilliant?'

The silence in the room startled her: *had she missed something*?

The long pause was broken by the elderly moderator who delivered a sharp 'Hmmp.'

Without a word even been spoken it was immediately clear to everyone including Ashley that she had done something wrong. Although her normal impulse now would have been to run like a rabbit at a dog track, she wasn't herself due to the stresses and hassle of the previous week. For some inexplicable reason her internal response mechanism switch flipped dramatically from flight to fight, 'Ah, come on now, what is it with you guys and your "*Hmmm*" and the gloomy faces: we all have to deal with bereavement, but you have to move on. You told your funny drinking stories, mine was better: it's time for you to stop wallowing in your self-indulgent melancholy'.

Up to this point the silent pauses had been short. Now, as the seconds ticked past it began to unnerve Ashley.

She was utterly confused but still in more in fight than flight mode, so she continued: ‘In my work I deal with death a lot, for you as a group maybe can I just say, negativity doesn’t really help in the long term.’.

The woman replied: ‘I’m sorry, there seems to be some confusion. The point of this group is absolutely not to revel in drinking stories, it is to use the twelve steps to move away from that whole abyss that you seem to be living in. We can all see you have an alcohol and perhaps a drug problem, but this lack of insight and denial won’t help your recovery.’

Ashley had a eureka moment and realised why her catwalk into extroversion had crashed like a five-year-old trying high heels for the first time. She wavered, everything in her life up until now, suggested she should apologise, run or faint. Perhaps all three together, but she still had some circulating adrenaline and recklessness, and a new take on life.

‘So, I guess I’m in the wrong room, this isn’t the “*Dealing With Bereavement*” class I was looking for… you guys are obviously busy so I’ll get back to work, but if I could just get you to sign here to say I attended a patient discussion group?’

The rest of the day she spent in a fog just getting through the clinic and talking to patients, but her heart wasn't in it. To raise her spirits before she left for the evening she went to intensive care to see her splenectomy patient. He was lying on his bed with lines and monitor leads in all directions, but he was awake and looking at something that his mother was showing him on her phone. Ashley didn't interrupt them but looked at the screen and seeing that all the numbers were good she left for the bar.

Chris was late, in the half-light she sat up on a high stool at the bar. She scanned the chrome beer taps and the rows of bottles on shelves surrounding the till. Beer wasn't doing it for her anymore.

'Double Jameson, thanks'

It took a few seconds for the heat to rise up from near her diaphragm and swirl around the back of her throat. *That's what I needed.*

Chris's arrival interrupted her intimate appreciation of her second whiskey.

'Sorry I got held up, I was just finishing with the patients from on-call. I was up all night and spent today sorting them all out despite the efforts of radiology and anaesthesia to obstruct and delay everything.'

'Whiskey?'

'No, I'm too wrecked for that, beer maybe?' he yawned and leaned on the bar. His red rimmed eyes, stubble and lined face after a night without sleep made him look like the regulars in the bar who had been in since lunchtime.

Ashley ordered his beer and another whiskey. 'Anything good last night?'

'One appendix I did before midnight, the rest was dross. A few tummy pains, an obstruction in a palliative cancer patient, drunk RTA's and a fight with medicine who didn't want to take a geriatric because they felt vomiting once, must be a surgical problem. The usual…' said Chris.

'That's the problem with this job, you have to sort through so much to get to the good stuff.'

Chris sipped at his beer before yawning and resting an elbow on the bar he supported his chin with his hand. Ashley saw him looking at something and as she turned around she saw a shaven headed man with heavy stubble walking towards the bathroom door. He was wearing frayed denim jeans, a black t-shirt and his arms were tattooed. Something about the tattoo caught her eye, but he was too far away and gone through the door before she could fully appreciate it.

'I'll be back in a minute' said Chris as he eased off his stool and headed towards the bathroom.

Ashley sought some warmth from her glass and swirling the whiskey in her mouth she thought about tattoos. Maybe at the weekend, she would have a few hours on Saturday. Suddenly it came to her where she had seen that tattooed arm in a black t-shirt before, a sheep in wolf's clothing.

It took Chris a few minutes to return but when he did he hopped onto his stool and called to the barman. 'Whiskey, one for Ashley as well.' While waiting for the whiskey he drained his almost full glass of beer in one swallow. Placing a glass with a satisfying slap on the beermat he turned to Ashley. 'Why don't we go downtown, someplace livelier than here?'

She was feeling a little giddy with the alcohol, but Chris's new energy struck her as odd. 'Did you see that guy who went into the bathroom before you?'

'Who? No.'

'The guy with the shaved head and the tattoos, he came out immediately after you, were you talking to him?'

'No, there might have been someone there, I didn't notice. Why?'

'I recognised him, I treated him once.'

'Oh.'

'I remember him because when I saw him, he was handcuffed on the trolley. He had the two arms out to the sides and I thought his ink was unusual. That's why I recognised him tonight.'

'OK'

'Don't you want to know what was wrong with him?' she asked.

'Yeah, yes?'

'He was shot. It was a drug deal gone wrong.'

'Interesting, will I order a taxi, so we can go?'

'The police were looking for the bullet afterwards. They seemed to think he was a serious drug dealer' said Ashley.

‘Oh, right. Maybe that club Central Park?’

‘I want to try some, have you got any more?’

‘Ashley, no, I don’t, what are you talking about? We are not going there, even if I did, you can’t, it’s just …it’s not you, it’s not right for you.’

Chapter 24: The Sting

Chris and Ashley took their usual seats at the back of the lecture.

'Mary loves these big meetings where she gets to lecture the whole hospital staff. It's such an old school way to manage a hospital,' Ashley said.

They each had an orange paper cup of coffee and a Danish pastry. They had been drinking late at the bar every night they weren't working and needed the calorie hit in the mornings.

'Yeah, now I want a re-match on the bullshit bingo, but no cheating this time' Chris said.

Ashley shushed him as Mary and Professor Stone entered the room. She took her place at the lectern and Stone sat in the front row.

'Can everyone hear me?'

Nobody responded and, taking this as a positive response, she continued.

'Myself and Professor Stone have a number of housekeeping issues that we wanted to bring up for discussion with you all today. Firstly, heading into another Covid season we are planning to have the entire staff of the hospital vaccinated. This will be mandatory and we will be seeking vaccine champions who will ensure all staff in their department are vaccinated. Anyone not vaccinated by next week will be suspended without pay. Any questions?'

Dr Rossi stood up.

Chris elbowed Ashley 'This will be good, Rossi will blow her out of the water. Mary says it's for discussion and next thing it's mandatory and immediate suspension without pay.'

'I fully support this initiative and I think we all have a responsibility to ourselves, our patients and the hospital to ensure we are all vaccinated. I would be happy to volunteer as the lead for the surgical department to get this done,' Dr Rossi said.

Chris looked at her with the wide eyes of a stunned goldfish whose water has been topped up with Tequila.

'Thank you Dr Rossi. The next item on the agenda is in relation to drug misuse. This is a major problem in all healthcare institutions and a working group of myself, Professor Stone and Dr Attwood have put together a policy in relation to the medical staff. The key elements are that Serenity Hospital has a zero-tolerance policy for drug misuse. The possession or use of narcotics is incompatible with working in this hospital. Any possession of drugs or a positive drug test is incompatible with employment in our hospital. We will be conducting random searches of lockers, personal property and targeted drug testing of all personnel to ensure compliance. Just so we are all clear, zero means zero, any possession or positive drug test will equate to immediate dismissal. Any questions?' Mary looked around to see if she could focus her frosty gaze on Jeffrey.

Unable to pick him out, the silence was again taken as support.

Professor Stone, whose antenna were sharper than Mary's, picked up the silence as a sign of possible disharmony. 'Thank you Mary. I've represented the hospital on government and international groups in relation to this issue and can I just say that this is a critical issue for all healthcare organisations to address. Nobody is immune and nobody is above suspicion of drug abuse. We need to root it out and deal severely with perpetrators. That is why, with Dr Attwood's help, I have written the policy without appeal mechanism, or any way for crooked lawyers to prevent dismissal. Possession or use of drugs will mean instant, irreversible dismissal.'

The oppressive nature of this meeting was starting to grate on Chris. He leaned across and whispered. 'Ashley, is alcohol considered a drug?'

'Don't know about that, I'm not sure any of this testing is legal, but that box of cigarette papers and herbal tea and anything else, should probably go in the bin.'

The hostile looks and silence in the lecture theatre suggested that the new policy was about as welcome as a cell search in a jail.

'Sorry, just to clarify we are targeting this policy only at prescribers,' said Mary. 'It only applies to those who can prescribe drugs. So that means only doctors will be tested. We are aware of the need for patient confidentiality, therefore Dr Attwood is the sole medical supervisor, all tests will be anonymised and results will only go to him. He will have the sample numbers and only he will be able to relate the results to the individual doctor.'

All the nurses in the room, united as part of the white uniform power collective, nodded enthusiastically at the hypothesis that it was only doctors who were susceptible to temptation.

'Well, if there are no further questions. Excellent, thank you all for coming, as always my door is always open.' said Mary.

'Actually, you can't get near her office because of the number of people complaining about you,' Chris helpfully pointed out to Ashley as they left the lecture theatre.

Keeping to their usual pattern Rossi and Attwood stayed behind until they could talk alone.

'I think we're looking good, everything is in place. I liked your support for Mary there, team player and all that…you have got to be the most duplicitous, devious, the most underhand, simply the best' Attwood said.

'I know, it's obscene, I feel like I need to shower, but it needs to be done.'

'Are you certain? We can still pull back, the registrars aren't out of danger either, if this goes wrong.'

'I've wanted to do this for years and I know you don't think he was responsible for your wife's death but on so many levels he needs to go. We've gone this far, it will be hard to get everything lined up again if we don't finish it now.'

Chapter 25: Testing

Slow breaths, indistinguishable from sighs, and a tendency to lapse in and out of consciousness declared that Jack Salmon wanted to die. All of Ashley's tests, treatments and consultations no longer mattered. Marfan's syndrome had been a diagnosis, a battle to fight, something tangible to cling to in a storm. It no longer mattered; he had turned off the innate human instinct to always survive. He hadn't lived long, but he had used his time well: the family and friends around the bed, the yellow cigarette stains on his left index finger and the cirrhosis in his liver, were pointers to a life fully lived.

The evidence that proved the living well diagnosis was evident to all on the ward as they listened to the laughs, smiles and tears of the many who had visited his room as the final scene approached. Like a river, the flow and volume of visitors swelled as thunderclouds descended to mark the end of his run.

Ashley refused to accept his spiral descent to death. She put a central line into his jugular vein and squeezed fluid into him to raise his blood pressure. An adrenaline infusion gave him an external fuel source to keep him warm. Antibiotics, steroids and anti-inflammatories were added as part of the cocktail that doctors prescribed when they weren't sure what to do and ending up dosing the patient to treat themselves. She wrote up the orders at the nurse's station and when she got to the end she stopped and chewed the end of her pen to think if there was anything else she could do.

'Ashley, how's he doing?' said Dr Attwood whose approach down the corridor she had completely missed.

'Oh, Dr Attwood. Well, I've started adrenaline, his fluid balance is three litres positive, his white cell count is twenty, the liver function.....'

'Stop, stop. Let me ask again. How's he doing?'

'Well, I'm trying a few things.'

'Yes, I've seen that. But you know don't you? It's not your fault.'

Attwood threatening to take away Ashley's disguise of clinical activity prompted a flustered response. 'Well, yes, objectively, I mean. I've been looking after him for months. I know it's over'.

'Ok. Yeah, I trust your judgement. Just separate yourself from Jack, make your peace and let it go.'

Two manicured hands with rings and blood red nail polish slipped onto the desk beside them. 'Everything all right?' asked Dr Rossi.

'Absolutely' answered Dr Attwood. 'I need to talk to you.' He placed a hand on Rossi's elbow and propelled her away down the corridor to spare Ashley having to share the onset of her crying with spectators.

'Is she going to be OK?' asked Rossi.

'I really hope so, sometimes she's way too nice for the cut and thrust.' He looked left and right along the corridor before he went on. 'Anyhow we're on track. I floated the idea to Mary that the Consultants should lead by example, so she is going to have the first series of random drug searches to begin with our lockers and to test us all today. She went a bit *Fargo* on me and suggested we do the registrars as well, so I had to go along with that: we better just check.'

'Yeah, I'm thinking Chris, he wouldn't have weed or something else in his locker would he?' Rossi asked.

'He's probably OK, but we better just warn him, I'll get onto that right now. We don't want something stupid like that messing up all the work we put into this' Attwood said as he hurried away at a pace more commonly associated with a cardiac arrest call.

Dr Rossi walked down to Professor Stone's office just outside the ward and knocked as she put her head around the door. 'Professor, you are the last person on my list for Covid vaccination, why don't I give it to you now and I'll be done,' she said.

'Absolutely, where do you want me?'

The nurse placed the pre-loaded syringe on the trolley and left Stone and Rossi alone in the treatment room. He took off his suit jacket, rolled up his sleeve and sat down on the stool holding his arm out to the side.

'I just wanted to thank you for all your support Claudia, I'm sure I'll find a promotion for you in our new structure, once we get Jeffrey appointed. What do you think' he said.

'Absolutely, life moves on, we need to adapt.'

Dr Rossi picked up the syringe from the trolley and moved behind Stone. She understood precisely the bribe she had just been offered. Her preferred course of action now would be an *et tu Brutus* moment where she could stab this Caesar. However the law tended to frown on involuntary euthanasia of that kind. Her stabbing would have to be a much more precise injury. She wiped his shoulder with an alcohol wipe. She slipped the hand with the syringe into her pocket, dropped it, and exchanged it for a different one that she already had in there.

'Just a prick,' she said as she injected the clear contents into his arm. Not the full syringe: just enough that it would be in his system.

'You might feel a little woozy if you get a reaction, but it usually goes away within a few hours,' she said.

'Thanks Claudia. It's great that we are all working together. In the long term I want my legacy to be the new hospital development and I hope when we open the Professor Stone Institute that they will be a role for you there.'

'Professor, I'm flattered, I'll look forward to the day.'

Attwood didn't want to call or send a message that would leave a digital record in advance of the drug search. But he knew where to look and found Chris waiting for his flat white in the coffee shop.

‘Chris, I just wanted to let you know about something. I’m sure we don’t have a problem or anything. But there is going to be a random search of all the doctors’ lockers today, to look for any evidence of drug use. We’re not going to have any issues are we?’ Attwood asked.

‘Well, no, why, I don’t think so. No, definitely not’ Chris said.

‘Good man, but just, if there was any issue, there’s probably time to deal with it now, if you understand what I mean?’

‘No, really it’s fine, I’ll just go and help Ashley with the pre-op patients,’ Chris said.

Chris didn’t start to run until he was out of Dr Attwood’s sight. He wished he had been more careful. The bottle of Tropicamide he had used in Jeffrey’s contact lens solution was still in his locker. He couldn’t figure out how Attwood knew about it. If he had guessed that, then he maybe he knew that he had faked Jeffrey’s symptoms. He had been responsible for Jeffrey having an unnecessary MRI scan and a lumbar puncture, and if that got out he would be in serious trouble.

In the coffee shop Attwood helped himself to the flat white off the counter that Chris had abandoned in his haste to get to the locker room. He strolled down the corridor and met Mary Gallen with the hospital's chief of security.

'Dr Attwood, we are just going to do our first random drug search. Perhaps you can accompany us to the locker room? It would be good to have Consultant leadership' said Mary.

'Absolutely, delighted to help.' Attwood fell into step alongside Mary as they walked along the corridor. 'It's good to have this program started. Just in terms of the staff drug tests did you work out how to schedule that?' Attwood asked.

'Well, I was going to go with your suggestion of getting everyone together after the lunchtime educational meeting. As you said, having everyone in the same place and getting it all done in one go seems the best way.'

'Yes, I agree. Why not today? Let's just get it over and done with. I think it will improve morale all round when we get a clean bill of health' Attwood said.

'Excellent, I'll arrange for the occupational health nurses to set up a station beside the coffee shop for the blood tests.'

When they arrived at the locker room Mary and the security chief began open and inspect the lockers individually. Dr Attwood went into the bathroom to put his coffee cup in a bin. He found Chris at the sink washing out a contact lens case.

'Chris, I didn't know you used contact lenses,' he said.

'Well, no, not often… I just found this case on the floor and I was washing it out, I think Jeffrey might have dropped it' Chris said.

Attwood threw the cup away. Something told him it would be better to get Chris out of the way while the search was going on.

'You better give Ashley a hand to get this afternoon's pre-op patients ready. There isn't much time before the meeting at twelve-thirty.'

'Absolutely,' Chris said 'but I just need to look at my locker for a sec.'

‘Too late, Mary’s already in there, you better head away.’

Chris slouched away and Dr Attwood returned to the row of grey lockers. Mary was wide-eyed reading what looked like bank statements when the security man called her over to another locker.

He handed her the two glass ampoules that had been hidden inside a surgical facemask.

Mary took them, rolled one on its side to read the writing on the red-rimmed label and turned to Attwood.

‘Excellent, morphine. I think we’ve found the drug addict. Let me just see whose locker that is,’ she said and slammed the locker shut with what Attwood thought was an excessive crash designed for theatrical effect.

They both looked at the name and stood silently absorbing the information.

Mary reacted first. ‘Well, our policy is very clear. I’ll ask security to locate Professor Stone and remove him from the campus. It will be a police matter from there on’ she said emphatically.

'Mary, I agree, that's exactly what the policy says, I know it well, in fact as you know I wrote it. But this is Professor Stone, how long have you known him?'

'It doesn't matter, the policy is the policy. This is a matter of patient safety.'

'I understand. Just bear with me for a minute: what if that was planted there, if it not his. If he's really using opiates, then he will test positive in a drug test. If he doesn't test positive, then this could all be a major mistake. He could sue you personally for millions in damages.'

Mary contemplated the possibilities. She liked to be decisive in her management style, but thinking through the unintended consequences unsettled her. Patient safety suddenly wasn't as much of a priority when weighed against the possibility of her being sued.

'Well, if he tests positive, then there couldn't be any doubt,' she rationalised. She had added up the prompts given to her by Attwood and come out with the answer he had been fishing for.

'Exactly. Now personally, I think he will test negative and there will be a simple explanation for all of this. Perhaps we should say nothing, the meeting is in an hour, and we can test everyone on the way out and see what comes out in the wash?'

The locker that Mary had been looking at before she had been called away was still open and as Mary looked deeper into Professor Stone's locker Attwood wandered over and seeing on the top shelf two glass ampoules, one blue and one clear he quickly scooped them into the palm of his hand. He casually swung the door half closed and saw Chris's name on the front. Using the door as a shield he spied a small metal tin and a crumpled envelope and put them both into his inside suit pocket.

It was lunchtime before Rossi and Attwood got to sit down together in the lecture theatre and compare notes just as the presentation began. 'Is it done?' Attwood asked.

'Perfect, I *'vaccinated'* him and let's just say he felt no pain afterwards,' Rossi said.

The lunchtime lecture was a presentation on the management of colonic polyps. Attwood and Rossi sat together, far enough away not to be overheard by others as they spoke, with the speaker's voice in the background.

'She behaved exactly as predicted. It was almost like she was reading from the policy I drafted: she wanted security to drag him out there and then,' he said.

They paused, as Stone had just interrupted the presentation to tell an anecdote of how he had once operated on a patient with an enormous polyp. Rossi rolled her eyes at the story. It was the same version of a three act play she had heard on many previous occasions. A patient had a problem, he was the only surgeon who could operate on it, he took it out along with half his giblets and everyone lived happily ever after.

Once the presentation had concluded, Dr Attwood stood up and addressed the room.

'As you know, Serenity Hospital has adopted a drug testing program for medical staff. Just outside the lecture theatre there are two of the hospital occupational health staff who will take a blood sample from everyone. Thanks for your co-operation, as you know for confidentiality, the samples are identified by a number rather than a name: the results come back only to me. I will inform every one of their individual results by e-mail tomorrow morning'.

The doctors in the room all obediently filed out to comply. Stone led the way, lumbering into the tiger-trap.

Chapter 26: Test Results

The summons for Dr Attwood to come urgently to Mary Gallen's office arrived in a flurry of phone calls the next afternoon. He ignored the first two entirely. The third came two minutes later, before he could text the automatic *'Can I call you later message'* the fourth call vibrated the phone in his hand.

Dr Rossi laughed when he showed her the caller ID flashing on the screen. 'You're going to have to answer her at some stage' she said.

'I know, I know, it's just priceless watching this unfold from a distance.' He put down the phone, picked up his coffee and leaning back in his chair, put his feet up onto the desk.

The hum of the vibrating phone on the desk caused them both to laugh.

'Go on, answer it, she's clearly having a breakdown.'

'Alright' he dropped his feet to the floor and picked up the phone. 'Hello, Dr Attwood here…ok, I understand….yes…..absolutely, right away, bye.'

'She wants me to some over to her office urgently, the hospital lawyer is with her.'

'I'll wait here for you to find out what happened' she said.

'What's your rush? Relax, lets finish our coffee. Maybe in thirty minutes I'll wander over. She'll be mad as a bag of cats by then and much easier to guide in the right direction.'

When Dr Attwood eventually settled into his chair across the desk from Mary Gallen she was clawing at a letter on her desk. She flicked her head with its narrow lips and wide eyes over and back between Attwood and John Turnbull, the hospital lawyer, in the other chair.

'What are we going to do now?' she said resting her gaze on Attwood.

'Well, it's fairly simple. Professor Stone has tested positive in a drugs test, we need to follow hospital policy. He should be suspended pending an investigation, he needs an occupation health referral and we will await the B sample result to ensure there is no mistake. It's all set out in our document specifically to address this type of issue' said Attwood.

'Well, the letter from his lawyers is very hostile. They say our policy, let me read it for you .... is unfair, oppressive, denies natural justice, is discriminatory, heavy handed... they are very upset.'

Attwood shrugged. 'That's all fairly predictable. John, you approved the legal side of all of these policies, are there any issues?'

'Well, the policies and the review of them and of course the processes themselves are all theoretically sound, in the normal course of events. But if this went to court and we got one of the judges who has the same connections as Stone, we could come unstuck. He's very well known around this town you know.'

Mary clearly had felt that having had her policies approved in advance by a lawyer would have made them bullet proof. The removal of her legal bullet proof vest now further unnerved her. 'You mean he could win if he sues us?'

'Possibly, one can never tell. These things are never certain' said the lawyer with the vagueness of a man who wasn't keen for his previous approval of the policy to be viewed as binding.

Attwood in his best reassuring voice, the one that he usually reserved for just before he stuck a needle into someone, tried to settle everyone down. ‘It is a little ironic that Professor Stone’s lawyer is being critical of a policy that Professor Stone himself drew up.’

‘That’s a very good point’ said John anxious to highlight anything positive. Attwood didn’t trouble him with the fact, that while Stone always took credit for any policy or output of any group he was a member of, he rarely did any of the work. Attwood had crafted the policy and set the trap. Stone never attended any of the meetings and probably had never read the policy before approving it. The fact that he as Director of Clinical Governance had approved and taken charge of the policy was now uncomfortably backfiring on him.

‘We don’t need to do anything, just go with the process and let’s see what comes out in the wash. We’ve done everything correctly, so sit back let things take their course. We are not the ones who have done anything wrong. There is of course potentially a very serious patient safety issue behind all of this’ said Attwood.

‘There is one other thing. Professor Stone came to me this morning. He wanted to get the B sample independently tested, so we went to the lab and I gave it to him to get it tested at an outside testing centre' said Mary.

Dr Rossi was waiting in Dr Atwood office and when he got back she looked up eagerly. 'Well?'

He recounted the story and they both sat in silence for a moment.

'So, if I've got this right, by her giving him the B sample the whole thing will implode' said Rossi sinking her head into her hands. 'We got so close, I can't believe she messed it up. She always follows the bloody rule book like a slave, why on earth did she do that?'

'I know, usually the greater the ignorance, the greater the reliance on dogma and policy. You've got to hand it to Stone, he's a player. But look, I told Mary if she backtracked or withdrew now it would be an admission of error on her part. The lawyer bought into that, like all of those legal eagles he was useless in a real time situation.'

Rossi raised her head but with the look of a child who is going back to school after summer holidays. 'What else can we do?'

'Think about it Claudia, what's the game plan for this situation? I think it's pretty obvious' said Attwood.

'Well, we just need to take control of the narrative and disseminate it as much as possible before it's killed. So, we have a hospital under police investigation for missing morphine. We have a high-profile Consultant who has failed a drug test. Let's just get the message out as widely as possible and see what happens.'

'Ok, if he's explaining he's losing. So, it's not over, this has a bit to play yet' she said.

Chapter 27: The Start

The following morning Attwood led the round: Ashley, Chris, some anonymous medical students and the nurse followed and on entering the first room they met Louise Stark dressed and sitting beside her bed with her bag packed.

'I guess you are trying to tell me something here?' he said.

She smiled, she had come to hospital with appendicitis. She was finally ready to leave with a long scar on her abdomen and a near death experience.

'I'd like to thank you all for your help. That day that Ashley brought you to see me I thought I was going to die,' she said.

'Yes, Ashley did a great job to spot what was going on. Thankfully it has all worked out well,' he said.

She stood up slowly, her thin legs still getting used to lifting her body again. Her clothes were looser than when she had come to hospital but like the bruises on her arms, that too would pass 'I do have an issue with Professor Stone. I think he could have done better'.

'Louise, you are not alone in thinking that. But my understanding is that Professor Stone has retired from clinical practice. What happened to you won't happen to anyone else,' he said.

That was clearly news to the doctors on the round as they all shifted their gaze from the patient to Dr Attwood. Ashley and Chris's mouths simultaneously opened to display the full 'O' sign. There was no drum roll, no retirement party with a gold watch, no speeches featuring the highlights of Stone's three act plays.

In the next room Joy Dean was for the first time smiling in the bed. Attwood picked up her observation chart and saw a straight line for the previous twenty-four hours unlike the Wall Street like erratic movements of the previous two weeks. 'You look good, the infection is clearly resolving. Things are good, we should be able to get you out of here in the next day or two' he said.

'That's great, I'm so happy, thanks to all of you.'

Outside in the corridor in front of the group Attwood turned to Ashley and said, 'Great job there Ashley, you saved her life and gave her a chance when you removed that tumour.' The rest of the round proceeded in a blur and, when it was over, Dr Attwood took Chris and

Ashley to the end of the corridor, where Dr Rossi was waiting.

Ashley was the first to speak 'What happened to Professor Stone? Was it to do with Joy Dean?'

'No, nothing to do with that or the other cases, but it's quite a shock,' said Dr Rossi. 'Apparently, he tested positive for opiates in the drug test. They found morphine in his locker and with the subsequent positive drug test that was game, set and match. There simply isn't any other explanation for a positive result apart from him being a user. Ironically the hospital policy he developed with Dr Attwood leaves him no option other than to go.' She gave an innocent shrug of her shoulders.

'There was a little issue with the test, in that as usual it was divided into an A and a B sample. The A sample was positive, he talked Mary Gallen into giving him the B sample which he says he got tested off-site and it has come back as negative' said Attwood.

'So, he didn't test positive?' asked Ashley.

Attwood shook his head. 'It's not clear and the policy is problematic, so if he hadn't resigned it could have gotten very messy. But between them they created such a mess that the compromise is that he's been promoted to regional clinical director. It's an exit package, but that's fine, because it means he works out of the regional office, has no patient care role and is out of our hair permanently.'

'Chris, she was also curious about why you had Tropicamide, methylene blue and so much money in your bank account?' Attwood asked.

'Well, the story there is…'

'Stop, there are things we don't want or need to know,' said Rossi. 'You do know if you give that to someone it can turn their urine blue? And Tropicamide I guess might cause visual disturbances and dilated pupils…'

'That's interesting,' was the most neutral response Chris could come up with.

'Anyhow all of this means that we have to plan how we're going to staff the department into the future. We can reconfigure the salary that was used to pay Stone to create two posts and keep the jobs open for six months to allow you guys to get certified and come aboard,' said Attwood.

'Now that Professor Stone is gone, Mary is more amenable to discussion. The investigation and the disciplinary process is now dead in the water. Jeffrey isn't a good fit for what we want, so we have the ability to give both of you Consultant jobs,' said Rossi.

Chris nodded and raising his eyebrows he looked at Ashley inviting her to respond. She looked downwards and slid her left hand along the side of her neck before reaching backwards and grasping her long hair. She pulled the hair forward until it was all swept forward onto her left shoulder. As Rossi and Attwood got their first glimpse of the new tattoo behind the right ear, which itself was now carrying multiple studs, she simply shrugged. Her hair fell forward again and smothered the fleeting image of a green phoenix emerging from a background of wispy flames tinged with purple. 'Sorry, I'm just a bit distracted, most of my patients are getting better, but Jack Salmon is dying, I know it's for the best. But you know, all of this…it isn't turning out like what I'd imagined a career in surgery to be.'

Dr Attwood straightened his stripped navy tie and looked at Chris and Ashley, 'neither of you look very enthusiastic: that's OK, you don't have to make a decision now. I fully understand the pressure you both have been under for the last while. But there is one thing we do need to understand: between the two of you there were traces of test positivity for cocaine, benzodiazepines and alcohol on the drug tests. The levels were below those of an actual positive result and given the people you treat, operate on and are exposed to, this would all be consistent with contamination from your patients. Tell me, is my understanding correct?'

Ashley flicked her hair back, stood tall and from her vantage point of five foot six, she slowly replied. 'Understand? Wow…. with of all the deluded, the dying and the ones trying to die, who are worse, and the people who run this mental place. I'm not sure I'm the person to help you understand.'

Before they could come to any understanding a breathless nurse broke in, 'Excuse me Dr Brown, your patient down the corridor in room 2 is deteriorating, we need you right now'.

It was clearly over now for Jack Salmon. There was no pleasure, no comfort in those long gasping breaths. No coming back, no more jokes, no more conversation, nothing. The finality of the situation was echoed in the sombre silence of the family standing and sitting around in the room. Ashley didn't want the memory to be sullied by a difficult, unpleasant death. She didn't want him struggling for air, bubbling, choking and grappling with death until the end. It wouldn't be dignified for him and the experience would scar his family and their memory of him for ever.

This was a single moment of time in the universe of Ashley and Jack's lives, but one that would change their shared world. This moment mattered and time slowed to pay its respects.

Taking his hand she checked his IV line. She fancied he had lifted many a full glass in good company with that now slender hand over the years. Whereas in the months before today Ashley would have dissected the causes of cirrhosis and explored whether or not a transplant was an option, she was now intrigued by the life he had led, the people he had met, and the experiences he had enjoyed. She lingered on the experiences and pleasures of life and wondered if, when she got to Jack's stage, would she regret not having lived those experiences, and whether there was still time, or would her career ultimately suffocate her soul.

A chapter would close with his passing. It wasn't a sad story, it was a novel of the good the bad and what was left behind, which would only exist in the minds of those he'd known. Ashley looked in slow motion at the sad, resigned faces and, sensing the agreement she took the syringe of morphine from the trolley. She tippled a dose of morphine into his IV line. His breathing eased and slowed. He visibly sank a little deeper into his pillow and the lines of stress on his face relaxed. Ashley pressed a little more on the syringe and released him from life as easily as slipping the rope tying a boat to a pier.

The same cells, chemical elements and atoms remained, but life had drifted away. Ashley always wondered at this point what had changed. Beyond describing the mechanics of the fact that the heart didn't work, and he no longer responded to pain, medicine and science can't measure of capture or define the ethereal elements that evaporate with the ending of a life.

'Is he gone now?' asked his son.

'Not quite, he's in that space between life and death. Just on the edge'

'Oh, sort of deadish.'

Ashley turned and smiled at him. 'Yeah, that's a good way of putting it.' She took her stethoscope and listened for his heart. It wasn't there anymore. The family watched as she leaned over listening. As her hair fell forwards the tattoo hidden behind her right ear again peeped out. The red rim around the edge gave away its freshness. She stood up, slipped the half-full syringe of morphine into her pocket and placed a hand on the son's shoulder.

'He's gone now.'

She eased back as the family merged around the bed. Watching the scene unfold she leaned back against the wall and with her hands deep in her pockets she felt the half empty syringe. She clenched it, going to put it in the sharps bin, but then she hesitated and dropped in back into the depths of her pocket. She silently left the room. It felt strange to her that she was at ease, even satisfied to have eased Jack onwards. Attwood, Rossi and Chris were still talking when she walked down the corridor.

'Sorry, I was distracted earlier. I do understand. I know what it's all about. I'll do the job.'

Printed in Great Britain
by Amazon

43608199R00215